Romance
RYAN
Jesi Lea

Ryan, Jesi Lea.

Surreal Estate.

JAN 1 0 2019

WITHDRAWN

SURREAL ESTATE

JESI LEA RYAN

D1178226

RIPTIDE
PUBLISHING

Riptide Publishing
PO Box 1537
Burnsville, NC 28714
www.riptidepublishing.com

This is a work of fiction. Names, characters, places, and incidents are either the product of the author's imagination or are used fictitiously. Any resemblance to actual persons living or dead, business establishments, events, or locales is entirely coincidental. All person(s) depicted on the cover are model(s) used for illustrative purposes only.

Surreal Estate
Copyright © 2018 by Jesi Lea Ryan

Cover art: Lou Harper, coveraffairs.com
Editor: Carole-ann Galloway
Layout: L.C. Chase, lcchase.com/design.htm

All rights reserved. No part of this book may be reproduced or transmitted in any form or by any means, electronic or mechanical, including photocopying, recording, or by any information storage and retrieval system without the written permission of the publisher, and where permitted by law. Reviewers may quote brief passages in a review. To request permission and all other inquiries, contact Riptide Publishing at the mailing address above, at Riptidepublishing.com, or at marketing@riptidepublishing.com.

ISBN: 978-1-62649-855-6

First edition
November, 2018

Also available in ebook:
ISBN: 978-1-62649-854-9

SURREAL ESTATE

JESI LEA RYAN

RIPTIDE
PUBLISHING

For Cassandra—I love you just the way you are.

Mid pleasures and palaces though we may roam,
Be it ever so humble, there's no place like home
—John Howard Payne

TABLE OF
CONTENTS

CHAPTER 1
SASHA

Fall

I wasn't sleeping. No one really did when spending the night on a bench in a seedy park. Too easy to get mugged by a crackhead. Instead, I stared up at the starless Milwaukee night and lamented my lack of four walls and a roof. The three layers of clothes I wore warded off the autumn chill, but I worried what winter would bring. I could wander south like some of my brethren, but at the heart of it, I was a Wisconsin guy born and raised. This was my home, no matter how battered and bruised it left me.

"Hey, kid," called a scratchy voice in the dark.

I sat up and saw Willie's dark figure ambling toward me. The cold must've been bothering his trick knee, because he leaned a little too heavily on the shopping cart that contained all of his worldly belongings. He was old and mostly harmless, but I pulled my bag closer to me anyway. You couldn't be too careful out here.

"What's up, Willie?"

The old man sat down next to me on the bench, sending a waft of air, acrid with meth-sweat and filth, up around us. I switched to breathing through my mouth.

"Saw you playing your guitar on the bridge today. From the looks of your case, I'd say you hauled in at least fifty bucks."

It had only been twenty-three, but it was always best to downplay any cash I might have . . . even if it was only Old Willie asking. "It wasn't that much, and I spent most of it on dinner."

"Well, that's too bad. I know a guy we could pick up a half gram of crystal from real cheap. Turn around and double our money easy." He gave me the side-eye, checking for my reaction. I forced myself not to clench my teeth as I replied.

"No, thanks, man. I'm not into dealing. Besides, I don't have that kind of cash." I did, but the last thing I was going to do was drop what I had into a half-cocked drug deal. Suddenly, I wanted to get out of here, away from the drug talk. I might be in dire straits, but I'd never turn to dealing. I'd seen the toll that shit could take on not just the user, but their families, their friends, everything they touched. A shiver rolled up my spine.

I stood, slinging my guitar case onto my back and lifting my bag. "Nice seeing you, Willie, but it's cold out here. I'm gonna see if I can find hot coffee or something."

"Okay, kid. Try the gas station over on Twentieth Street. They should be open."

I gave him a pat on the shoulder and walked away. It took twenty paces before my nose cleared of his scent. I wasn't the freshest either, but at least I made an effort.

It was late, or early, depending on how you looked at it. I crossed the little park heading to the street. A cop car drove past me a little too slowly; the second time I'd seen it that night. At best, the cop would tell me to be on my way. At worst . . . well, I didn't want to deal with that. I wasn't drunk or high or causing trouble, and I was so tired of people treating me like a criminal just because I was poor. I needed to get out of this place, with its heavy shadows watching me, and remind myself there was such a thing as normal in this world.

The tiny, no-name city park gave way to nearly empty streets as I cut through the parking lots of gas stations and Asian groceries. The worn concrete buildings and closed corner bars still displaying old Schlitz signs in the windows were echoes of a time when the city had teamed with blue-collar jobs and a hope for the future. No one could be hopeful on this street now.

I rounded the corner into a residential neighborhood lined with mature trees and pre–World War II family homes. It was the kind of neighborhood where parents worked jobs with uniforms and punched clocks, and they trusted their latchkey kids to hold the fort down until they could get home with their buckets of fast-food chicken for noshing on in front of the TV. In other words, a lot like the neighborhood I'd grown up in.

As I walked past the sleeping homes, a soft hum woke up the sixth sense in my mind. When I was young, I'd manifested psychic abilities, and walking down a neighborhood street had excited me. I had an affinity for homes . . . well, all buildings really. And in turn, they had an affinity for me. They always seemed to know I could hear them.

The best way I can describe my gift is that human emotions imprint on the places people live, work, and spend time. The structures absorb those emotions, and I can read them. Mostly, I only sense a low vibration of warmth, affection, sorrow . . . But if the vibrations are strong, well, other things happen.

My range isn't wide, but in a populous neighborhood like this one, the vibes tend to mix together like an odd, harmonious chorus in my mind. Sometimes a place will resonate more strongly than the others, rising above as if in solo and calling out to me with its story.

As I neared the corner, a house with plastic toys lying in the yard beckoned me closer. I approached the porch steps and rested my hand on the railing, opening myself up to the energy of the wood beneath my palm. My breath hitched as the spirit of the house touched my soul and slowly filled me with its tenderness for the occupants inside.

In my opinion, contentment is a vastly underrated emotion. Happiness, true elation, is difficult to sustain long-term. You'd either cross over into mania or you'd get so used to the feeling that your internal benchmark would shift, making it seem ho-hum. Which is actually sad. Contentment, on the other hand, is like a long feeling of *okay*. A sigh for the soul. Things might not be perfect in your life, you might have a micromanager boss or a persistent ache in your back, but overall, your life is going swell. The bad moments won't keep you down, and you retain your capacity for appreciating the good ones.

A light deep within the house came on. Someone getting up for an early shift or maybe just taking a piss. I adjusted the guitar on my back and continued down the street. I passed an elementary school and rounded another block. I was thinking of splurging on an Egg McMuffin when I felt it. A tug in my chest.

I turned to see what had pulled at me. Across a short expanse of overgrown yard was a large, stately colonial. Thick vines climbed the brick and clung to the mortar, giving the home an ominous quality in the darkness. But the sense coming from it didn't feel dangerous, only abandoned. The house called to me with a mixture of loneliness and desperation. I held my hand out, letting the cool vibrations roll over my skin.

Come inside.

I strode up the walk, unable to ignore the call. The neglect made my body feel hollow. The windows on the lower level were mostly boarded over with plywood. A niggling sense of heaviness on my left arm steered me, causing me to skirt the porch and go around the side instead. There, the vines climbed over the windows and choked the gutters. I reached the backyard with its foot-long grass and giant bushes that blocked the rest of the neighborhood from view. It wasn't four walls and a roof, but the privacy of the backyard lent a feeling of safety that I'd rarely experienced since taking to the streets.

Come inside.

I stepped up onto the rear porch and the nearly rotten wood gave way slightly to my weight. I opened the rusty screen door and tried the knob on the inner door. Locked tight.

Come inside.

How? I might be able to play almost any instrument set in front of me, but picking locks was not in my repertoire. I could track down Five Finger Felix (not his real name, but he answered to it) and ask him to come back tonight to help me break in, but no. If he knew there was a big, vacant home over here, he'd have it overrun with squatters by the end of the week. No one ever accused Felix of being discreet.

My side felt tingly and weighted again. I let the house steer me where it wanted me to go, stepping off the porch and rounding to the left side.

Come inside.

The heaviness vanished, and I stopped. I glanced down at a small basement window, and then bent to get a closer look. It was tough to see with the dark shadows cast from the lilac bushes, but a barely perceptible, otherworldly haze around the window forced my eyes to focus on it. There was no glass in the rotting frame, only a sheet of heavy black plastic. I pushed on the sheet. It came away easily, the adhesive on the old tape long dried out.

I slipped the guitar off my back and set it on the ground next to my pack. I was thin enough to have no problem fitting through the tight space, but was it such a good idea to venture in? No telling what hid in the black void of the basement.

Come. Inside.

I couldn't turn my back on the house now. Bad idea or not, it needed me.

I wiggled out of my jacket, not believing I was doing this. Breaking and entering wasn't my style. Then feetfirst, I sank down on my butt and scooched forward. I sat there for a moment, legs dangling inside, unable to sense the bottom of the black abyss. Then, with a deep breath, I steeled my nerves and dropped in.

CHAPTER 2
NICK

Spring

"This place is a real shithole."

I cuffed my brother lightly on the side of the head. "Shut it, Damey. She's got good bones. And if all you're going to do is bitch, you can walk your ass back home."

My excited fingers fumbled with the rusty door lock, while Damien picked at the peeling paint on the crumbling porch railing.

"These vines are going to be a bitch to scrape off."

"Yeah, it's not going to be fun, but I can't have the place looking like the Addams family lives here."

"Steven's gonna be pissed that you bought this place without him. What's the point of having a brother for a realtor if you aren't going to use him to take care of these things for you?"

"The bank auction was today, and Steven's still in South Beach trying to recapture his youth with the Spring Breakers. I didn't have time to wait."

"Why the hurry? Didn't think you'd even want to get back into house flipping after what happened before."

"The market's recovered."

"But has your bank account?"

I ignored the question and pushed open the door of the early 1900s colonial. A waft of musty, stale air and dust motes greeted me. The last rays of the setting sun slanted through the dirty windows, illuminating original hardwood floors and a hand-carved mantel piece. The place was more beautiful than I'd hoped, and my face split into a huge grin.

"Look at this!" I said, practically bouncing over to the mantel to trace the intricate scrollwork. "They don't make things like this anymore. A little scrubbing and staining, and it'll be good as new."

Damien kicked at one of the fallen bricks from the fireplace's facing. "Yeah, it's great."

"I'll have to put a gas insert in. Buyers don't like dealing with the maintenance of wood-burning fireplaces. Come on! Let's find the kitchen."

A set of French doors separated the living room from the dining room. Most of the glass panes were broken, but the wood was in great shape. "Check these out! They just need some new glass and stain. Don't think I'll keep them here though. This wall has to go to create an open-floor plan. But wouldn't they be nice in the master? I could use them to separate the sitting area from the sleeping area."

"We haven't even been upstairs yet, and you're making plans for the master bedroom? How do you know it has a separate sitting area?"

"This place is huge. If it doesn't already have one, I'll make one. Use your vision, Damey! Don't you see the potential here?"

"Potential for bankruptcy . . ." he muttered.

I pretended not to hear him, my mind spinning with renovation plans as I assessed the home's condition. Damien sneered at the cracked plaster, obviously wondering how his broke-ass brother planned to pay for the repairs. *None of his fucking business.*

We came to an abrupt halt in the kitchen doorway. All the air in my lungs expelled in a long whistle.

"Damn, Nick. That's not good." Damien groaned.

The ugly remains of a seventies remodel gone wrong was bad enough. The property had been abandoned for several years, so I'd known I'd have to update the place. But the layer of green mold coating the walls, ceiling, and the cabinets was thick enough to mow.

"Either a roof leak or a busted pipe somewhere upstairs," I speculated, stepping forward to see if I could spot where the moisture was coming from. "I'll have to get the mold remediation guy out in the morning to test and make sure it's not toxic, but I don't see any black mold, so we should be okay."

Damien pulled the edge of his T-shirt up over his mouth. "I'm outta here, man. I'm allergic to that shit. See ya at Mom's Sunday."

"Wimp."

Damien waved his middle finger behind himself as he strode out.

I was glad he'd bailed. Hadn't wanted him to come in the first place, but since he lived right around the corner, I couldn't exactly have hidden the fact that I'd purchased the abandoned property. Especially once he saw my Cooper Remodeling truck parked in front. The nosy bastard hadn't even stopped to tie his shoes before he'd come running over. Ten bucks said he'd call Steven within five minutes to tattle on me.

I reached down to switch off my phone. The last thing I needed right now was another brother lecturing me, even if it was out of concern. I wanted time to revel in this amazing house that I'd gotten for a steal.

I let my eyes unfocus a little so I could see past the furry mold and peeling linoleum. The room was huge! I could add an island and still have space for a nice breakfast nook by the large, southern-facing windows. New quartz countertops and dark-stained cabinets, and it'd be perfect.

Off the kitchen was a decent-sized bathroom with hookups for a washer and dryer. Good. An old house like this might have one of those creepy basements with only the rock foundation for walls and home to a thousand spiders. Potential buyers would hate having to drag their laundry all the way down there. A nice laundry area would give me an advantage in selling the house for a profit.

I was about to seek out the basement when a shuffling noise came from upstairs. I paused to listen. Squirrels? It was common for the rodents to nest in the attics of older homes. The yard had several overgrown trees with branches close enough to the roofline to make that possible.

The shuffle noise sounded again, this time accompanied by the soft creak of a floor board.

Could someone be in the house? No way. I'd walked around the foreclosed property and peered in as many windows as I could before making a bid on it. The place had been locked up tight. Must be an animal. Probably a bastard raccoon. I was halfway up the stairs to investigate before I remembered the crowbar I'd left in the back of the truck.

"Whatever you are, fucker, you better not have rabies," I called out, hoping the sound of my voice would scare it off.

I reached the top of the steps and peered into the first bedroom. Nothing but yellowing wallpaper.

Then I pivoted toward the next room and came face-to-face with a man.

"Holy shit!" I leaped back and raised my fists.

The stranger lifted his hands as if surrendering to the police. "I don't have rabies."

"Who are you?" I yelled, still trying to catch my breath. "Why are you in my house?"

"Sorry. I didn't think anyone owned the place."

Without taking my attention off the guy, I did a quick scan of the room beyond. It was obvious from the layers of sleeping bags in the corner, stacks of clothes, and neatly arranged personal items that he'd been squatting here for a while.

"You armed?"

The guy's eyes widened, and he dropped his hands. "No! I have a few plastic knifes over there next to the peanut butter jar, but that's it. I swear."

Sure as shit, the guy had the makings for sandwiches sitting on a box in the corner.

I eyed the squatter. He was young. Early twenties maybe? Just a kid. He was as tall as me, but thin. I had thirty pounds of muscle on the guy easy. The tension in my neck eased. If he wasn't armed, the kid was no threat.

"Look, I'll go. I just . . . Let me get my stuff." He ran his hand through the nest of dark hair and narrowed his eyes at his belongings. No way would he be able to carry it all with him unless he had a car.

"How'd you get in here?" The question came out harsh with the adrenaline still coursing through my system.

"Uh, basement window," he said absently, as he slipped into a pair of worn combat boots. "The first time anyway. Now I come in through the balcony."

A small balcony at the back of the room looked out on the backyard. The overgrown trees were just right for hiding an intruder from the sight of neighbors, not that there were many neighbors who could see this side of the house. The old Milwaukee neighborhood backed up to a wooded city park. The privacy of the backyard was one of the home's selling points.

The squatter snatched a large pack from somewhere and began jamming clothes into it. He'd need at least three of those bags for all his stuff.

Not sure what to do with myself, and unwilling to turn my back on him just yet, I studied him. His hair was overgrown and bushy and knotted with curls, and his face hadn't seen a razor in a while, but he appeared clean enough. The water was shut off in the house, so he must be getting regular showers somewhere else. His face was pale, and he had to keep pushing that hair out of his eyes so he could see what he was doing. Shit, he looked nervous, maybe even scared. I'd seen his type before. Guys who were down on their luck and had few, if any, options. Back when my company was flipping houses all the time, I used to hire guys like this, day laborers, to assist on jobs. As long as they were sober, I'd been happy to throw some work their way.

"Hold up." I sighed. When the guy didn't stop his frantic packing, I reached out to touch his sleeve. "I said, hold on a minute."

He glared at where my hand rested on his forearm before he stepped away. "You're not gonna call the cops, are you? I didn't damage anything. Okay, I smoked in the house once in a while, but honestly, that's it."

"What's your name, kid?"

His eyes narrowed on me. "Sasha."

"What kind of name is 'Sasha' for a dude?"

"Russian Jew."

"Really? What's your last name?"

"Michaels."

"What kind of name is 'Michaels' for a Russian Jew?"

"The kind whose grandfather decided not to saddle his future kids with 'Mikhailovich' when he left the Soviet Union."

"Good call."

Sasha rubbed a shoulder, and then bent to snatch up one of the many blankets that made his bed on the floor.

"I'm Nick. Nick Cooper."

Sasha grunted and began folding.

"You got somewhere to go, kid?"

"I'm twenty-four years old. Not exactly a kid."

"Well, do you?"

He gave a small headshake, and glanced out at the falling twilight. "Might be room over at the United Methodist shelter. I'll have to find a place to stash my things first, though. Last time I was there, some assholes made off with my shit while I slept. Only reason they didn't get my guitar is because I was curled up with my arm around it . . ."

Sasha motioned to where a beat-up guitar case leaned against the far wall. He averted his eyes from me.

"How long you been staying here?"

Sasha shrugged. "A few months. More like six. Again, I'm sorry. I didn't know anyone owned the place. It's such a lonely old house. Figured I'd be long gone before anyone came around."

"An out-of-state bank owned it. I just bought it today. They don't let people tour foreclosed properties before purchase, so I didn't know you were here."

"You bought a house without seeing the inside? That's . . . risky. Have you seen the kitchen yet? The place looks like a science experiment gone mad."

"I saw it. It's fixable. I was going to have to gut the kitchen anyway. I'm going to renovate the place and sell it."

The ghost of a smile touched Sasha's lips. "Really? I mean, that's cool. That you'd fix it up and not just knock it down to build a parking lot or something."

"No parking lot. They don't make homes like this anymore." I knocked on the plaster wall. "You know, with character. A new kitchen, some cosmetic work, and it'll make a good family home again."

Sasha trailed his fingers down the nubby plaster wall gently. "Yeah. She'll be happy to get rid of that kitchen."

She? Uh, okay. In any case, the guy seemed to have genuine affection for the old place. Could he see the same potential in it as I did? If so, maybe I should keep him around. I could use someone on my side when Steven the Great finally showed up to tell me what a mistake I've made.

I leaned in the doorway and crossed my arms. "What're you doing for light here without electricity? Candles?"

"I have a camping lantern. One of those where you turn the crank a bunch of times and it stays lit for about ten minutes. I don't need much light anyway. I go to sleep early so I can get up for work in the morning."

My brows shot up. "You have a job?"

"Uh, yeah," he answered sarcastically. "I work the opening shift at a coffee shop on National Ave during the week. And I do some busking around town for cash. Once in a while, I'll play in a bar gig or a coffee shop or something, but that's not regular."

"So you work, but you're squatting in an abandoned house? Why?"

Sasha scowled at me again, and I stifled a grin.

"I'm trying to save money, all right? Do you know how hard it is to afford rent in this town on your own? Not to mention, every landlord wants two references and a credit check. Baristas and buskers don't exactly rate as the most financially stable people with the credit bureaus. I'm doing the best I can."

I raised my hands. "Sorry, man. Not judging. Just trying to understand."

Sasha's scowl faded as he reached for a sleeping bag. He smoothed out the wrinkles and began to roll it with the precision of a well-practiced Boy Scout. Suddenly, I felt like an asshole for making the guy leave. He wasn't hurting anything. And I'd heard terrible stories about sleeping in homeless shelters. Shit, if it weren't for my family's support when my business had gone bankrupt and my ex-wife moved out with her share of what was left, I could've ended up on the streets myself. But what was I supposed to do? I couldn't let a homeless guy stay here. What if he trashed the place?

In his haste, Sasha bumped his knee on the box he was using as a table and knocked a plastic bottle half-filled with water over onto the hardwood floor.

"Oh, shit! I'm sorry!" He grabbed a threadbare bath towel draped over the radiator to sop up the mess. He scrubbed the area. When the towel was soaked, Sasha slipped off the flannel shirt he was wearing over a T-shirt and used it to finish the job.

"Dude, you don't need to use the shirt off your back. It's just water."

Sasha didn't look up as he gave the wood planks one last wipe. "There isn't much lacquer left on this floor. If I let it sit here, the wood will discolor."

He said it so earnestly that I swallowed hard to stop from telling him that every floor in the house would need to be redone anyway. It touched me that he had taken such good care of a house that wasn't his. Not quite believing what I was about to say, I said, "Hey, it's getting late, and obviously you aren't cooking meth in here or anything, so I guess there isn't any harm in letting you stay the night."

Sasha clutched the wet cloth to his chest. "Really? You'd let me stay? Why?"

I shrugged a shoulder. "You don't have anywhere to go. And if you got all your things snatched in a shelter, I'd feel like a dick for making you leave here."

He eyed me with suspicion. After a moment he asked, "And what do I have to do for it?"

"For what?"

"For being able to stay the night. What do I have to do for it?"

"Nothing, man. It's too late in the day for me to start any work now. Just get some sleep, all right?"

He averted his eyes from mine and took in the room. "Thanks. I have to work in the morning, but as soon as I get off, I'll come by and get my things."

"I should be around in the afternoon. Feel free to use the front door. I don't need you breaking your leg climbing that tree and suing me." I knocked my fist on the doorframe. "Well, I want to finish looking around, then I'll be out of your hair."

I was halfway down the hall before I understood what he'd been asking.

CHAPTER 3
SASHA

The glow of the camping lantern had long faded, leaving only the silvery moonlight to illuminate the room. I didn't need it anyway. I'd been lying on the pallet of blankets and staring at the ceiling for hours. The house buzzed with nervous agitation, making my mind anxious. I should've been trying to come up with a game plan for where I was going to sleep tomorrow night, but instead, I was overcome by the intense emotions rolling off the walls.

"Oh, House, you have to calm down. I can't think." I sat up wearily, wishing I had a cigarette. Plus I needed to piss. Normally, I'd go off the balcony into the lilac bush below, but hell, I had permission to be here now. I could use the back door and piss in the bushes like a civilized person. I stood, my bones creaking too much for my age, and made my way downstairs.

Nick Cooper was a surprise. Not just because he'd showed up out of the blue and scared the shit out of me, but because he hadn't run my ass out of here with a pitchfork. I still wasn't sure why he'd let me stay. Judging by the muscles bulging from that T-shirt, he could've kicked my ass into next week. Whatever his reasons though, I was glad for them.

At the bottom of the steps, I turned left into the living room. Of course, I knew the room was empty, but that wasn't what I saw. Before me was the ghostly image of a comfortable family room with clean, but dated, plaid furniture and a plant stand filled with African violets. The fireplace crackled with a fresh log, its promise of warmth making my bare arms break out in goose bumps. As always, there were no people in the vision, only the evidence of their presence . . . a folded-open *TV Guide* on the coffee table, a Motorola console record player with unsheathed John Coltrane albums lying out as if the listener would return any moment. I'd seen this particular scene before. It was from a time when the home had been especially happy, and it liked to revisit those days over and over.

I clenched my eyes tight, hoping the vision would clear. It didn't. The energy in the house was too strong tonight. She didn't like it that Nick bought her without seeing her first. It was like he didn't really give a shit about her at all. Made her nervous. And when the house was nervous, I felt it like a flutter in my chest. It had helped when he said he planned to sell to a nice family, but what if the house didn't like them? She didn't care for toddlers coloring her walls with crayons or moody teenagers who took their aggression out punching holes through her plaster. Worse, what if no family wanted the old home, and Nick had to sell to a group of young guys who brought in a Kegerator and had parties every weekend like that group in 2002 had done? It longed for quiet, respectful occupants.

"Relax, House," I whispered, petting the cool wooden banister. "Be happy that you're getting a makeover."

I made my way to the back door off the kitchen, carefully avoiding the furniture that I'd be able to walk right through. The visions weren't usually this vivid. Sometimes I would go days without seeing anything, only feeling the psychic pulse of the walls around me. That was what had called me to this place to begin with. The old house had been so lonely, it had practically begged me to move in. Okay, it didn't actually talk to me with words. That would be crazy. But the place made its wishes known just the same.

I tugged open the back door and stepped onto the concrete stoop. I opened my fly and turned to do my business. The night air was cool. Too cool to sleep outside. What the fuck was I going to do? The few hundred bucks I had stashed away wouldn't buy me a week in a motel. Kenny, the baker at work, had intimated several times that I was welcome at his place, but the thought of having to suck the fat fuck off for the privilege of sleeping on his pot-scented couch made me sick.

Nick Cooper on the other hand . . . I might be willing to go to my knees for him if he'd let me stay here until he sold the house. Those full lips and that intense stare had about killed me. Dude was a fine specimen of man. Unfortunately for me, my gaydar hadn't given the slightest ping when he'd stood in the room.

I tucked myself away before I got hard and had to do something about it.

Back in my room, I checked the time on my pay-as-you-go phone. Not quite midnight yet, but I needed to be up before the sun to make it to work by six. If I wasn't so desperate for cash, I'd call in tomorrow and work on my living situation. For the millionth time, I thought about my zayde's—my grandfather's—place in Oak Creek, the home I'd grown up in. I'd still be living there if he hadn't died, and his whole meager estate hadn't passed to my deadbeat mother. The only way she'd let me stay there now is if I agreed to give her my paychecks to feed her drug habit. I'd rather sleep under a bridge than spend one night under her roof.

I drew my guitar out of its case and arranged myself on my simple bed with it perched in my lap. I strummed the strings in an absentminded tune, hoping to soothe both myself and the house. My eyes drifted closed as I picked away with my calloused fingers. Behind the dark lids, I saw Nick's face again. His whiskey-colored eyes and granite jaw, those full lips, begging to be bit. Without consciously meaning to, the tune dropped into a slow, sultry swing. I hummed along in a wordless melody until the house calmed, and the night overtook my restless mind.

CHAPTER 4
NICK

"Good thing the power's off," I mused, fingering the knob and tube wiring in the attic. "The place is gonna have to be completely rewired and brought to code."

"Got it," my intern, Kelly, replied as she entered the costs of an updated electrical system to the budget spreadsheet on her tablet. "One hundred twenty amp?"

"Nah, make it two hundred. Won't cost that much more, so we might as well do it right. The good news, we won't have to reinsulate the whole attic. Looks like just the spot on the rear side where that leaky vent is."

I'd found the source of the moisture in the kitchen easily enough. An old ice dam must have loosened a few of the shingles around a roof vent, allowing rain water to trickle in and down the inside the walls. I'd bet money there was mold behind the tub surround of the upstairs bathroom also. I wouldn't know for sure until I demoed it all out though.

Damn, the place was going to be an expensive fix. Not to mention, it would take all my free time for the next couple of months. I couldn't afford to pay my regular crew to help with the work. I needed them on the few remodel jobs I had that would actually pay my bills. No, if I wanted to flip this house, I need to do as much of it on my own as possible. Damien would help. He owed me a lifetime of brotherly debts. I might even be able to rope Steven into rolling up his sleeves for some manual labor, if he wasn't too pissed off that I'd bought the house behind his back. I still hadn't returned his angry voice mail.

"And have you made a decision on replacing the roof?"

I shook my head. "No, the shingles are at least twenty years old, but they're holding up. I'd love to replace it, but there are more pressing concerns. I'll just fix the spot by the vent. I think the rest is good for another five years."

"Okay. If that's it, I'll work on calculating the budget. Nick, this place is going to cost a fortune. I hate to say it, and I know that you always say you need to take some risks in this business, but you may have gotten in over your head here."

Jesus, not another person getting down on me for my decision. Why couldn't anyone else see the potential here? A 2,700-square-foot house filled with original architectural details, for only $65,000? No way could I lose. I just had to be smart about how I spent my money.

"I know it's a lot, but we can do it." I flashed her a grin that I hoped was more reassuring than nervous. "Don't worry. I'll text you if I think of anything else. Oh, and be careful with the finishes. It has to look quality, but I can't afford to spend a lot on things people can't see."

Kelly sighed. "High-end on a Walmart budget. Got it." She turned toward the stairs and let out a squeak.

Sasha had peeked up over the railing. "Sorry. Just wanted to let you know I'm here to get my stuff."

Seemed all the guy ever did was apologize for taking up space. Didn't know why that bothered me, but it did. "No need to apologize. Sasha, this is Kelly, my intern."

Kelly closed the cover on her tablet and gave Sasha a look she never bothered to give me, and I fought to stifle a grin. "I know you. You're in that band who used to play the college bars. You went to Marquette, right? I graduated last year. I thought I saw you around campus a few times."

Sasha's cheeks reddened, and he averted his gaze uncomfortably. "Uh, yeah. I used to go there. I'm gonna get my bags now, Nick."

Sasha turned to leave, but Kelly wasn't done with him. "I'm in grad school at Concordia. Interior design."

I had to admit I was curious about the guy. So when Kelly followed Sasha, I did too.

"Do you still play?" Kelly asked, practically stepping on his heels. "I'd love to see you perform again."

Sasha entered his room and resumed the packing he'd begun the night before. There were two more ratty duffel bags on the floor beside the sleeping bags. "The band broke up."

Kelly did one of those flirty pouty things with her lips, but it was clearly lost on Sasha when he didn't bother to glance her way. "That's too bad. You guys were good."

"What kind of music?"

"Alternative rock. Some pop," she answered for him. "He has an amazing voice. Plays guitar too. You should've seen them do that song 'Some Nights' by Fun. They always ended their sets with it. He'd have the whole place rocking and singing along."

"Just a bunch of bullshit covers, mostly," Sasha said, obviously uncomfortable with the praise.

"Kelly, can you excuse us? I need to talk to Sasha."

Kelly shot me a hurt glare at the dismissal, but since I gave her so few direct orders, and she really needed me to give her a good evaluation for her course grade, she couldn't exactly complain. She reached in her purse and withdrew one of the business cards she'd had printed up for her future interior design business, and held it out to Sasha. "Next time you play—anywhere—let me know."

My eyes caught on the way she allowed her finger tips to graze his hand as he took the card. For some reason, her blatant flirtation irritated me, but it appeared to be one-sided. Kelly strode out the door with a little extra swing in her step, but Sasha had already turned back to stuffing his clothes in a bag.

Once she was gone, I cleared my throat. "A band, huh?"

Sasha ignored the question, and I started again.

"Did you find a place to stay?"

He peered up at me from where he was kneeling on the floor. "Not really, but my manager said I can keep my things in the storeroom for a few days, until I come up with a plan."

"So you're going to the shelter?"

He shrugged. "Maybe."

I'd never been inside a homeless shelter before, and in my mind, I pictured it like an Army barracks, but more crowded and dangerous. Something happens to men when they are riding the edge of rock bottom, when they have nothing left to lose. That was no place for a young guy to be. Did he have no one to give him a hand?

"Can you swing a hammer?" I heard myself ask before my brain fully realized why I was asking.

Sasha sat back on his heels and looked at me skeptically. "Why?"

"I was thinking . . ."

He raised his brows and nodded for me to continue.

I decided to just lay it all out there. "Look, I have a tight timeline and not enough money to get this house fixed up and sold. My crew is busy working on actual paying jobs, so this place is going to depend on me and whatever I can scare up for weekend labor from my brothers. I can't pay you much, but if you're willing to give me a hand, I'll let you stay here."

"You serious?"

Was I? Maybe hiring some street kid was a stupid idea, but desperate times and all that. "Yeah. I need to be completely done within seven weeks. That's not long, but it would give you more time to make a plan."

"I've never done construction before."

"Do you know how to follow orders? If so, I can teach you enough to make you useful."

He paused, clearly kicking the idea around in his mind. "I work at the coffee shop from six to two most days. I can be here and ready to go by three."

"Works for me. I have to spend my mornings checking in on my other jobs anyway."

Sasha looked at his half-packed bags, then stood up. "Guess I can put all this back."

"Sorry to jerk you around. If you have time now, I can show you the things that need to be demoed first, so we can get started right away tomorrow."

"Yeah, sure."

I led Sasha downstairs, feeling oddly self-conscious. *Did I really just invite this stranger to stay in my house and offer him a job?* I'd have to make sure he didn't steal my tools and pawn them for quick cash. No. No, this guy didn't give me that kind of vibe. He was just down on his luck. Like me. And I'd be smart, lock everything up each night.

This better not come back to bite me in the ass though.

"So the first thing we need to do is gut the kitchen," I said, waving toward the nasty room. "I have a dumpster being delivered in the morning. Everything has to come out. Cabinets, appliances, that ugly-ass sink. Most importantly, anything with mold on it. I had someone out this morning to test it, and thank fucking god it's not toxic, but still, it's nasty shit to breathe, so I don't want you working in here without a mask on. I have a whole pack of them in my truck that I'll bring in. When we do the actual demo, we'll use respirators. Got it?"

Sasha nodded.

"And I want to remove this wall. Open it up to the dining room and create a more open space."

"Uh, you'll have to be careful with that. That's a support wall."

I narrowed my gaze at him. "How do you know?"

"Well, under that plaster is solid brick."

I examined the wall. No holes in the plaster. All the moldings securely in place. What, did he have x-ray vision?

"Again," I repeated slowly, "how do you know?"

"Used to watch HGTV with my grandfather. The only reason I can think of for a brick wall in the middle of a house is if it's doing something to hold the place up."

My jaw tightened. "See this?" I pressed the flat wall. "This is plaster. Unless you're Superman, you can't see through it. How do you know what is under the plaster?"

Sasha looked at his feet.

I knocked on the plaster with my fist. It didn't sound hollow. Curious, I went out to my truck and returned with a crowbar. I struck the plaster hard enough to create a spiderweb crack, then pried a small section of the lath away. Sure enough, there was brick under it.

"For the last time, tell me how you knew."

"Lucky guess."

I wasn't buying it. How did this guy who knew nothing about construction know there was a giant brick wall in the center of the house? I examined it on both sides. Aside from the one hole I just made, the brick was completely hidden. What in the hell was I missing?

Sasha cleared his throat. "If you want to knock down walls, maybe you could open up the one between the living room and the dining room. The brick wall spans the length of both rooms, so you could remove the plaster off and use it as ... What do they call those things?"

"An accent wall?"

"Yeah, yeah. An accent wall."

I set aside for now how Sasha could possibly know anything about the brick wall hidden under plaster and allowed myself to picture what he'd described. A brick wall spanning the length of the two rooms would make the place appear larger and more cohesive. The exposed brick would also highlight the home's character. It wasn't something you'd be likely to find in a cookie-cutter ranch house.

"Yeah, man, that could really work."

Sasha didn't meet my eyes. Something was off about this guy, but damn if it didn't increase my curiosity about him.

I patted him on the shoulder. "Good idea. Now, let's figure out what to do about the other side of the house."

We walked back to the front door. At the bottom of the staircase and to the right was a row of three dark, cramped rooms. Presumably some large family from the past must have divided the area to make bedrooms, but it looked ugly as hell. The walls in all three rooms were covered in hideous yellowed wallpaper with an acorn pattern on it. There were few things in life I hated more than scraping wallpaper.

"I'm planning to take down the walls between these rooms too, and making another living space."

"A library," Sasha said before biting his lip. "Sorry. I just think the front part could be a family room, but the back part a library. You know, with built-in bookshelves or something."

I'd been expecting to have to replace the furnace and water heater, but surprisingly, they were only about ten years old. I could afford to add some shelves. "Not a lot of light in the back though."

"No, but there used to be another window back there that someone bricked over. You could open it up again."

He was right. I'd noticed the bricked-over window when I'd examined the exterior prior to the auction. I wandered back to the dim room, with Sasha following. "Good point. And I'm thinking about cutting in another door here to open it up to the kitchen. It'd make a big difference in the flow."

Sasha ran his hand along the wall and smiled. "This place is gonna be amazing when you're done with it. I always thought it was such a shame that it was sitting neglected."

Finally, someone who could see the potential in the old place! I knew I'd gotten a good feeling from this kid.

"I can't afford to get all new windows, but I'll have to replace that one." I pointed to a small window with cracked glass and a frame covered in dry rot. "If we're going to open the old window back up, I might as well cut this one bigger to match. The morning light will flood this room. Can't you just see someone reading their morning paper and drinking coffee in front of all those books?" I pulled out my phone to text the changes to Kelly so she could adjust the budget.

"Yeah, perfect! Kind of makes me wish I could afford to buy the place when you're done with it. So what are your plans for upstairs?"

I glanced up from my phone. "The bedrooms are okay, but the bath situation needs work. I'm hoping to keep the existing tub and refinish it, but I want to replace all the tile and the sink. Install a new vanity. For the bedrooms, I'll refinish the floors, change out the light fixtures and repaint everything. I think a master suite would increase the home value higher than that tiny fifth bedroom does though, so I'm going to convert that into a new master bath and walk-in closet."

"And you're going to have this all done in seven weeks?"

My gut tightened. It was a fuck-ton of work to get done in such a short time frame, but I didn't have a choice. The home had to be sold ASAP in order to meet my loan obligation.

"I don't plan to get much sleep."

"Hope you have more help than just me."

"I have two guys working for me who will take care of the jobs lined up for my remodeling business. That will free me up to spend most of my time here. I'm licensed in electrical and plumbing, so I can do most of that work myself. My brothers and a couple of buddies will help on the weekends; maybe I'll pick up some day laborers when I can. I'll let Kelly handle the interior decorating details. She loves to shop with my money, but she's surprisingly thrifty. I'll probably hire out the landscaping. I hate that shit. And I have you."

"Yeah, me."

"I'll pay you," I quickly added. Didn't want him to think I was using him. "I can only afford minimum wage though. That cool?"

Sasha nodded. "I'm just glad you're letting me stay. The extra cash will come in handy after my eviction."

"Sorry about that, dude, but I have to sell this place if I'm going to recoup my expenses, you know? Oh, and I had the water turned on today. Gas too. Not sure where you've been showering, but the one in the downstairs bath works now. So does the toilet."

"Sweet! Your lilac bush will appreciate that."

I raised one brow at him. "Do I want to know?"

Sasha grinned. "Don't worry. It was number ones only, I swear. Anything else and I walk down to the BP station."

"Good to know. Well, I have to run, but I'll be around when you get off work tomorrow. Here." I slid a key off the ring in my pocket and handed it to Sasha. "Lock up when you leave."

"I still have plenty of daylight left. Got something I can start on right away?"

"Yeah, start peeling these fucking acorns off the walls."

CHAPTER 5
SASHA

I t wasn't the best shower I'd ever had, but you wouldn't know it from the way I stood under the spigot grinning like an idiot. Since I'd taken to the streets last year, I'd been sneaking over to the Marquette campus a couple of times a week to shower in the locker room. Sometimes I'd grab a workout, if there weren't too many people around to notice me. I had a school ID that was only slightly out of date, but no one ever checked it. Even so, the endless hot water and the occasional jock-boy eye candy didn't beat being able to shower at home and go straight to bed all clean.

After Nick left, the wallpaper had come off easily. I'd used the glue loosening solution he'd left to soak the sheets, then peeled them from the walls in long strips. Got all the exterior walls on the right side of the house done before the sun went down. I didn't bother with the interior walls since they were going to be demoed anyway.

I had to admit, it was kind of nice to do some manual labor. Walking around with Nick listening to his plans for the house had been cool too. He'd had this excited spark in his eyes as if he could really see past all the deterioration to the house's full potential. I half wondered if he saw visions from the home's heyday as I did. But no, Nick wasn't a psychic; he was something better. I only saw visions of things from the past, things that had actually existed and took no imagination on my part. But Nick's mind could envision things not yet real. He could see the potential beauty in the home. And given how excited he got when talking about it, I had no doubt he could make his plans reality.

When the water ran to lukewarm, I got out and dried myself with the one towel I owned, then draped it around my waist. In the fading light of the camping lantern, I examined my face in the medicine cabinet mirror. I wasn't one of those guys who could grow a full beard all manly and shit. It was more like some wonky-looking sideburns with a lopsided goatee. I should trim it up one of these days. And I couldn't remember the last haircut I'd had. Maybe I'd take a few bucks from the money Nick was going to pay me and stop into the cosmetology school for a trim.

My phone buzzed on the closed toilet lid with an incoming call. Not recognizing the number, I debated answering it, since I was low on minutes. But my curiosity won out.

"Hello?"

A tinny recording replied, "This call is being made from the Milwaukee County House of Correction."

"Sasha, baby. It's Mom."

The recording then asked me to press number one to accept the call. My finger hovered over the number a moment before I sighed and pressed the button.

I didn't bother to disguise my groan. "What do you want?"

"Is that any way to talk to your mother?"

"You're in jail?" I didn't have time for her bullshit. I was tired and wanted to get to bed.

"It was a misunderstanding. They say I have outstanding warrants or something. I'm sure it'll get cleared up in court tomorrow. But listen, I need your help."

"I don't have any money to bail you out."

She scoffed as if it were so preposterous that she'd call me for money, even though it was usually what she wanted from me. "I have money, Sash, but it's at the house. I need you to go over there and get it, and bring it down to the jail for me."

"I don't have a key, remember?" She'd unceremoniously stripped me of it last year during our last epic fight that had ended with her latest boyfriend bleeding and me out on my ass.

"You don't need one. Jerry should be home."

"Who's Jerry?"

"This call is being made from the Milwaukee County House of Correction," the recording repeated.

"He's my fiancé."

If I had a dollar for every "fiancé" my mother had ever had, I wouldn't be homeless. "Why don't you call him, then?"

"The phone at the house's been off for a while. There was a mix-up with the bill. You know how hard those phone company people are to deal with."

"So you want me to go over there and tell this Jerry guy to bring your money to the jail?" I really hoped her boyfriend could run her errands. It'd take three buses and several hours to get there and back to get to Oak Creek this time of night. A taxi would be faster, but would cost money I didn't have.

"I don't want Jerry to know where I keep my cash. I want you to get it without him seeing. Tell him you need something from your old room. He'll let you in. I've told him all about you, baby."

Nice, trusting relationship there. I should tell her to kiss off, but every time I did, I saw my zayde looking down on me all disappointed like. The old man had always had a soft spot for his only child, and I'd had a soft spot for him, so go figure. I glanced at the time on my phone. Shit, it was past eight o'clock already. If I did this, I'd be up all night.

I sighed. "Still keep your cash in the same place?"

"Yeah. Thanks, honey. I appreciate it."

"How much do you want?"

"I think five hundred will get me out of here tomorrow. My lawyer said the rest can go on a payment plan."

"Fine." I hung up and barely resisted throwing the phone against the wall. Knew I shouldn't've answered it.

I changed into clean clothes and tied my wet hair into a knot at the back of my head. I could catch a bus down on National Avenue. Then, assuming Mommy Dearest had an extra few bills in her stash, I'd let her buy me a cab back.

The street was nice and quiet in the dark. It was one of those working-class neighborhoods typical of Milwaukee, shabby but not ghetto. A decent place to live if you couldn't afford the burbs.

When I got to the bus stop, I took a seat on the bench and lit a cigarette, settling in for what might be a long wait. I didn't smoke much, mostly because I couldn't afford seven bucks a pack, but I'd bummed a couple off a girl at work today after I'd done her the favor of waiting on her ex-boyfriend so she could hide in the back until he was gone.

Turns out I didn't have to wait long. Before I was half done with my cigarette, a familiar truck pulled up beside the curb in front of me.

The passenger-side window rolled down to reveal Nick. "Waiting for a ride?"

I nodded.

"Get in."

"That's okay, man. I have to go to Oak Creek tonight. I'm sure that's well out of your way."

"I got time. Get in." The lock clicked open.

My pride wanted to refuse, but hell, I didn't want to have to sit on the bus all night. I knocked the cherry off and stuck the rest of the extinguished cigarette in my shirt pocket before climbing in.

Nick turned down the rock station he'd been listening to. "What's in Oak Creek?"

"Have to pick something up at my mom's house."

I didn't miss the surprise on his face. No doubt he figured a homeless guy wouldn't have family in the area. I was glad when he didn't ask for details.

"Thanks for the ride. Were you just lurking around the neighborhood?" I asked, smiling to take the bite out of the question.

"My brother Damien lives over here. We were watching the Brewers game, but they're getting their asses handed to them, so I left early."

I knew next to nothing about baseball, so I didn't have anything to add. Instead I stared out the window for several minutes of uncomfortable silence.

"So you went to Marquette? What did you study?"

I suppressed a sigh. I wasn't good with the whole get-to-know-you small talk thing on a good day. Now, I was tired and more than a little frustrated to be called away from my bed. But the guy was giving me a place to stay and some honest work, so I needed to play nice.

"Secondary education with a minor in music. Dropped out after my third year when I ran out of money."

"A music teacher. That's cool. I only went to tech school."

"At least with tech school you can get a job that pays enough to support yourself."

"Gonna go back? To school?"

My laugh came out as a derisive snort. "My current lifestyle doesn't really allow me to spend thousands of dollars on tuition."

He was quiet for a minute before changing the subject. "I've been broke too, man. My company used to be a lot bigger. I did new construction as well as house flipping. But when the housing bubble burst, it took me with it. Had to declare bankruptcy and everything."

"But you weren't homeless." My tone came out a little harsher than I'd meant it, but if comparing war stories was how this guy wanted to bond, I didn't want any part of it.

"No, I wasn't. But only because my brother Steven and his boyfriend let me sack out in their guest room for a year while I worked to get my shit together."

Well, if he had lived with a couple of gay guys, I could be reasonably certain that my new boss wasn't a homophobe. That was a bonus. "Another brother?" I asked. "How many of those do you have?"

"Just the two. Steven's a year older than me. He's a realtor, and is currently pissed at me for buying that house without waiting for his sage advice. Damien is a few years younger. He owns a bar not too far from the house."

When we got to Oak Creek, I directed Nick to my old neighborhood. We pulled up in front of the ranch house; the only light coming from inside was the glow of the TV. At least this Jerry guy was still awake. I just hoped he wouldn't be an asshole about me coming over. Nick got out of the truck with me, and I wanted to protest, but it might actually be good to have some backup.

"So this is where you grew up?" he asked as we crossed the street.

"Yeah. It was my grandfather's house. He raised me. My mom got it when he died, and we don't get along so well."

I knocked on the screen door and waited. Some cursing came from inside, and a moment later a thin guy in a wifebeater answered.

"What?"

"I'm Rina's son. I need to get something from my room."

"Rina ain't here."

"I know. She's in jail. She sent me here to get some paperwork for her."

He seemed like he wanted to slam the door in my face, but a glance at the big guy behind me apparently made him think better of it. "Whatever." He turned and walked back to his seat on the couch where he took a hit off a joint and stared blankly at the television.

Nick surveyed the room. Embarrassment warmed my neck seeing how dingy the place had gotten. Clutter overflowed every available surface, and the carpet had that flattened food-crumb look that came from months of not being vacuumed. If I let my eyes unfocus, I could see faint traces of the home I grew up in. I blinked them away. It hadn't been like this when my zayde had been alive. Now the place smelled like weed and dirty laundry. Well, it wasn't the rotten-egg smell of meth cooking, so that was something.

To Nick, I said. "Wait here. I'll be back in a minute."

He nodded and crossed his arms menacingly, and I was thankful he was on my side.

I hurried down to my old bedroom in the basement, and my breath caught. Okay, technically most of my things were there, but the room was trashed. It didn't take much imagination to guess that my mother had ransacked it at some point searching for drugs or money or anything she could sell. My stereo was gone, as was the small tube TV that had been on top of my dresser.

I placed a hand on the wall and let the emotions of the home tell me their story. My eyes drifted closed for a moment. When I opened then again, the room was overlaid by a vision of the past. The bed was in the same spot, but was made up with Simpsons bedding. A pile of Legos littered the floor beside my toy box. It was obvious the house missed the time when I was a little boy. Unlike the vibe I'd gotten from Nick's house, this one hadn't ever been happier than when we'd had the neighborhood kids running in and out, filling the place with gleeful noise.

As much as I hated the way I'd been kicked out of this home, I knew I'd never be able to give it the family and kids it longed for.

Part of me hoped my mother would get sick of living in the burbs and sell it. As a family home in a good school district, it had to be worth enough to support her for a long time. Okay, so it was the house I'd been raised in, but really, nostalgia only took me so far. I'd rather see it in the hands of a new owner than watch her let it slowly deteriorate. Selling would be a win-win for both her and the house.

Then something shifted in the house's mood. The nostalgic vision of my childhood faded away, and negative energy rolled into my body. Tension set my teeth on edge and caused my shoulders to stiffen. I wanted to lash out at someone. Kick those deadbeats out and change the locks so that fucking meth whore couldn't come back.

I dropped my hand from the wall, shocked that my old home could be filled with so much rage. If I didn't get what I came for and leave soon, I was afraid I'd lose it and toss Jerry out on his ass, and I didn't feel like ending up in the slammer with my mom tonight. It was one of the reasons I liked staying in Nick's house so much. She might be a lonely old thing, but she was happy I was there, and she let me be.

"Sorry, House," I whispered. "I'd help if I could."

I righted an overturned chair and dragged it to the closet, where I pushed one of the tiles of the drop ceiling out of the way and felt around until my fingers brushed against an old Teenage Mutant Ninja Turtles lunch box with its handle missing. I pulled it out and sat on the bed. When I was a little kid, my mom started hiding things in the ceiling of my closet. It was an idea she got from my zayde. He hadn't talked much about his life in the Soviet Union under Stalin, but presumably things had been pretty bad, because he'd passed down a heathy dose of fear and mistrust to both of us. He used to have hidey-holes all over the house where he'd secreted away cash, important papers, and anything else he'd thought was too important to leave unprotected. When I was a teen, I used to make a game out of trying to find all his stashes. Likely, the first thing Mom did after the funeral was comb the house from top to bottom searching for her inheritance. Anyway, her hiding spot in the top of my closet was the one place she'd known my zayde wouldn't think to look for drugs. The lunch box was our secret, and I'd been so proud that she trusted me with it that I'd never told on her.

I peeled back the crusty duct tape, barely sticky anymore from the years of use, and lifted the lid. On the top were Mom's important papers—birth certificates, a couple of letters from some long-ago boyfriend. My dad? Who the fuck knew. Beneath, mixed in with my baby teeth and mismatched earrings was the typical paraphernalia, but no drugs. There seldom were any in the box. If Mom had drugs, she'd rather take them than save them.

I spotted the thick roll of cash wrapped neatly with a rubber band, but my eye was drawn to a faded brochure on the bottom. Woodland Acres Rehab Center. The seams in the paper were worn and brittle from being opened and refolded hundreds of time. I knew. I'd been the one who'd slept with it tucked under my pillow when I was a kid, and I'd pulled it out on my more melancholy nights and dreamed of a time when I might have the money to send my mom. She must have found it while searching my room. Why hadn't she thrown it out? Had she ever looked at it and dreamed of getting clean? Maybe. The truth was, when she was sober, she was a reasonable person. Too bad the addiction had such a strong hold of her that I rarely got to see that side.

Leaving the brochure be, I slipped the band off the money roll and counted. Seven hundred and thirty bucks in small denominations. I tried not to think about what my mother had had to do to earn that money as I counted off the five hundred she needed. I also pocketed the thirty bucks so I could offer Nick some gas money and buy myself a sandwich for my trouble.

I was placing the lunch box back in its hidey-hole when the house sent a vibration down my arms. Just then, I heard a gunshot.

Nick.

CHAPTER 6
NICK

Sasha had disappeared down the basement steps, leaving me with the stoner who was laughing inappropriately hard at an episode of *Family Feud*. Seriously, the PG innuendoes just weren't that funny.

What in the hell was I doing in Oak Creek? All I'd wanted when I left Damey's house was to spend some quality time with my pillow. When I'd first driven past Sasha, he'd been walking down the street in his own little world. Did he know that when he walked, he sort of bounced to the music in his head? It had made me wonder what song was going through his mind to make him move that way. I'd gone a couple of blocks past before my curiosity had made me turn around. There was something about the guy that piqued my interest. It was more than just feeling sorry for him. It wasn't pity at all. Sasha had an inner strength that transcended his lot in life. It shone in those steely gray eyes of his.

And how the hell did I know what color his eyes were? *What's wrong with me?* I was acting like I had a crush on the kid. No way. I mean, sure, I wasn't blind. He was a good-looking guy. And sure, I'd been a little attracted to guys before . . . like a hundred years ago when I'd been in high school. But other than whacking off to fantasies of the assistant football coach, I'd never acted on it. I bet if people were honest, they'd all admit to considering what it would be like to bat for the other team. I dug chicks, so it wasn't like I was gay. Maybe I was a little bit bi. Or more likely, it was just the weirdness of having a total stranger living in my construction zone making me curious about him.

Where was he anyway?

I didn't have time to ponder it further, because just then another emaciated guy came stumbling out from the back of the house. His skin glistened with cold sweat, and he was tweaking on something, his movements all jerky and uncontrolled. But that wasn't what had my heart stuttering into a gallop. It was the black gun he waved out in my general direction.

"Vince send you? You got my money?"

I held my hands out as if trying to calm a feral cat. "Hold on, dude. I don't know any Vince. You can put the gun down."

The guy on the couch glanced over. "Put that away, dumbass. He's a friend of Rina's kid."

Dumbass looked back and forth between me and the guy on the couch, which caused his body to sway unsteadily on his feet. "He's got my money, Jerry!"

"He doesn't have your fucking money. You're amped up and hallucinating. Chill out and put the gun down."

Dumbass didn't lower his arm, but started crying instead. Big fat tears streaked down his sunken face.

"Jesus," Jerry groaned, reluctantly getting up off the couch. "Relax, would ya? Give me the gun." He reached for his hand, and Dumbass snapped around to aim directly in Jerry's face.

"Don't touch me."

Jerry stepped back, hands up. "Sorry, man. Just trying to help. Why don't you put the gun down, and we can talk about it?"

Shit was getting too fucking real in here for my comfort. I scanned the situation, searching for an opening to get the gun away. I glanced back toward the kitchen where Sasha had gone through a door down to the basement. What if the guy went after Sasha? The hair on the back of my neck rose, and my protective instincts kicked in. I had to get that gun away before Sasha got hurt.

I needed Dumbass to get distracted with something else. I could overpower him, if only he weren't pointing at Jerry. A moment later, I had an idea. It was a bit childish, but the guy was high enough that it might work. *Here goes nothing.*

"What's that?" I called out, pointing toward the darkened kitchen.

Dumbass swung the gun and pulled the trigger, shattering the window over the kitchen sink.

I lunged forward, tackling the guy to the ground. He smelled of sweat and something acidic, and it did queasy things to my stomach. In a half-hearted attempt to keep the gun from me, he stretched his arms above his head, but I dug my fingers in the soft underside of his wrist and used my other hand to strip the weapon away. He writhed on the floor under me, wild like a caged animal. I didn't want to hurt him, but couldn't reason with him in his inebriated state. I flipped him over, reared back, and punched him square in the jaw twice, knocking him out.

"What the fuck?" Jerry yelled. "Why'd ya have to butt in like that? I had it under control."

I ignored Jerry's ranting and sat back on my heels, panting with adrenaline coursing through my veins. What the hell had I been thinking? Thank fucking god Sasha hadn't come up those basement steps at the wrong moment and stepped right into the path of that bullet.

"Nick!" Sasha called out as he ran upstairs. His face went white as he spotted me kneeling over the unconscious man with the gun in my hand.

"It's okay." I popped the magazine out of the gun and gave everything a quick rub with my shirt to get my prints off. Somewhere outside a dog was losing its shit from the noise. "No one got hurt, but we better go before one of the neighbors calls 911."

Sasha was at my side in an instant, dragging me to my feet. I dropped the gun, and we ran to the truck with Jerry swearing behind us.

The shakes overcame my hands as I tried to shift and buckle my seat belt at the same time, failing miserably at both.

"I got it," Sasha said, buckling me in. "What the hell happened back there?"

I didn't answer, just drove off, heart pounding, intent on putting some distance between us and that gun before my breakdown set in fully. When I spotted a crowded Target parking lot ahead a few minutes later, I swung into a space at the back, slammed the stick into neutral, and stomped on the e-brake. Then I folded my arms over the steering wheel and dropped my head with a shuddering exhale.

We sat listening to the engine idle for a few minutes while my heart slowed to a normal rhythm.

Almost too soft to hear, Sasha whispered, "I'm sorry."

"Not your fault," I muttered.

"Whatever happened back there, I shouldn't have brought you into it."

I rotated my head to the side. Sasha was clearly freaking out. He gnawed on his thumbnail and his eyes were bright with agitation. I reached over to pat his arm, and he stiffened. Rather than pull back, I grasped his forearm.

"Don't you apologize for those pieces of shit. That wasn't you."

"You could've been hurt!"

"But I wasn't. Look at me." I turned his chin so he had no choice but to meet my gaze. In the shadows of the parking lot, his gray eyes appeared black, full of fear and concern, and I felt a sudden tug in my chest. My hand drifted back to my side, the ghostly feel of his soft beard still on my fingertips, and my mouth went dry.

I cleared my throat. "You didn't know those guys, did you?"

He shook his head no.

"Did you suspect there were going to be psychotic tweakers in there waving guns?"

"Not the guns, but with my mother and her friends, the psychotic tweakers were a definite possibility. I didn't think anyone would mess with you though. You look like a guy who can take care of himself."

I paused before asking the next question, hoping Sasha wouldn't take it badly, but I had to ask. "Are you into that shit? The drugs? That wasn't what you went there for tonight, was it?"

He reared back against the door, hurt written all over his face. "Fuck no! I've watched my mom struggle with addiction my whole life. I don't need a PSA to know what happens to a brain on drugs. Never touched the stuff. I don't even drink."

"Sorry. Didn't mean to offend you, but I needed to make sure."

"No, I get it." He sighed. "My mom's in jail. She used her one phone call tonight to ask me to go over there to get her bail money. She doesn't exactly believe in bank accounts."

"What's she in jail for?"

He shrugged. "Who knows? Said they picked her up on an old warrant. Probably prostitution or breaking probation for something. If it was for dealing again, she wouldn't be expecting to get out tomorrow."

Prostitution? I wasn't stupid. I knew that was a thing people did. But no kid should have to think of their mother in that way. I made a mental note to hug my sweet, boring mom next time I saw her.

"I'm sorry, Sasha."

"For what? For my loser mother? Look, I've had this conversation a million times. I know I'm not her, all right? Every school counselor I ever had went to outrageous efforts to drill that into me. But I guess I understand if you look at how I'm living now and ..."

I waited, but he didn't continue. He just stared out the windshield in the direction of the Bed Bath & Beyond, clearly not really seeing anything in front of him.

"Hey, the only thing I see is a guy down on his luck who could use a little help. I don't know your story, but you seem all right to me. Plenty of good people come from shitty parents, so I'm not judging. Hell, I have great parents, and you should've seen me a couple years ago after I lost my first business. It hurts to fall off that ladder toward the American dream. And you, you're just starting out in life. You're nothing but potential. You'll figure it out, and then you'll be on your way."

He was quiet a moment. "Wow, Nick. That was so ... inspirational." Then he broke into a chuckle.

"Fuck off," I replied, giving him a light slap upside the head. "So did you get your mom's cash?"

"Yeah."

"Okay. Then let's deliver it and go home. We both could use some sleep."

CHAPTER 7
SASHA

A huge dumpster sat in the driveway when I got home from the coffee shop the next day. A couple of guys on ladders ripped vines off the side of the house, making huge piles at their feet. Inside, the walls vibrated with anxious psychic energy, raising the hair on my neck. I followed the banging to the kitchen, carefully avoiding walking through the phantom furniture strewn about the rooms. Nick and another guy had respirators on and were beating the hell out of the place with sledgehammers, laughing like little kids on a beach stomping on sandcastles. Remembering what Nick had said about breathing in mold, I lifted the hem of my shirt up over my nose.

The muscles of Nick's arms and back bunched and stretched impressively with each swing, and I was content to just stand there and watch him move. He lifted the heavy hammer and brought it down with a crushing blow onto a countertop, making the whole unit shudder away from the wall. He reached for the broken wood and pulled, tossing the pieces on a debris pile near the door.

"You've got an audience, bro," the other guy called out. He gave me a playful wink before turning back to the hole he was banging in the wall.

Nick rounded in my direction, but before I could say hi, his gaze dropped to my waist and roamed over the exposed skin of my abdomen before raising to meet my eyes. The heat of that look blazed a trail straight up my body. Startled, I dropped the edge of my shirt from my face.

"Uh, you shouldn't be in here without a respirator," Nick cautioned, no longer meeting my gaze. He stepped past me awkwardly, and I followed him to the living room. He bent over a giant toolbox and tossed me a heavy, black mask. "Here you go. I'm leaving this package of disposable masks here too. In an old house like this, it's smart to always wear a mask during demo. I haven't run into any asbestos yet, but that doesn't mean it's not here somewhere."

I nodded and held the mask over the lower half of my face, trying it out.

"You ready to get dirty?" As soon as the words were out of his mouth, the smile faded from his eyes and color flooded his cheeks. "Work, I mean. Ready to work? Um, yeah."

I fought off a grin and put him out of his misery. "I have to change my clothes first."

"Sounds good. Whenever you're ready."

I watched him walk back toward the kitchen, and admired the way his tool belt tugged the waist of his jeans down just right.

Jesus, Sasha. Stop lusting after your new boss. Landlord. Whatever.

I went upstairs to change. Maybe I was lonely. Living on the streets made sex either inconvenient or dangerous, especially if you were gay. Most of my encounters were hurried handjobs in grubby alleys or behind trees in late-night city parks. Shelters were absolutely off limits for sex. Not only did it go against the house rules and the sensibilities of the church volunteers, but coming on to the wrong person was a good way to get bashed. I'd once seen a guy get beaten and stabbed in a communal shower. He'd lived, but had lost a kidney from the knife wound. Kid had been young too. Not even eighteen. Anyway, after that, I'd known enough to play it straight around people whose only option to assert dominance over others was through discrimination and violence.

In my room, I changed into my oldest pair of jeans and a threadbare Nirvana T-shirt from Goodwill. I wound my hair into a knot so it wouldn't get tangled with the respirator's elastic band.

The house was so anxious, it made my teeth buzz. I pressed my palm to the wall, letting the energy course through me. My eyes drifted closed. "This work is a good thing, House," I said in a barely audible whisper. "You've been through changes and updates before. It won't be anything like those assholes in the seventies. I have a feeling you're in good hands with Nick."

Back when I'd first moved in, the house had felt like this too. Once it had realized I was going to stay, it settled. But since Nick bought the place, the mood swings had been worse than a hormonal teenager's. I didn't need the house interfering with my concentration while I worked. There was only one way to dial it back. I opened my mind, letting the energy fill me. I allowed the house to have its say for a moment before I latched on to my inner calm and slowly willed the house down to a light hum.

After a few minutes, my limbs felt both heavy and buzzing with energy. I shook them out and opened and closed my fist a few times. Altering the emotions of a space always did funny things to me. Thankfully, the demolition work would burn off some of the energy I'd absorbed.

When I returned to the kitchen, the guys were tossing large chunks of mildewed wood and plaster out the back door into a wheelbarrow.

"Sasha, this is my brother Damien. Damien, Sasha." Nick waved between us.

Damien slid his hand out of his work glove and shook mine. "Nice to meet you. I've seen you walking around the neighborhood. Figured you lived around here somewhere."

"Hey," I replied, not knowing what else to say.

The family resemblance was there in the eyes, but Damien's hair was longer and lighter than Nick's close-cropped style.

Nick flung another piece of plaster into the wheelbarrow. "Damey, can you dump this? I'm gonna get Sasha started on finishing the cabinets."

"Aye, aye, Capt'n." Damien gave Nick a mock salute and wheeled the rubbish down a makeshift ramp.

Nick handed me a hammer the size of a baseball bat. "All these cabinets need to come out. Uppers and lowers. The sink too. I already unhooked it from the pipes, so no need to be careful about it."

I lifted the hammer, testing its weight in my hands, and then I dug deep to retrieve the old gym class memories from our softball unit. I rotated into a batter's stance with the hammer perched over my shoulder.

"Whoa, hold up there, Slugger. Let me show you how to do that without throwing your back out." Nick sidled up beside me, so close I could smell the light spice of cinnamon gum on his breath. He wrapped his large hand over mine and moved it so it was up close to the head. His heat, even so briefly, made my blood rush.

Nick continued, a wobble entering his voice, betraying some lingering unease that his confident words couldn't contain. "Standing sideways is a good way to take out your shin. You want to face the counter head-on." He placed his hands on my hips and tilted them parallel with the countertop. His firm grip sent a warm shiver down my back. His hands seemed to linger a second longer than they needed to, but maybe that was just my imagination.

I blinked and tried to clear my head. "Oh, okay."

"Now, lift it up over your shoulder like this and push it so it falls. The hammer is heavy enough to generate its own force. You're only guiding it, see?" We took a few practice swings. "You're a pro now. Have at it."

When Nick stepped away, I took a deep breath to clear the cinnamon from my nose. Then I gripped the hammer and unleashed my sexual frustration on the cabinets.

A few hours later, Nick shoved a bottle of water in my hands and said, "Take a break."

The kitchen had been torn down to the studs. In the far wall, there was a new opening for a doorway into the future library.

"I'm developing new respect for people who work construction in July." I was soaked in sweat, and it was only April.

Nick smiled at me over the push broom he was scooting across the floor. "Thanks."

"Where'd your brother go?"

"Over to his place to get cleaned up. He has to work. Friday nights are busy at the bar. They do a really good fish fry." He paused. "Speaking of, if you got something going on tonight and need to bug out early, feel free."

It took me a moment to realize what he was getting at. "Oh . . . no. I don't have any plans."

"What?" He leaned on the broom handle, grinning. "Figured a good-looking guy like you would have a social calendar filled with the ladies."

"Nope." I took a quick sip from my water. "No guys either."

There. It was out now. Not that I was ashamed of being gay or anything. I'd come out of the closet at fourteen, literally. My zayde had been the janitor at my high school, and he'd walked in on me and a kid from my math class making out in the supply closet during lunch period. Although to be honest, I think he'd known before then. But it was different with new people. I never knew when to do the big reveal. I mean, when was the last time a straight guy walked up and blurted out how much he liked fucking women? It wasn't exactly appropriate dinner conversation.

"No guys either? You're bi?"

"No, I'm all the way gay. That a problem?"

Nick made another distracted sweep with his broom. "Course not. I wondered if you leaned that direction anyway when you didn't take to Kelly."

"Kelly? The intern?"

Nick let out a soft laugh. "Yeah, man. She was dealing out some of her best moves, and they were sailing right over your head. She's pretty cute too."

I rolled my eyes. "Then you date her."

He scrunched up his nose. "No way. Not interested. Besides, I'm too old for college girls."

"Yeah, you're ancient. What are you? Fifty? Sixty?"

He lifted the broom over his shoulder and made like he was going to smack me with it. "I'm thirty-nine."

"Dang. That's old."

"Break's over. Get back to work."

We labored until the diminishing sunlight forced us to call it a night. Then Nick produced a couple of cans of soda from a cooler, and we sat on the back steps letting our sweat cool in the evening breeze. I loved sitting outside this time of year, before the mosquitos woke up from their winter slumber and ruined everything.

Nick popped open his can and sipped the foam off the top. "As soon as the demo's done, I'll rewire the house and get some electricity in here for you."

I leaned back on my elbows and tried to pick the stars out from the glare of the city lights. "I'm getting by okay. It's nice now that the water's on."

"I bet." He paused. "Have you given any thought to where you're gonna go when this is done?"

Yes. It was all I'd thought about for days. "Still weighing my options."

"Well, my brother Steven gets back from vacation soon. He might be able to help you find an apartment in your price range. The company he works for has a department that handles rental property management too. That's how I found my place. It's just a studio, but it works for me."

But would I be able to find something in my price range that wouldn't also be so filled with negative energy that I'd want to crawl out of my skin? That wasn't exactly something a realtor could help me with. I decided to change the subject.

"So, no Mrs. Cooper waiting for you at home tonight?" Now, why the hell did I have to ask that? It was none of my business if the guy was married.

Nick smirked. "Not anymore. The former Mrs. Cooper is now living in Shorewood with Husband 2.0 and her brand-new twin baby girls."

"Shit. Sorry."

"Don't be. Sometimes things don't work out. We weren't happy together. Now she has everything she ever wanted."

"And you? Do you have what you want?"

He sighed. "I'll get there someday. You got anyone special you have your eye on?"

"Nah. I don't make the best boyfriend material at present. Not a lot to offer someone."

"I don't know about that. There's more to a guy than just a bank account and a swanky apartment. The right person would see past all that." His eyes met mine, startling me with their intensity. "You're a good guy, Sasha Michaels. Smart. Hardworking. I hear you're plenty talented too. This place is only a pit stop on your incredible journey."

My chest tightened, and my gaze fell to those thick lips. I wanted to worship that mouth for saying such beautiful things to me, and then bite it hard for making me hope.

I stood abruptly. "Guess I haven't met the right person yet, then." Having this conversation with a straight guy was a surefire way to drive me into Unrequited-Crushville. "I'm gonna grab a shower and hit the sheets. See you in the morning."

CHAPTER 8
NICK

For the rest of the weekend, I put the pedal to the metal and channeled all my energy into demoing the house with Sasha and Damien. For a rookie, Sasha really seemed to understand the house and how all the materials fit together to form solid construction. His idea about exposing the brick wall in the dining and living rooms was genius. We'd gotten all the lath & plaster knocked off. All it needed now was a little tuck-pointing, and it'd look fantastic. It was nice having an employee who did everything I asked and caught on quickly.

And we were getting along great. Sasha was easy to talk to, and surprisingly funny. He had a talent for doing celebrity impressions and had me laughing Sunday afternoon with his mock radio show hosted by Christopher Walken and Matthew McConaughey. I swear the guy was magnetized. I found myself constantly glancing over to check on him, as if he were some fascinating, but wild, creature that might disappear any moment. Maybe it was because I knew that as soon as this project was over, I'd likely never see him again. Or maybe he was simply a welcome distraction, something other than the fuck-ton of work on my plate to obsess over. Either way, my body sensed him in the room, and I gravitated to him without consciously thinking about it.

Monday afternoon, Damien and I stripped the old knob-and-tube wiring. He'd agreed to donate his labor to me if I would buy him the Extra Innings TV package so he could record and watch his games. That deal worked fine for me since it meant I could crash at his place and watch them with him on his giant TV of Overcompensation.

I'd just sent Damien off to take a load of scrap metal to the recycling plant when a familiar voice called out, "I go out of town for two weeks and you can't seem to keep yourself out of trouble."

I looked down from the ladder I was perched on to remove a light fixture, to see Steven stood in the doorway of the master bedroom wearing a gray suit and a new tan.

"Aren't you worried about skin cancer?" I asked as I passed the light cover to him so I could climb down.

"Nope. It's a spray tan."

"Like those kids on *Jersey Shore*?"

"Bite me." He waved a leather-bound portfolio at me. "I ran some comps for you, since you didn't bother asking me before you bought this heap."

"I ran my own comps."

"Sure you did. And I redid them the right way. Come here."

Steven leaned on the windowsill, extracted several papers. "The good news is you didn't overpay on the purchase price."

"Ha! Told you I got a deal."

He shot me a glare. "Oh, you got a deal all right. The problem will be making enough money on the sale to cover all the cash you're sinking into it and still eke out a profit. Houses in this part of town just aren't performing well. Check out this place." He stepped up beside me to show me the first listing. "It's five blocks away and similar in size. Completely updated. And see what it sold for?"

Steven circled the bold number with a red pen as if I was too stupid to read an MLS sheet.

"Yeah, but that house is located on a six-lane street and has no yard. Who wants to live there with little kids? Did you see my yard out here? Private, wooded. A mom could send her kids outside and not worry about them having to play Frogger with cars every time their ball gets away."

"True. But this place has a Jacuzzi tub with a marble surround."

I tossed the screwdriver I'd been holding in the general direction of the toolbox and rubbed my stubbled face with my palms. After a moment, I said, "I'm adding a master bath. I can put in a Jacuzzi."

"With what money, Nick? You don't have two nickels to rub together, and I know no bank loaned you this much."

I struggled not to clench my fists. "I found an old retirement account that I forgot I had and cashed it in."

"So you're lying to me now? Is that how you want to play this?"

"Don't worry about the money. I got it covered. I'll just have to massage the budget to incorporate some higher-end finishes."

"You can't massage blood out of a turnip, Nick."

"That doesn't make fucking sense."

Steven stuffed his comps back into his portfolio and stomped to the door. "Whatever you say. When you're ready for a reality check, let me know."

I listened as he descended the stairs and slammed the front door.

"Shit!" I groaned, leaning over with my hands on my knees. I needed cash. At least another ten grand on top of the hundred I'd already borrowed. I'd known that before Steven had showed up with his paperwork. I'd even known how to get the money. That was the bad news.

Steven might be able to loan me the money if I asked after he had a chance to cool off, but I couldn't do it. After my business tanked, I'd lived with him and his partner, Tod, for over a year. Steven had been cool with it, but I knew what a strain having me around had put on his relationship. Tod and I didn't exactly get along. No, I'd sponged off Steven enough for one lifetime. And Damey didn't have any extra cash. Both his house and the bar were mortgaged to the hilt. My parents? They were retired and living on a fixed income. No way. I'd have to borrow and find a way to tack it onto my existing loan.

"Uh, Nick?" Sasha stood in the doorway wearing his black coffee-shop clothes. "I didn't mean to eavesdrop. Got off early. You okay?"

I stood up and tilted my head to the side until my neck popped. "Sorry about that."

"Wanna talk about it?"

"Who me?" I scoffed. "No. I don't know."

"I'm here and willing to listen."

He seemed so damn earnest standing there with those big eyes. Sweet. Like beneath the hard life and the bad mother still existed a pure soul. It made my chest hurt.

What? Am I a fucking poet all of a sudden?

"How much did you hear?" I asked.

"All of it, I think. You're in financial trouble, aren't you?"

"You could say that."

Sasha straightened his shoulders. "Okay. How can I help?"

A humorless chuckle escaped me. This homeless guy wanted to help me out of my financial quagmire? How cute.

"Don't give me that look." Sasha glared. "I might be poor and in a shitty situation myself, but I'm not stupid. I see how you dance around the subject of money every time anyone brings it up. If you won't tell your brothers where you got the money to buy this house, I'm sure it came from a shady place. And hell, I know all about shady places. I also suspect you're in over your head. So if you ever decide you want help getting out of this situation from someone who isn't going to judge, from the one person who actually believes in this project besides you, let me know." He pivoted to leave.

"Hold up," I said before he made it to the door.

Sasha turned, eyebrows raised expectantly. Unless he was secretly sitting on a fortune and dying to invest it in a business that had failed once already, he wouldn't be much help, but I did appreciate the fact that he was the only person who wasn't lecturing me on my stupidity for taking this project on.

"Sorry. I don't mean to be a dick. I'm just . . . stressed."

Sasha gave a small nod.

I hadn't had a decent night's sleep since I'd gotten into this mess. I might be able to get more cash, but paying it back would be another story, and my anxieties were about more than my credit score. My insides twisted at the idea of having to go ask for additional cash.

"Fine, you wanna help? Why don't you get changed and take a ride with me? I gotta go see someone, and you can keep me company on the drive." It was probably a stupid idea to bring him with, but there was something about having Sasha around that settled me. I'd just leave him in the truck while I ran inside.

"I can do that."

Sasha headed to his room, and I shot Damien a quick text letting him know I was running out for a while, and I'd leave him a key in the mailbox.

A few minutes later, Sasha and I climbed into my truck, and I turned north. I popped a stick of cinnamon gum in my mouth and outlined what I needed to do.

"So, I'm gonna need a minimum ten grand, fifteen if I want to do the house up right. I should be able to tack it onto my existing loan. What do you think of this? I'll upgrade the master bath from my original plan. Put in a jetted tub. Maybe custom tile work too. We could even echo the tilework in the downstairs bath. I know a guy who'll give me a good price."

"Sounds good."

"Kitchens and bathrooms sell houses, so I'll have to add a few embellishments to the kitchen as well. Maybe a really cool backsplash. I could buy standard cabinets and add some sleek hardware and molding to make them appear custom."

"There's a stack of old tin ceiling tiles up in the attic that used to be in the kitchen. Maybe you could paint them silver and use them for a backsplash. It would look good, and wouldn't cost you anything except a can of spray paint."

Sasha watched the city go by through a beat-up pair of aviators. I could ask him how he knew the tin ceiling used to be in the kitchen, but the mysterious little shit would probably clam up again.

"Good idea. Keep 'em coming. I need to make as much money on this house as possible. The interest on my loan is ridiculous, and I hope to clear enough profit at the end to secure financing from a reputable lender for my next project."

We turned off Interstate 43 into a neighborhood run down with age and neglect. The beauty of the mature trees contrasted with the boarded-up and condemned buildings. Some had For Lease signs on them. Others looked like the owners must have given up and t urned them over to the crackheads long ago. The area was safe enough during the day, but it wasn't a place you wanted to hang around after dark unless you were a local.

Past the railroad tracks, I pulled the truck into the weedy parking lot of a brick building with windows of blackened glass and bars.

"What is this place?" Sasha asked.

"Diamond's Gym. Owned by Frank Diamond. He's both the unofficial mayor of this neighborhood and a guy you never want to end up on the bad side of."

"So which of his sides are you on right now?"

"I always stay on his good side. Frank currently holds the under-the-table mortgage on our house."

Sasha's eyes widened, and he looked like he wanted to say something, but I opened my door and said, "Stay here and lock the doors. I'll be back in a bit."

I hopped out and headed for the building. Halfway across the lot, Sasha jogged up to my side.

"Thought I told you to stay in the truck."

"And I thought I told you that I'm used to dealing with shady people. No matter how big you are, you shouldn't have to do this yourself. This guy some kind of a mobster?"

I shrugged. "Something like that."

Sasha visibly winced as we stepped through the door. The cavernous room smelled like sweat and stale cigar smoke—the state public-smoking ban didn't apply a guy like Frank, especially in his own place. Fluorescent lights hung on chains over the regulation-size boxing ring, shining down a greenish glow on sparring fighters below. Around the periphery of the large room were various workout stations with punching bags, free weights, and dubiously maintained cardio machines.

A thin African American woman sauntered up with a bored scowl on her face. "Here to box?"

I shook my head. "Not today. Need to see Frank. He around?"

"He's busy."

It was the standard answer. Whether Frank was in the middle of something or not, those who wanted an audience with him would have to wait. "Can you tell him Nick Cooper is here to see him when he's free? I don't mind waiting."

She sniffed and walked off, presumably to pass on the message. I touched Sasha's shoulder and led him beside the middle ring where two welterweights were going at each other, their coach shouting abuse from the ropes.

"Have a seat," I said, sinking down onto an uncomfortable metal chair. "It may be a while."

"You're a boxer?"

I shook my head. "I train in martial arts, just for fitness though. Did a few amateur competitions when I was younger, but after my last concussion, the doc told me I should stop if I didn't want to risk ending up with a scrambled brain. It was through the fights that I met Frank."

"Do you work out here?"

"Nah, this place is a dump. I have a membership over at Roufusport."

Sasha glanced at the lumps of my biceps. "It's working for you. I took you for a football player or something."

"I'm not really into playing team sports. I was one of those rambunctious kids who had too much energy and was always getting under my parents' feet, so my mom tried to enroll me in Little League and soccer. But I hated having to rely on other teammates all the time. I'm pretty competitive and wanted to be in control over whether I was going to win or not. So, one of the coaches recommended martial arts, both as a solo activity and one that would teach me some patience. Thank god Mom enrolled me when she did, otherwise I'd have probably turned into a juvenile delinquent."

"Martial arts, huh?"

"Yeah. Started in a youth jiujitsu program and progressed up the ranks."

In front of us, the coach began waving his arms and shouting, "Above the belt, Lipowski! He wants to father kids someday!"

"What about you?" I asked. "Play any sports in school?"

"No sports. I spent most of my after-school time either with the school band or in my friend Justin's garage pretending we were rock stars."

I leaned in toward him to block out the screaming coach. Maybe if I got Sasha talking, it would take my mind off having to go to Frank with my tail between my legs. "Tell me about your music."

He hitched his leg up on the chair and turned to face me, and the commotion of the gym faded. "What do you want to know?"

"You were in a band. You guys break up or something?"

He sighed. "Yeah, something like that. Long story."

I looked around the gym. "We have time. Frank loves to ice people out. Makes him feel like a big man."

"Okay . . . well . . . my friend Justin and I started playing together when we were in junior high. We both played guitar, and while I was the better singer, Justin was the one with most of the writing talent."

"Thought you said you just did covers."

He shrugged. "When we played college bars we did a lot of covers. People like music they already know and can sing along to. We'd sprinkle in some of our own stuff now and then, and always managed to sell a few demo CDs at our shows."

"So then what?"

Sasha ran his palms over his lightly bearded face and groaned. "I don't know. I guess it's the same story a lot of failed bands have. We started to get a little success around town. That combined with the pressure of college and everything else got to us, and Justin just couldn't handle it."

"Your friend Justin from high school? You were still performing with him?"

"Yeah. When college came around, his parents insisted he go to Marquette for engineering—you know, something practical. The only thing I ever wanted to do was perform. There were better schools out there for music, but I followed Justin anyway. I thought I needed him. People always saw me as the front man because I sang and took the lead on stage, but it was always Justin's band. He chose and arranged the music, wrote the original songs, booked our gigs."

"Kind of like Keith Richards is the leader of the Stones even though Mick's the front man."

"Yeah, I guess."

"Sounds like a lot of responsibility for a young guy. Engineering's no cakewalk. What'd he do? Quit the band?"

Sasha's brow creased as if the memories were still too raw. "It was the end of junior year. I'd gotten a call from the hospital telling me my grandfather had died. Heart attack. And I needed a ride over there, so I went to Justin's place to see if he'd take me. I found him on the floor of his bathroom with a needle in his arm."

"Fuck . . ."

"He was alive and everything, but completely useless. I was so angry and sad and just fucking numb. I couldn't deal with him. So I took his car keys and left. The next day when I brought the car back, we got into it. I mean, he'd been around my deadbeat mom almost as much as I had. He'd been there the night I came home to find her naked on the floor and foaming at the mouth. If anything would turn a person into a teetotaler, that should have done it. But he gave me all these excuses about the pressure he was under with school and the band, and how he only needed something to help him relax."

"Most people who need to relax take a trip to the beach; they don't turn to intravenous drugs."

"No shit. I knew he drank and smoked weed now and then, but if he didn't do it around me, I didn't care. But heroin? I told him I couldn't be anywhere near that."

"He refused to get clean?"

Sasha got a sheepish look on his face. "Don't know. I didn't stick around to find out. The only real parent I ever had had died, and my loser mother was already carting off everything of any value in the house to the pawn shop. I had a partial scholarship, but most of my tuition and expenses were still being paid for by my zayde before he died. I couldn't focus on Justin and whatever bullshit he was trying to feed me. All I could think about was that I needed money and quick. The dorms were gonna be closing soon, and I refused to go back to the house with my mom and her loser friends there. So I asked Justin for my share of the band profits. We'd been saving for a year to buy studio time to record an album, so there should've been over ten grand in the account. Maybe I was so emotionally fried from all the shit with him and my zayde dying, but it took me a few minutes to catch on to the nonsense coming out of Justin's mouth. The money was gone."

"Let me guess . . . the drugs?"

"Probably. I don't know. Looking back on it, he must have been using for a while. But I was so used to following Justin's lead. I trusted him with the band's bank accounts. I should have realized something was up when bars that we'd always played at in the past didn't want us anymore. It got to where I hardly ever saw Justin outside practice. When I'd ask him to hang out, he'd give me excuses about how he was too busy studying and stuff. He'd lost weight and seemed tired, so I figured he was just stressed out. His program was tough, so I didn't question it. I suppose a good friend should have."

"His issues were not your fault, man."

"Not the drugs. I know that, but god, I'm such an asshole."

I stiffened. "Why are you the asshole?"

"Shouldn't a real friend stick around and try to help? Even someone as far gone as my mother deserves help if she wants it, but

I wasn't thinking that way at the time. What if I could have done something for him?"

Without thinking, I reached out to clutch his shoulder, just a brief touch meant to reassure a friend, but it made my chest tighten unexpectedly. I tried not to think about that as I drew my hand away. "You were in no position to do anything for him. Sometimes when life turns to shit, we have to pick and choose our battles based on immediate need. I'd say figuring out a place to live and how to take care of yourself was your priority."

He scoffed out a humorless laugh. "And look what a bang-up job I've done with that."

I opened my mouth to argue, to tell him that he was doing the best he could, and he shouldn't be so hard on himself, but just then the woman called out, "Cooper. Frank'll see you now."

I wiped my sweaty palms on my jeans as I stood. "Stay here."

Again, he ignored me and started to follow.

"Seriously, Sash," I said, putting out a hand to stop him. I dropped my voice low. "These are not the kind of people I want to bring you around. It's not safe."

"No, Nick. I told you. I've had it with letting my people down. If this guy is that bad, you need someone in your corner. Let it be me."

"Can you all deal with your lovers' quarrel later?" the woman asked. "People working around here don't have time to waste waiting on you."

"Whatever," I muttered, addressing them both. I needed to convince Frank to loan me more money without spooking him into calling in the loan early. Rumors about what happened once a person got on his bad side were scary, but surely they were inflated. He was a business man, not the boogey man. Still, maybe bringing Sasha in would be helpful. Another witness couldn't hurt.

As we followed the woman back to Frank's office, I whispered to Sasha, "Don't say anything. I'll do the talking."

CHAPTER 9
SASHA

This wasn't like any gym I'd ever been in. The vibe of the place was all kinds of ominous.

I followed Nick down a dim hall and into a smoke-filled office. My throat tickled with the smoke, and I suppressed the urge to cough. The room was lined with trophy displays and framed photos of different boxers, some autographed. I didn't know enough about boxing to be impressed.

Nick must've thought I was a whiny ass. I hadn't meant to go so maudlin on him with all that Justin crap, but it had been a spectacularly bad day. And it hadn't helped any to go into a building filled with such disturbing emotional energy. I had to keep pinching my thigh to keep myself on the chair. Luckily, the violent tone was more of a need for physical exertion, and not born from anger. I didn't think I could handle that today.

I'd told Nick I'd gotten off work early, but the truth was, after the meager lunch rush, my boss, Bill, had called me into his office to "talk." That's never a good sign, but when he closed the door, I'd known it was serious.

"Sasha, you're a great worker, but ever since Dunkin' Donuts moved in down the street, our sales have tanked. We're overstaffed, and since you have the least seniority, I'm going to have to let you go."

I hadn't listened to whatever else Bill had said. My brain had already been shuffling through my options and thanking the heavens that Nick had come along with his remodeling work when he had. Only instead of using that money for my future apartment fund, I'd have to use it to eat. And anyway, Nick's work was just temporary. *How in the fuck am I ever supposed to get ahead?*

All I'd wanted to do was get home and talk to Nick. I knew the guy was tight on cash, but I'd been hoping to convince him to give me more hours. Even if he didn't have the money to hire me on full-time, he might be willing to recommend me to another contractor. I didn't mind the work, and with my affinity for houses, maybe I could put my talents to use elsewhere too.

I hadn't gotten the chance to ask him, though, because as soon as I got home, I'd discovered Nick was in as much financial trouble as me. Who was this Frank Diamond? Some sort of loan shark? A drug dealer? Whoever he was, I'd have to pull my shit together quick, because I was about to meet him.

Standing inside the door was a guy who looked like he ate steroids for breakfast. He gestured us in without speaking. Inside, a bald toad of a man sat in a large leather chair behind a heavy desk covered in ashtrays and paperwork. Frank Diamond.

He stood and offered his hand. "Nick Cooper! How's it hanging?"

My sight twisted, and I saw a ghostly blood splatter on the wall to the side of Frank's desk. My gaze traveled down to a phantom puddle on the floor. I swallowed the rising bile in my throat and willed myself not to stare at it.

"Hey, Frank, this is my friend, Sasha. He's helping me with the house."

My stomach did a little flutter being introduced as a friend and not just an employee. I was crushing like a thirteen-year-old, and that shit had to stop. I made a silent vow to work on my social life.

"Nice to meet you, Sasha." He examined me through his pop-bottle glasses. "You box?"

"No, sir."

"You have the right physique for it. Muscular, but not bulky. Long reach. You ever want to try it out, you come by and see me. Have a seat, boys."

We sat in the cracked vinyl chairs across the desk, which presumably were purposely low so Frank could glare down his nose at us.

He turned back to Nick. "How's the house coming?"

"Good," Nick replied a little too cheerily. "Demo is done and electrical's almost completed. It's gonna be beautiful."

Frank's protruding eyes drilled Nick, and his benign friendliness turned scary. "Let's just hope it gives us the return on our investment that you projected."

"Don't worry," Nick replied, clearly trying to pretend he wasn't intimidated. "You'll get your money back. And that's what I came to talk to you about. You know these old houses, once you open them up, you find additional damage that drives up the costs."

"What kind of costs are we talking about?"

"Another fifteen grand?"

Frank leaned back in his chair and took a puff on his cigar. "That's a lot of unsecured debt you're adding on top of the hundred I already gave you."

"At the interest you're charging, it's easy profit. At only sixty-five grand, I got a hell of a deal on the place. If I put fifty into it, I can sell it for two eighty or three hundred easy."

"*If* you can sell it."

"You know my brother is one of the best realtors in the city. Trust me, the property will move."

Frank steepled his fingers. "I don't know, Nick. This investment is making me nervous. I don't like being nervous."

"Don't worry about it, Frank. Especially now that Sasha agreed to help. He's got a real vision for houses." Nick kept talking—probably to distract from the strangled sound I'd made in my throat. "He saved me a boatload of money by suggesting this cool accent wall in the downstairs. It's going to really enhance the vintage character of the home, which means we can expect higher offers come sale time."

Frank examined me through narrowed eyes. "You partners now?"

I sat dumbly, not sure of what Nick wanted me to say.

"No, but a couple of weeks ago, I twisted his arm to come work for me. He knows his shit." I just bobbed my head and tried not to look like I was going to swallow my tongue. "So you see, your investment is safe. We plan to not only finish on time, but we'll make the place even more incredible than my original plans."

Frank's expression was unreadable. After a long moment, he said, "If I do this for you, I'll need to renegotiate the terms."

Nick tensed. "Figured as much. What are you thinking?"

"The current deal is twenty percent interest due in twelve weeks. I'll give you the extra money, but the interest on the entire amount goes up to twenty-five percent."

"Still the twelve-week timeline?"

Frank paused, as if trying to make Nick sweat. Finally, he nodded. "You can have your twelve weeks, but that's it. I like you, Nicky. Don't make me have to show you what happens to late payers. I'll have the cash ready for you tomorrow."

Nick stood grinning. "Great! Text me when to come pick it up."

"One more thing."

"Yeah?"

"Next time you see Marty Weise, tell him I wish him a speedy recovery."

A muscle in Nick's jaw ticked. "Marty?" he gulped. Like really for real gulped. "Sure, Frank."

I followed Nick out of the facility, rushing to keep up with his hurried pace. We got into the truck, and Nick pounded the steering wheel with his fist. I kept quiet. Giving him time to process whatever the hell it was that I'd missed in there.

After a moment, Nick turned the ignition and pulled out onto the street. The uncomfortable silence grated on my nerves.

"Who's Marty Weise?"

He squeezed the steering wheel in his fists. "A guy from my gym."

"Is he sick or something?"

He coughed out a humorless laugh. "Nah, he was jumped a few weeks ago by a couple guys with baseball bats. Shattered his jaw, broke both arms, and banged up his spleen beyond repair, so they had to remove it." He stopped for a red light, then shot a glance at me. "I guess that was Frank's way of warning me not to renege on our deal."

"Jesus fuck, Nick! Frank did that to him? What are you doing getting involved with people like that?"

Nick's face was pale, and his jaw ticked. Finally, he said, "Marty was an idiot. I'm sure he made bad loans with unachievable terms. I have a plan to pay back my debt, and once I do, I'm out. I should make enough on this place to have a good down payment for my next project."

I still didn't like it. "Hey, man, I know you need cash, but you don't have to do this if you don't want. We can find another way to get the money."

That made him laugh for real. "Oh, we will? How?"

I didn't need to think about it. We both knew I had no ideas. If I did, I wouldn't be crashing in an abandoned house. "I don't know. You're a smart, capable guy. I trust that you could come up with another option." I paused. "I'll help."

Nick didn't laugh as I'd expected him to. He just sighed and turned the truck toward home.

CHAPTER 10
SASHA

The sun was still up when Nick left. He said he needed to run errands, but I'd seen how agitated he'd been since his meeting with the loan shark, and I didn't blame him for ducking out early. It scared the shit out of me that he was so involved with these people. But then, why did I care what Nick did anyway? Maybe this was a sign that I needed to get over whatever thing I had for him and concentrate on my next plan to crawl out of my homeless hole.

I paced my room, restless and angry. Not having to get up for a job in the morning meant I had no incentive to make it an early night, so I slung my guitar on my back and hopped a bus down to Water Street. Weeknights weren't the best time to go busking, but I could pop into the bars along the strip to see if they were hiring bar backs.

I lucked out. A big Broadway musical was playing at the Marcus Center, which had a modest crowd of dressed-up yuppies milling around the street. I propped open my case on the corner and tossed a couple of bucks in to prime the pump. Then I strummed the strings a few times, reacquainting myself with the feel of my instrument before launching into an acoustic version of "She Moves in her Own Way" by The Kooks. The bouncy beat always worked well to get people's attention. When it was over, I slid right into an Ed Sheeran medley.

At the end of every song, a few people would step forward to drop a dollar or two into my case. I'd smile and nod gratefully, flirtatiously with the women as long as there didn't appear to be a man around.

I was just finishing a raucous version of The Lumineers' "Ho Hey," with the crowd singing along merrily, when someone announced the show starting. A few more dollars dropped in my case as the crowd funneled inside. I scraped the bills out and jammed them into my pockets to count later.

"You're good," said a man standing off to the side.

He casually cruised me, so I gave him a once-over back. He was older than me . . . older than Nick even . . . but he wore his age well. The silver in his hair made his blue eyes bluer. His body was on the thin side, but the designer jeans were tailored to show off his assets. He wasn't as sexy as Nick, but not bad.

"Thanks. You headed in to the show?" I asked, nodding toward the theater.

"No. Just walking down to the brewery for a drink. Care to join me?"

"I don't know . . ."

"Come on. One drink. If you're not into it, you can leave. No hard feelings."

The guy did have amazing eyes. And a nice smile. I slung the guitar case over my shoulder. "Only if you're buying."

He smiled. "Sure thing."

I fell into step beside him, and we walked the block down toward the Water Street Brewery.

"I'm Trevor. You?"

"Sasha."

I shook Trevor's offered hand. His skin had a softness to it that I associated with office workers. Nick's hands would be calloused. *Stop comparing him to Nick!* With effort, I excised Nick from my thoughts and turned my attention to Trevor.

Inside the brewery, a handful of patrons sat at the bar nursing pints of beer. Trevor waved to the bartender and led me to a wooden booth along the back wall. He was obviously a regular.

A pretty waitress took our drink orders, and I was pleased that Trevor ordered a beer instead of some pretentious wine. He looked surprised though when I asked for a regular ice tea.

"You're not underage, are you?" he asked, seeming genuinely worried.

I smiled. "No. I just don't drink. Alcoholism runs in the family, and I don't like to tempt fate."

He relaxed at that, and we made small talk until the drinks arrived. Trevor was a finance guy, but he also served on the board of directors for a local LGBT center. He was new to the dating scene after the recent breakup of a long relationship. He owned a condo here in the city, a cabin in Door County, and a vacation home in Florida.

In order words, he was way out of my league.

I played along anyway. I told him I lived on the south side (truth), attended Marquette (true in the past tense), and that I planned to be a music teacher (not even remotely true anymore). He acted sufficiently interested, and by the time he finished with his second beer, we were getting along rather well. I didn't feel the same spark that I did with Nick, but at least Trevor batted for my team.

"What happened to your arm?" he asked, reaching out to run his fingertip lightly over an ugly purple bruise on my forearm. His concern was touching.

"Oh, nothing. I've been helping someone remodel an old house, and I banged it on something when we were tearing down the walls."

"It doesn't hurt?" he asked. He circled the bruise again with his finger.

"Only if I press on it. Why?"

Trevor drew his hand back and grinned. "Just making sure you're okay."

"If you think this one is bad, you should see the one on my leg."

Trevor ran his fingers up and down the neck of the bottle. "Wanna get out of here?" he asked with the hesitation of a guy out of practice.

Did I? Trevor was nice. Seemed to have his shit together. And the longer I hung out with him, the more attractive he grew. I didn't see anything long-term with him, but there was nothing wrong in showing him a good time.

"Yeah, I'd like that."

Before we left, I made a quick pit stop in the restroom, where I stuck some quarters into a machine and got a condom and a single-serving packet of lube. I didn't care how together this Trevor was, I never went to a party unprepared.

When I returned, Trevor was standing at the bar settling our bill. His jean-covered ass was sexy as hell with him leaning forward on his elbows, his one foot propped up on the rail below. My cock twitched in anticipation. *Fuck my sleeping bag on the floor. Fuck being homeless. Fuck lusting after straight guys.* My pulse increased with the desire to welcome Trevor back to the joys of single life.

I sidled up behind Trevor, placed my hands on his waist, and leaned into his ear. "Want to show me your place?"

His body tightened, and his ass rocked back slightly. I rolled my hips forward, mimicking his response, and letting him feel my growing erection against his crack. I bent my head to place an openmouthed kiss on his neck.

"Fuck yes," he moaned.

I grabbed my guitar and followed him outside, where he hailed a cab. While the driver stashed my guitar in the trunk, I climbed into the back with Trevor. He immediately pulled my mouth to his. The guy could kiss, but he tasted like beer, which I found a little gross. I tried to ignore the taste by concentrating on the sexy spice of his cologne.

We were still making out like teenagers when the cab stopped in front of a high-rise condo building. Trevor paid while I retrieved my guitar.

Inside the elevator, Trevor hit the button for the fifteenth floor, and then shoved me against the wall, sucking on my neck and collarbone. I looked across at the reflection of us in the darkened glass. I pictured Trevor's arms with larger, harder muscles, his back broader, his hair darker. Would Nick be an aggressive lover? *I bet he would be.*

Shit, I had to stop thinking about Nick.

The elevator *ding*ed at our floor, and I followed Trevor down a short hall to his place. He unlocked the door with a brass letter *C* on it, and I stepped into an *Architectural Digest* spread come to life. But before I could admire the open-floor plan or the large leather furniture, a tingle rolled up my spine and made me feel like an animal caught in a trap. I pressed my hand to the entry wall to steady myself and was flooded with dark emotion. The building couldn't be more than ten years old. No way should there be so much negativity accumulated unless something really bad happened here. Many repeated somethings.

Trevor dropped his keys on the entry table and walked over to the open kitchen. "Can I get you a drink?"

"Uh, no." I hoped he didn't hear the hesitation in my voice. Where was all this heaviness coming from? "How long have you lived here?"

"About eight years. My partner and I bought in when it was brand-new."

Lie. There had been no partner. Don't ask me how I knew. My vision flashed, and I saw the same room but different. There appeared to have been some sort of altercation. Tipped over furniture, a shattered glass coffee table, a potted plant flung against the wall leaving a trail of black dirt stuck to the textured drywall. For the millionth time, I wished I could see people in my visions. *What the hell happened here?*

As soon as I thought it, the vision morphed into a different scene, making me momentarily disoriented. Again, same room, more disorder, but focused on the kitchen this time. Broken dishes, a spilled bottle of red wine soaking the rug, the refrigerator door hanging open.

Get out. Get out. Get out.

"Are you okay, Sasha? You've gone pale." Trevor ushered me farther into the room and gestured for me to have a seat on a stool at the breakfast bar.

I shook my head to clear the vision. "Sorry. Low blood sugar."

"No, I'm sorry. We should have ordered food at the bar. I can fix you a chopped salad. I went to the farmers' market yesterday and bought loads of fresh vegetables." Trevor circled the kitchen island and reached for a knife in the butcher's block.

Get out. Get out. Get out.

No fucking way was I eating anything he made for me. I wasn't a hundred percent sure what the danger was yet, but this didn't feel right. The violence in the atmosphere was so different from the boxing club. There, the room had been filled with physical exertion and the pain that came from a hard workout. Here the violence was . . . sexual.

"Um, no. That's okay. I think I might actually be coming down with something. My sister had the flu earlier this week. I better go."

I headed over to the door, but before I could twist the knob, Trevor rushed up behind me and pinned me to it, twisting my bruised arm behind me. "You never mentioned a sister when I asked about your family."

Was he still holding the knife? I couldn't tell. Which meant I couldn't fight back or I'd risk getting shanked. My mind raced back to our conversation in the bar. Shit, he was right. I'd told him I was an only child. My heart was speeding, but if I wanted to get out of here, I had to play it cool.

"Hey, ease up, man. She's a stepsister. Less than that actually. The daughter of my mom's boyfriend. But we grew up together off and on."

He relaxed enough for me to turn sideways, but I still couldn't see if he held a knife in his right hand. The blue eyes that seemed so warm before had turned hard as steel. They were the eyes of a predator. "I don't like to be lied to."

I gave him what I hoped was a natural-looking smile. "I didn't lie," I lied. "We're not technically related, so I didn't think to mention her."

Get out. Get out. Get out.

Trevor dragged his visible hand along the side of my face. "Good. You do look pale though. Maybe I should run you a bath. You can relax while I fix you something to eat." He reached behind me to the dead bolt and turned the lock. The *click* of the tumbler set my teeth on edge. A feverish heat swept over me, leaving me stuck somewhere in the middle of fight and flight.

Trevor hustled me deeper into the condo, through a dark master bedroom and into a huge bathroom with a tub the size of a small swimming pool.

My vision rolled into another horrific scene. Worse this time. Handcuffs dangled from an exposed pipe in the shower, a leather flogger lay on the floor, and sexual aggression filled the air. A little kink play was one thing, but this . . . Nothing about it felt like consensual games.

Get out. Get out. Get out.

Trevor turned the water on, testing the temperature with his hand, and then squirted scented bath oil in.

"Now let's get you undressed."

Still half-disoriented from the onslaught of vibes, I turned away from his reaching hands and leaned on the vanity counter. That was when my gaze fell on the ghost of a strange object on the counter. There was a thin metal rod attached by an electrical cord to a controller. I squinted through the fog of the vision to read the writing on the remote. *Fetish World's Electro Shock Penis Sound.* Unable to hold back any longer, my gut turned, sending the remains of my ice tea splattering into the basin.

"Oh, honey! You really aren't feeling well, are you? I'll take care of this."

Trevor leaned around me to turn the sink tap on and used the glass beside his tooth brush to splash water over the mess. Then, he set a cap-full of mouthwash for me on the counter. My legs shook with disgust and fear. I half sat and half fell onto the edge of the tub.

I didn't know if it was the puke or what, but Trevor eased up on the lechery. "Let me get you some water."

His footsteps trailed away. Once I was reasonably certain he was gone, I let out a shuddering breath and frantically ran through my options. Was I strong enough to fight the guy off and get out of here? Not if he had a knife, and not with me feeling as shaky as I was. Even if I could get to a window or balcony, we were too high up for me to go anywhere.

Frustrated, I drew myself up to the counter and lifted the blue mouthwash. I swished and spit, to get rid of the vomit taste in my mouth. *What in the hell am I going to do?* I still had my phone. I pulled it out and started to dial 911, but stopped. What would I tell the cops? That I'd picked up a guy in a bar and now was getting visions of blood splattered around his apartment? Shit.

I dialed Nick instead and sat back down on the edge of the tub.

He picked up on the second ring. "Hey."

"Hey," I whispered. "I need help."

"Is there a problem at the house?"

"I'm not at home. Look, I don't have a lot of time here. I'm sort of trapped in this creepy guy's condo, and I'm scared. Can you come get me?"

There was rustling over the line, and I hoped it was Nick springing to action. "Where are you?"

I gave him the address that Trevor had given the cabbie. "Fifteenth floor, apartment C."

"Is there a doorman?" The ignition of his truck sounded in the background.

I knelt down in front of the vanity to check under the sink for a weapon of some sort. Nothing but a stack of towels and a couple of spare rolls of toilet paper. "No, but the front doors are locked. Think you can get one of the other residents to buzz you in?"

"They damn well better let me in. Does he have a gun?"

"Don't know. All I saw was a knife, but he doesn't know I'm onto him yet. I told him I wanted to leave, but he wouldn't let me go. And now I'm feeling sick—"

"Sasha? Can your stomach handle pasta?" called Trevor. I had just enough time to stash the phone in my pocket before he stepped into the bathroom. "Oh, honey, why are you on the floor?"

"Sorry," I said, letting him help me to my feet. "I got woozy."

He started peeling my shirt from me. "You'll feel better once you've had a soak in the tub and some food in you." I raised my arms so he could yank the T-shirt off. "Fuck, Sasha, you are exquisite." He ran his too-soft palms over my chest. "Your skin is like velvet. And you're unmarked . . ."

He leaned in to nuzzle my neck. I had to grip the edge of the sink to keep from pushing him away. *Unmarked*? Was he talking about tattoos or something? I remembered his fascination with my bruise, and I shuddered.

"Um, what was that about pasta?" I asked, hoping to get him to give me space and buy time for Nick to get here.

Trevor drew back, still clutching my hips. "Oh, I'm sorry. I shouldn't be all over you when you're not feeling well. Let's get some food in you, and I bet you'll perk right up. I have tortellini in the freezer, and I can heat up sauce. Sound good?"

I nodded and tried my best to look like the thought of eating didn't make me want to hurl. "Yeah. Sure."

Trevor stepped away. "Need help getting undressed?"

"No. I'm good."

"Okay, then. Enjoy your bath." He kissed me on the mouth before leaving. "Oh, and leave the door open so I can hear you if you need me."

When his steps retreated, I snatched the phone out again. "Still there?"

"Yes," Nick hissed.

"What should I do?"

"Play along with him. I'll be there in less than ten. Don't hang up the phone. I want to be able to hear what's going on."

"Okay."

"And Sasha?"

"Yeah?"

"Don't let that fucking asshole touch you."

I placed the phone on the counter and set my T-shirt over it. Hopefully the material would be thin enough for Nick to hear. I finished checking the cabinets and the linen closet for anything I might be able to use to protect myself. I picked up a can of hair spray and thought about squirting it in Trevor's eyes. Something like a spark lit up my mind as I envisioned how deliciously painful that would be. His eyes would turn red with the sting, tears would pour down his face as his body attempted to flush the chemicals away.

I dropped the can on the floor and squeezed my eyes tight. No, I couldn't let the emotions of the condo overcome me. Trevor might be an aggressive jerk, but I didn't want to hurt anyone. I dredged up an old memory of the dog I'd had when I was eight. Sparky. He was an old stray lab that had followed me home from the playground, and even though I'd only had him for a few months before he died, that dog was the closest I'd ever come to being in love. I focused on the feeling of lying in my bed next to him on a Sunday morning. Stroking his fur. Slowly, the urge to hurt Trevor subsided. For now. If I didn't get out of here, it'd be back.

I heard footsteps in the hall, but couldn't tell if they were headed my way. Shit. He'd be pissed if he had to tell me to get in the tub again. Nick had told me to play along, but taking my clothes off would make me more vulnerable. I had to hope he wouldn't take too long.

Not knowing what else to do, I shucked the rest of my clothes off and climbed into the water. It was a little too hot for my taste, and the smelly bath oil coated my skin with slippery slime. I shut the tap off. I wished Trevor would have given me some bubbles. I hadn't had a bubble bath since I was seven years old, but at least they would shield my nakedness.

A few minutes later, Trevor returned with a glass of red wine. Seeing me sitting cross-legged in the middle of the giant tub, he shook his head. "You really don't know how to relax, do you? Come here. Lean back. That's it."

He knelt down on a folded towel and stroked my hair. "Why don't you dunk your head?"

"I don't want to get that oil in my hair."

"Ah, I bet these curls are temperamental."

I nodded and tried not to cringe at his touch. The desire to snap his fingers off swelled in me, and I focused my thoughts on old Sparky again.

Trevor raked his gaze over my naked form now stretched out the full length of the tub. The predatory look was back, and I had to force myself to stay still and allow the violation of his stare.

"Damn, Sasha, your body is a dream. I wish I could get in there with you. Maybe slowing down for food is a good idea though. A quick fuck isn't going to be enough."

"How's dinner coming?" I asked, not really caring, but needing to get him off the subject of sex.

"It'll be about twenty minutes yet. Long enough for you to have a nice soak." He reached in to give my flaccid dick a stroke. I twisted out of his grasp, and he leveled a glare at me. "I thought you liked me?"

"Sorry. I just . . . I need some time to get back in the mood."

He removed his hand and wiped it on the towel. "Okay. After dinner, then." He stood and left the glass of red wine on the side of the tub. "I know you said you don't drink, but one glass of merlot will help settle your nerves. I'm going to check on dinner."

Once he was gone, I slumped back in the tub again. "Fuck, Nick. Hurry up."

CHAPTER 11
NICK

Getting into the building had been easy. I'd pressed buttons until a tinny voice had answered through the speaker.

"Yeah?"

"Police," I announced. "Buzz us in."

Either my gruff voice had been convincing, or the person on the other end of the line really hadn't given a shit who they let into their building, because the door buzzed right away.

When I reached the fifteenth floor, I rapped on the door of apartment C. I stood there with my toolbox in hand and what hopefully was a bored expression on my face. Inside, I was seething. The thought of someone hurting Sasha had me wanting to claw out of my own skin to get at them. Him being in trouble had me bordering on a rage that I hadn't known I had in me. How could anyone want to harm Sasha? He was kind and thoughtful and smart. It made me sick that someone wanted to hurt him. There was something about the guy that had my protective instincts jacked up to ten, and I wasn't leaving here without him, even if I had to take this door off its hinges. I took a calming breath and knocked again.

There was movement at the peephole, then a gray-haired guy cracked the door open, leaving the chain in place. "Yes?" he asked, clearly irritated.

"Maintenance. Unit below yours is getting water raining from the ceiling. You busted a pipe in your bathroom."

He looked me over, and I prayed he wouldn't realize no working plumber would ever show up to a job wearing workout clothes and gym shoes.

"There's no water in my bathroom. I was just in there."

"Of course not. That's because it's running down inside your walls and spraying all over your neighbor's unit. If you don't let me in to fix it now, you're going to have to explain the liability claim to your insurance company."

The man slammed the door shut and removed the chain. "Fine. Come in. But give me a minute. I have a guest in there bathing."

I resisted the urge to deck the guy and go retrieve Sasha myself. Barely. "Hurry up. I need to get to that pipe."

The guy strode to the back of the unit, obviously pissed off. Nothing in the place appeared to be out of order. The pot on the stove was going to boil over any minute, but I didn't care enough to turn the burner down for him. I fished my phone out of my pocket and listened through the still-open line while the man hustled Sasha out of the tub.

"No need to get dressed. Just put my robe on."

A fresh wave of adrenaline flooded my veins, and I squeezed the handle of the toolbox. After decking this perv, I wanted to sling Sasha over my shoulder and cart him out of here.

The guy returned with Sasha, who was wearing a paisley bathrobe. He carried his clothes in a tight bundle against his chest. Seeing he was unharmed, I let out a sigh of relief.

"That all your stuff?" I asked Sasha.

He nodded. "And my guitar's by the door."

"Get it, and head to the elevator." I set my toolbox on the floor and made a show of cracking my knuckles. Sasha did as he was told, and I stood like a sentry, protecting his path to the elevator.

"Wait a minute," the old guy said. "What's going on here? I thought you said there was a leak?"

I didn't say anything, just stared at him with eyes narrowed to slits.

"Sasha, wait—" As the guy tried to get by me, I grabbed his shirt collar and slammed him against the wall, the force knocking a framed picture askew.

"The next time a guy tells you he wants to leave, you sure as fuck better hold the door open for him. Got it?"

The momentary confused expression cleared, leaving behind eyes filled with hate. "He called his boyfriend? Christ! The kid came on to me!"

My jaw clenched at the thought of Sasha wanting this creep. "And he changed his mind. Simple as that. If I ever see you within a hundred feet of him again, you won't be conscious long enough to regret it."

I shoved the guy toward the sofa, where he landed across the back in an ungraceful heap. Then I picked up my toolbox and strode out the door to where Sasha stood holding the elevator. I jabbed the ground-level button over and over until the doors closed. After we descended a couple of floors, I pressed the Stop button, causing an alarm to sound.

"Get dressed," I said, careful not to look anywhere but the floor so I wouldn't inadvertently see the reflection of Sasha's nakedness. I tightened my fists to keep my hands from trembling. Now that we were out of that apartment, my conflicted emotions had me wanting to either lash out at him for being so stupid or hug the shit out of him.

"Done," Sasha said, and the contrite tone ripped through my anger and made my chest constrict. I pushed the button to start the descent again, then whirled on Sasha.

"Jesus, Sasha, are you okay? He didn't hurt you?"

"I'm fine, but he scared the shit out of me."

"What were you doing with a guy like that?"

"I . . . Well . . . he seemed nice."

"If you want to hang out with someone nice, don't go home with a stranger. Call a friend or something. Or, hell, call me."

Sasha's lip twitched. "Uh, Nick. I don't think you're into my way of being nice."

"Don't assume shit about me."

I stepped forward, tangled my fingers in those loose curls, and smashed my mouth on his. He gasped, and I took full advantage by licking in along his tongue. What started out hard and frustrated and scared, downshifted into tender as he began to kiss me back. He tasted like cigarettes and man. Who knew that was such a heady combination? The hair of Sasha's patchy beard felt strange on my face, so that even with my eyes closed, I knew who I was kissing. And fuck, it was hot.

Sasha's essence filled me and made my heart race. It had only been a week since we met, but I felt like I'd been waiting for this kiss my whole life.

In the back of my mind, I registered the elevator doors opening on the empty lobby and then closing again. I didn't care. I was too busy taking all my fear and worry out on Sasha's mouth, sucking and biting. Sasha gave as good as he got, reaching around to my ass and drawing our bodies close, sending delicious friction to my cock. I gave an experimental pump of my hips, and Sasha groaned.

"Jesus, Nick."

I gazed into his molten eyes, still clutching his tangly curls.

"Don't freak out on me, Nick."

"Not freaking out," I murmured. "Just looking." And I wasn't freaking out, not yet. Maybe not ever. If I were being honest with myself, I'd half wanted him since that first day of demo. I'd feared the image of him leaning against that doorframe holding his shirt up like an invitation was permanently burned onto my retinas. And yesterday when he'd been carrying heavy scraps of wood out to the trash, I hadn't been able to tear my gaze from his lean arm muscles all corded and strained.

My reaction to him had had my brain spinning in a thousand directions. At first, I'd chalked it up to not having dated anyone in while. But why this guy? Why now? Maybe it was that he was the only person who truly believed I'd be able to pull off this risk with the house. I loved it that he was as excited as me when talking about my plans to restore the place. Could this attraction simply be my need for someone to trust in me?

I ran the side of my thumb along his jaw.

Sasha was . . . beautiful, I guessed. Lips kiss-swollen. Eyes bright with lust. Was it weird to think that about another guy? So what if it was? I wanted . . . I didn't know what I wanted. Just him. I wanted him. And I wasn't sure what to do with that.

The elevator doors opened to the lobby again, this time revealing an old lady and her dog wanting to get on. I reached for the toolbox at my feet and stepped out, and Sasha followed, guitar case strapped to his back. I grinned as he rolled up the bathrobe and chucked it behind a potted fern. Good. I didn't want that prissy thing in my truck.

My truck sat in the parking lot at an angle. I hadn't even attempted to stop between the lines. Sasha didn't comment, just tossed his guitar in the back and hopped into the cab. It took three stabs to get the key into the ignition. I pulled out of the parking lot and turned in a random direction.

An uncomfortable silence settled between us, so thick it could have fogged the windshield. We were both stuck in our heads, but I couldn't tell if Sasha was thinking about that incredible elevator kiss like I was or about the creepy apartment.

Okay, so maybe I was freaking out a little. Who wouldn't? I kissed a guy! And, truth be told, I'd liked it.

I wasn't completely ignorant about these kinds of things. I grew up in a house with Steven, who was the only out-and-proud kid in our high school. And our parents were actual card-carrying members of PFLAG. Damey and I'd had the most liberal sex education of any of our friends, and while it had been embarrassing to talk with our parents about it at the time, I now knew enough to understand that sexuality was more complex than just gay and straight. I thought that was why when I had felt attraction to guys in the past, it hadn't sent me into some weird spiral where I questioned everything about myself. I'd just figured if I never acted on it, that meant I was straight.

The hard-on in my pants would disagree.

CHAPTER 12
SASHA

I woke in my makeshift bed when the first rays of dawn slanted through the curtainless windows. My lips curled into a lazy smile at the memory of Nick kissing me in the elevator the night before. Damn, it made me half-hard just thinking about it. I'd been hoping for a repeat when he'd dropped me off last night, but no. He'd only muttered something about seeing me tomorrow before he'd hightailed it out of here.

I couldn't blame Nick for being trippy over the whole thing. This one time my band had been performing in a bar near school, and afterward some drunk chick, who'd been all upset about her boyfriend, had planted a sloppy, lipstick-flavored kiss on me. Shock had kept me from pulling away instantly. I'd stood there, not knowing how to get her off me without upsetting her further. When her tongue had begun to lick at the seam of my lips, trying to get them to open for her, I'd taken that as my cue to gently push her away. It'd been horrifying and slightly nauseating at the time. And then for the next week, it would hit me at odd times that a *woman* had kissed me.

I wondered how Nick felt. I had assumed he was straight, what with the ex-wife and everything, but had I misjudged? He'd been the initiator and an enthusiastic participant. Very enthusiastic.

As awesome as that kiss had been, I knew better than to hope for a repeat. Nick probably regretted it already. What if things were strange between us now? What if he didn't want to be friends anymore? Better work on my exit strategy.

I groaned as I stood, my joints creaking and popping. Sleeping on the floor was getting old, despite the two sleeping bags piled beneath me for padding. I needed a bed. But before a bed, I needed a place to call home, even if it was only a rented room somewhere. Nick and whoever he could scare up for a crew wouldn't arrive for another few hours, but when they did, I'd have to tell him about getting laid off from the coffee shop. Shit, if he didn't think I was a loser already, he would then.

I picked up my discarded jeans from the floor and rooted around until I found the small roll of cash I'd made busking last night. Thirty-eight bucks. Not bad for an hour's work on a Monday night. I did some mental math. Adding this to what I had in my stash, my last paycheck, and the two weeks' severance pay that Bill had promised me, brought my total worth to just under eight hundred dollars. Enough to rent a small roach-infested room down at the Michigan Inn, a pay-by-the-week, gentlemen-only boarding house for derelicts and drunks. It was owned by a local nonprofit, and a hundred bucks a week got you a room decorated in the worst of the seventies that smelled like stale booze. Each floor had a shared restroom with large community showers. Not a place a gay boy like me would feel comfortable dropping the soap. As much as the thought of living there disgusted me, it would be better than sleeping under an overpass. And if I hoped to get in, I'd have to get my name on the waiting list today.

It was too early to call, so I went about showering and getting ready for the day. Back in my room, I sniffed the jeans that I was starting to think of as my work jeans since laboring on the house had made them so holey that they weren't much good for anything else. They were dirty, but hadn't quite crossed the point where they could stand up on their own, so I could get one more wear out of them. I added laundry to my list of tasks to do later.

I wandered the house chewing a dry granola bar, trying to find something to work on until Nick got there. Without someone to give me directions, I was still sort of useless on a jobsite. And thanks to his insisting we clean everything up at the end of every workday, there wasn't even stuff for me to straighten. Well, there was one thing I could do.

I walked to the skeleton kitchen and took a cross-legged seat on the floor. The morning sun streamed in the eastern window, illuminating the fairylike dust motes in the air. Resting my fingertips on the bare hardwood planks, I opened my mind to the rhythm of the house, forming a mental bond of perfect communion.

The house had the same slightly wounded feel that she'd had since Nick began working on her, but she wasn't as anxious as last week. There was an air of acceptance in the vibrations, as if the house was finally giving its permission for the rehab. I knew from past experiences that a home could make things difficult for occupants if it wasn't happy. I'd seen wood railings that dry rotted before their time, floor boards that buckled under the slightest exposure to moisture, window frames that sprung seemingly spontaneous leaks. Keeping this house calm and happy would go a long way toward the success of the renovation.

In my mind, I visualized and meditated on each room individually, sending soothing and positive thoughts as I did. The house loved it when I did this, so much so it almost purred under my ministrations.

When my thoughts reached the south-facing bedroom, vibrations niggled in my mind. I slipped deeper into the meditative state to investigate. In my mind's eye, I could see a red sore spot on the rear wall of the closet near the floor. It wasn't clear what the problem was, but there was definitely something going on there. *Show me,* I insisted, but only that glowy red came through.

"Sasha!"

The voice startled me back to myself. I opened my eyes to see Nick leaning in the doorway, arms crossed and concern on his face.

"Sorry," I said, shaking off the house connection. "What?"

"I asked what you're doing. Why aren't you at the coffee shop?"

"No work today. Hey, come with me a sec. Bring your crowbar." I needed to check out that closet to see what the house was trying to show me.

Nick fetched the crowbar from his toolbox and followed me up the steps to the south bedroom. I flung open the closet door and knelt, running my hand over the nubby plaster of the wall. Nothing felt odd or out of place with the wall itself, but that same sore vibe ran up my arm when my fingertips grazed the spot.

"You need to open up this wall."

"Why? I can't go around opening walls. I can't afford to re-drywall the whole place."

"Trust me, all right? Open the wall from here to about here. If you don't find anything, I'll pay to patch it myself."

Nick stared down at me with one eyebrow popped up in curiosity. Finally, he sighed and said, "Move out of the way."

I stood back and watched, curious myself, as he knocked a hole in the wall and broke through the wooden lath. Nick used the flashlight app on his phone to peer in. After a moment, he turned and gave me an incredulous stare.

"How'd you know?" he demanded.

I swallowed hard. "Know what?"

"About the broken drain pipe."

I didn't know what to say, and it must have shown on my face, because Nick grasped my wrist and drew me down to look for myself. I peered into the hole at the underside of the bathtub in the next-door bathroom. Nick's phone shone light on the pipe running out of the bottom. Sure enough, there was a jagged, rust hole the size of a quarter in the galvanized metal.

"First time someone took a bath or shower in there, the entire downstairs would've flooded."

"Uh, sorry."

"Sorry? I had no plans to open up this wall, Sasha. It'll cost me a couple hundred dollars to switch out this pipe, but that sure as shit is better than the thousands of dollars a leak would've caused."

I grinned stupidly, thankful to the house for warning me of the problem. When Nick frowned at me though, my grin faded.

"So I'll ask you again, and you better tell me the truth: How did you know?"

I moved to stand, but his hand clutched my forearm, keeping me in place. My brain scanned through my mental rolodex of plausible excuses, but blanked.

"Um . . . lucky guess?" It came out as a question, to which Nick shook his head, clearly not buying it. "Look, I have to get going. I have an appointment this morning."

"This isn't over," he warned. "We're gonna talk about this."

"Yeah," I replied, staring at him pointedly. "We have a lot to talk about, don't we?"

He let go of my arm and turned his gaze back to the hole in the wall, not meeting my eyes. "Fine. We'll talk later. About everything."

I walked across to my bedroom, gathered my dirty clothes up into a ball, and stuffed them into a duffel. I usually took my guitar to the laundromat with me, but not today. The neighborhood folks doing their laundry appreciated the free entertainment, but I had other errands to run and didn't want to mess with dragging the big case around.

I felt a little guilty about using last night's awkwardness to make my escape, but dang, I needed some time to figure out what I was going to tell him. The only person who'd really known about my visions had been my zayde. He'd used to tell me stories about his home village in western Russia, what is now Belarus. He'd been raised on the folklore and superstitions of the old country. A place where the witchlike descendants of the Baba Yaga were thought of as a fact of life. Tales of people who had visions and could read minds were common. When I'd gone to him as a child to tell him about the strange emotions and visions I'd been having, he'd set me on his lap and assured me I was fine. Then he'd told me of his sister, who used to visit people's dreams, and of his mother, who'd claimed to read people's emotions. He encouraged me to test the limits of my abilities and see what they could do. He'd explained to me that it was a hereditary gift, and I should nurture it. But at the same time, I should guard it, because many people would not believe what they couldn't see.

I didn't know Nick well enough to guess at his reaction if I told him the truth.

The laundromat down on National was empty apart from the ever-present old lady who owned the place sitting at the counter. Behind her was a row of single-use detergent boxes and tiny fabric softener bottles. She looked up from the zipper she was sewing into a pair of pants and grunted.

I dropped a couple of bucks on the counter. "Can I have a box of detergent please?"

She grabbed a red box from the shelf behind her, slapped it on the counter, and tossed my money into the till as if it were dirty or something. She was always like this. If there were any other laundromat within a mile of this place, I'd take my business elsewhere.

I found an empty machine as far from her as possible and dumped my clothes in, not bothering to sort. Then I slipped my jeans off and tossed them in as well. If anyone came in and took issue with my boxers, they could shove it.

While I waited for my clothes to wash and tumble dry, I used the several-years-old phonebook, which was chained to the broken pay phone on the wall, to look up numbers. First, I called the Michigan Inn. The man who answered wasn't too optimistic about me getting a room before the end of summer, but I gave him my name for the wait list anyway. If Nick sold the house and I had to sleep under a bridge for a while, at least the weather would be reasonably nice.

Next, I phoned around to the various employment agencies where I had résumés on file to ask for an update on new jobs. Each harried and hurried person I spoke to directed me to the job boards on their websites. Like I had a computer.

When the dryer's buzzer rang, I slipped into my warm jeans and folded the rest of my clothes into the bag. If I was going to continue working with Nick, I needed a few more sets of work clothes. With my bag slung over my shoulder, I walked five blocks south to the Dig & Save Outlet. The place was filled with giant bins of wrinkly, unsorted clothes, and ten bucks would buy you whatever you could fit into a brown paper bag. T-shirts were easy to find, and I snagged a few of them, but it took an hour of hunting before I found two pairs of jeans in my size. I needed underwear too, but I'd rather go commando than buy someone's used boxers. I'd have to remember to stop by Walmart.

I walked out of the store holding my bag of musty-smelling clothes. I would have to wash them before they could be worn, but a trip back to the laundromat just didn't appeal. Instead, I ducked into a neighborhood grocery and bought some store-brand detergent so I could wash them by hand in the sink at home.

I rounded the corner to the house and slowed at the sight of a strange minivan parked in the driveway behind Nick's truck. Stuck to the back of the car was a weathered rainbow bumper sticker that read, *I'm an LGBT ally. I use social media. And I vote!*

What the hell?

I opened the door and saw Nick talking with a tiny lady with dyed black hair. When they turned toward me, I was struck by the resemblance of their eyes.

"Well, hello, dear. You must be Sasha." She shot a sideways glance at Nick. "*Damien* has told me so much about you. Now, set that down." She rustled my shopping bag from my arms, wrinkled her nose at the stench, and set it on the floor beside her luggage-sized purse. "Look how skinny you are! Nick, the least you could do is feed him. Come now. Sasha. I brought sandwiches. Let me fix you lunch."

Nick smiled apologetically as his mom half dragged me into the kitchen, where a large cooler sat. She reached in and lifted out an individual-sized bottle of milk and a cellophane-wrapped ham sandwich, both of which she shoved into my hands.

"Now, I've got string cheese, baby carrots, and grapes in here." She held up a gallon-sized Ziploc bag to show me. "And if you'd like dessert later, there's homemade chocolate mousse in the Tupperware."

"I'll take some of that," Nick said, stepping forward.

His mother smacked his hand. "Oh, no, you won't. You have plenty of food. Poor Sasha doesn't even have a kitchen to cook in." Turning to me she said, "Now, I have a pot roast in the Crock-Pot at home. You're invited to our place for dinner tonight. No arguments," she ordered when I opened my mouth. "Nick, have him there by six thirty. Don't be late. Have a nice day, boys."

And with that, the little woman breezed out the door. A moment later, her van started and she drove away.

I turned to Nick, still holding the milk and sandwich in my hand. "She's scary."

"Don't I know it," he groaned, scrubbing his hand over his shorn hair. "Oh, that was my mom."

"So I gathered."

"She can be a little . . . excitable."

"Ya think?"

Nick chuckled. "You gonna eat that?"

"I'm afraid not to. I'll share the mousse with you, though."

"Sweet."

We stood in the kitchen and ate in silence. The sandwich was good, and when I checked out the cooler, I saw three more. It touched me that Nick's mom cared whether I ate or not. My own mother didn't give a rat's ass about my well-being. Hell, she'd never even thanked me for bringing her bail money.

I never had been the type to be jealous of my friends' parents. I'd known my shitty mom wasn't my fault, and my zayde had always taken good care of me. Still, it surprised me when parents extended their kindness to me.

After lunch, Nick removed the interior doors and stacked them in the driveway. There, he set me to work stripping the paint from them while he left to meet Kelly at Home Depot. The plan was to refinish all the original woodwork with a natural stain. Stripping decades of layered paint was smelly work, but easy enough, and it allowed me a chance to think. The daydreaming must have worked, because the wisp of a melody floated into my mind. Before I lost it, I retrieved a notebook from my room and wrote it down with a rudimentary treble clef with five lines extending out to place the notes. I kept the notebook beside me for the rest of the afternoon, jotting notes on lyrics as I worked.

It felt good to write again, even though I didn't have Justin with me to help. We'd made a pretty good composing team back in the day. I was good at dreaming up odd bits of melodies and lyrics, and he had fleshed out the harmonies and arranged the music for the various instruments. Basically turning my amateur idea into a real song. For the millionth time, I thought about forming a new band. And for the millionth time, I dismissed the idea. I needed to be practical and focus on surviving. Making music wasn't something you did for the money.

With another door finished, I set it against the garage to dry and began prepping one to strip, when I misjudged my footing and knocked the can of turpentine, splashing my notebook. I could only watch as the liquid blurred the new song beyond all recognition.

Fuck my life.

CHAPTER 13
NICK

"Shit," I muttered, seeing both of my brothers' vehicles parked outside my childhood home.

"What's wrong?" Sasha asked from the passenger seat. The whole way over I'd been acutely aware of his presence. It was unnerving, and my reaction to him was frustrating the hell out of me. For his part, Sasha didn't seem the least bit nervous around me. But then, maybe that was because he was all pale and shit with the idea of seeing my mom again.

"Nothing. Just that my brothers are here, which means Mom's making some kind of family occasion out of this."

Sasha groaned. "Maybe this is a bad idea."

I unbuckled my seat belt and opened the truck door. "Oh, for sure it's a bad idea. But I don't think either of us want to suffer the punishment if we bail. Promise me that you won't hold my family against me, okay?"

"I don't really do so well in large groups of people," he said warily.

"No worries, man. They're decent . . . well except Steven's boyfriend, Tod. He's a tool, but he'll probably go to great lengths to ignore both of us, so it'll be fine."

We walked in the front door and were met with the usual cacophony of my family. Dad and Damien were sitting in front of the TV in the living room arguing over the Brewers/Cubs game. Damey had decided as a kid to support Chicago sports teams. In the beginning he had done it to be contrary to our die-hard Wisconsin dad, but over time, he'd genuinely turned into a Chicago fan. Damien always had to be the rebellious one. I stayed out of it.

When they saw us enter, both stopped sniping at each other and greeted us warmly.

"Hey," Damien said, pulling Sasha into a one-armed bro hug.

"Uh, hi."

"Sasha, this is my dad, Bob," I said, making the introduction. "Dad, this is Sasha." I wasn't sure what else to say. My brothers had clearly told my parents about Sasha and the circumstances that had him living in my empty house. I hoped they wouldn't make Sasha uncomfortable by making a big deal out of it.

"Nice to meet you, son," Dad said, shaking Sasha's hand. "I hear you're working with Nick on that dilapidated old house. My wife tells me you boys have your work cut out for you."

"Yes, sir."

"'Sir'? Nah, call me Bob. Everyone does. You like baseball?"

Dad clasped Sasha's shoulder and steered him into the living room. Sasha flashed me a panicked look. I only shrugged and excused myself to tell Mom we were here.

In the kitchen, Steven stood over the stove with his tie loosened and shirt sleeves rolled, stirring gravy in a saucepan. Must've come straight from work. He was the only one of us boys who enjoyed cooking, which automatically gave him bonus points in the race to being Mom's favorite.

"Oh, good, you're here!" Mom said, wrestling with the knotted cord of the carving knife. "Where's Sasha? You brought him, right?"

"Yes, Ma," I replied, leaning in to kiss her cheek. "He's with Dad and Damien, watching the game."

"Oh, good. I better say hello. You unwind this and carve the meat."

Mom shoved the carving knife at me and left the room. I untangled the cord and plugged it in beside where an enormous, steaming roast sat on a carving board.

"Sounds like Mom has a new project," Steven teased.

I rolled my eyes. "Why'd you guys have to tell her about Sasha? The last thing he's gonna want is her nosing around trying to adopt him."

"I didn't tell her. Damey did."

I grunted, not caring who told, just praying Mom didn't end up scaring Sasha off.

"Where's Prince Wiener?" I asked, mentally crossing my fingers that he'd had to work late or something.

Steven glared at me. "*Tod's* out on the back porch making some calls for work."

Sure he was. More like he was using that as an excuse not to have to associate with my family, so he wouldn't pick up our blue-collar germs.

"Can you do me a favor and try not to antagonize him tonight? He's been under a lot of pressure lately, and we haven't been getting along so well. You don't know how much I had to beg to get him to come tonight. When you act like a dick to him, I have to deal with the fallout at home for days."

"I don't know how you put up with him. He treats us all like something he scraped off the bottom of his shoe. You're an okay guy. You could do better."

Steven sighed but didn't argue. He knew I was right. Tod (aka Prince Weiner) was the grandson of a global sausage and hot dog mogul. The family-owned company had bought and merged with several other food companies over the years, making it a favorite on the Forbes list, and placing the family firmly in the top one percent. Tod worked in the family business, but doing what, I wasn't sure. The whole year I'd lived with him and Steven, I'd only ever heard him talk about *doing* lunch with this bigwig or another, and name-dropping famous people who he claimed to know like his mouth had a persistent leak. I had no idea what Steven saw in him.

I carved the roast and arranged the slices of meat on a serving plate, while Steven poured the gravy in Mom's etched silver thing that looked like a jinni lamp.

"Jesus, she didn't break out the good china, did she?"

"You know she did," Steven replied in a singsong voice.

"Sasha's gonna hate this," I grumbled, carrying the platter into the dining room, where the table was set like the Queen was coming for dinner. Steven followed with the gravy and a giant bowl of mashed potatoes.

"Dinner's ready," I yelled in the direction of the living room.

"Really, Nick!" Mom scolded. "Must you shout? I raised you with better manners."

"Sorry, Ma." I rubbed the top of her head in a way that she pretended to hate.

"Stop that. Come on, help me bring in the rest of the food."

Mom had gone overboard as usual. Green bean casserole, steamed corn, homemade biscuits, two desserts. Even with the extra leaf in the table, there was barely enough room for our plates. You'd think it was a holiday rather than a random Tuesday in April.

I sat next to Sasha, giving him a reassuring pat on the shoulder. His return grimace made me wince.

"You okay?" I whispered.

He nodded once and took a sip from his ice water.

Everyone took their seats, Mom claiming the other side of Sasha so she could "get to know him." Tod wandered in and parked himself next to Steven, opposite me. His expression was the usual combination of bored and put out.

"So, Sasha," Mom started, offering him the bowl of potatoes. "Tell us about yourself. Where are you from?"

Sasha's body stiffened, and he cleared his throat before speaking. "Oak Creek, ma'am."

Mom beamed, probably at his good manners, and gave me a pointed look. "And do you still have family there?"

"Yes, my mom." He took another drink of his water and didn't meet her eyes.

"Enough with the twenty questions, Ma," I interjected. "Can't we eat now?"

So, we did. As usual with our family dinners, everyone talked over each other in a weave of conversation threads. Sasha only spoke when asked a direct question, but he slowly seemed to relax.

He ate like he hadn't had this much access to food in months, and I felt bad. Maybe he hadn't. Sometimes, I provided lunch while working, sub sandwiches or pizza or something, but considering he was working for practically nothing, maybe I should be a little more generous.

"Saw the guitar case in your room," Damien said, waving his fork at Sasha. "Kelly said you played Summer Fest a couple years ago."

Sasha swallowed his mouthful of potatoes and nodded. "Yeah. But it was at like eleven thirty on a Wednesday morning. I think there were only about twenty people there, and most of them were our buddies."

"But, man, Summer Fest! All the greats have played there. You still play?"

"Nah, the band broke up."

"I host some live music in my bar. You should come by and check it out sometime. Maybe you could play for us."

"Uh, sure. I'd be happy to."

When Sasha tucked back into his food, Damien gave me a quick wink. I grinned back. My brother could be a pest, but he had a good heart, and Sasha could use another friend.

Things appeared to be going fine until dessert, when Tod finally gave in to Mom's persistent questions and put away his phone, which he'd been obsessively checking throughout the meal.

"I hear you were out west last week while Steven went to Florida with his friends, " Mom said. "Was it a work trip?"

"Yeah, San Fran. My father is working on a contract with AT&T Park to supply their concessions. The Giants hosted a charity dinner for childhood cancer or something, so he thought someone from the family should attend."

"That sounds nice. Did they raise a lot of money?"

Tod shrugged. "Enough, I guess. It was five thousand dollars a plate and sold out. Robbery for overcooked filet mignon, if you ask me. But Darren Criss sat at my table, so I suppose that was worth it. He's so funny!"

Mom glossed over the name drop, either because she didn't know who Darren Criss was or she didn't care. "I've always wanted to see San Francisco. It sounds romantic with the hills and the fog and the—"

"Swarms of vagrants? Really, Carol, the place is literally infested with them. I could barely leave my hotel without being accosted for money or drugs. I don't understand why the city can't round them all up and ship them somewhere. I hear Alcatraz isn't being used."

Silence fell over the table, and Sasha's forkful of chocolate cake froze midway to his mouth. I balled my fists up, ready to leap the table and bash that fucker Tod's teeth in. Steven gave Tod a not-so-subtle kick under the table.

"What?" Tod exclaimed indignantly. "They really are a blight on a perfectly beautiful city. I mean, I feel for them, I really do, but what are our tax dollars paying for anyway? I'm just glad the hard freezes in Milwaukee help to drive them down south."

Sasha set his fork down. "Excuse me. Your restroom?"

"Top of the steps, honey," Mom answered, giving him an apologetic smile.

As soon as Sasha was out of earshot, I erupted. "How fucking dare you, you arrogant prick!"

"Not cool, man." Damien glared at Tod. "Sasha's a nice guy. You didn't need to be a dick to him."

Dad set his cutlery down. "That was uncalled for, Tod."

"Tod, I'm ashamed of you." Mom shook her head. "I will not tolerate rudeness at my dinner table."

Only Steven, with his face frozen in pale horror, sat silent, staring at Tod with his mouth hanging open.

I leaped to my feet and pointed at Steven. "If you value his ass so much, you better get him the fuck out of here before I lodge my foot in it."

Steven stood and tugged Tod with him, giving me an apologetic frown. I didn't forgive him. I only hoped this would convince him it was time to dump the asshole. As Tod was hustled out the door, there was the barest hint of a smirk on his face, and I made to go after him, but Damey's viselike grip on my arm held me back.

When the front door closed, I shook his hands off. "I'm gonna check on Sasha."

The only bathroom in the house was upstairs by the bedrooms. I ascended the steps two at a time. My knock on the bathroom door was louder than I'd intended.

"Sasha, open up."

"It's not locked." He sighed.

I opened the door to find Sasha sitting on the edge of the tub, his elbows resting on his knees. He appeared completely defeated, and I had to grip the towel rack to keep myself from catching up to Tod and rearranging his face.

"I'm sorry, Sasha. I told you he was an asshole, but I never would've brought you here if I thought he'd act like that."

Sasha gave me a sad smile. "I know. And I shouldn't let it get to me, but it does."

"Of course it does! You shouldn't have to put up with being insulted like that. You're a good guy and a hard worker. I'm lucky I found you, you know? I'm just so fucking sorry I subjected you to that."

"Not your fault. People are like that everywhere. I should be used to it by now. Before I found your house, I used to sleep in parks and under overpasses. You think I don't know what a 'blight on the city' I was? How I probably will be again in a couple months? I saw it in the faces of every person who passed, even when they pretended not to see me."

I closed my eyes and tried to will away the image of Sasha being looked down on by mobs of strangers. Despite my martial arts training, I wasn't really someone who solved problems with my fists, though tonight had me rethinking that. I wanted to wipe the condescension off the faces of everyone who'd ever dared treat Sasha that way. How could they not see him for the person he was?

"You're not a blight on anything," I said in all sincerity. "You . . . You're amazing. So full of . . . I don't know . . . light? I don't know what it is, but you're not like anyone I've ever met. And I swear to you, I will never sit back and let someone treat you as less of a person again."

Sasha stood. "Don't worry about it, okay? Can we get out of here now? I sort of hit my limit of being social."

I clasped his arm and fought the urge to pull him in for an embrace. We still hadn't discussed what happened last night, and forcing myself on him now probably wasn't such a good idea.

"Okay. Let's say goodbye. I'm sure Mom will want to know you're all right."

CHAPTER 14
SASHA

We left the house, arms loaded with foil-wrapped leftovers. Nick's parents had apologized profusely for Tod's insensitivity, but it wasn't their fault, and really, their words had just made me feel more embarrassed. It wasn't until I climbed into Nick's truck that I felt better. I let out an audible sigh and sank into the seat. I didn't get any vibes from vehicles, probably because people didn't spend enough time in them to psychically imprint on them. But the upholstery smelled like Nick, and that was nice.

I wasn't sure where Nick was driving, and I was too apathetic to ask. The whole day had been kind of awful for me. First, Nick had had a couple of day laborers with him when he returned from the store, so we never had our big talk. Then there had been his family. Don't get me wrong . . . they were great people, but the combination of their wide-open-arms welcome and the happiness rolling off the walls had made me even more self-conscious that I didn't belong. I'd just started to get a little comfortable when that asshat had started in on his rant.

We were riding along Lake Michigan when Nick spotted a small parking lot beside the beach and pulled in. He turned the engine off and stared out at the black water. He opened and closed his mouth a couple of times, as if he didn't know what to say.

"Mind if I smoke?" I asked.

"Oh, sure," Nick replied distractedly and hit the buttons to roll our windows down.

I dug my pack and lighter out of my chest pocket and lit up, careful to aim my exhale outside. When Nick didn't speak, it became clear that I'd have to say something. The stuff at his parents' house was too fresh, and I didn't want to rehash it, so I decided to tackle the other elephant in the truck.

"So, you ever kiss a guy before?" It wasn't the most graceful way to break the ice, but it did cut to the heart of the issue. Maybe I'd been wrong when I'd pegged him as straight, but with the ex-wife and all . . . Did that make him bi, then, or was he one of those gay guys who, for one reason or another, hid it?

Nick snorted. "No! Have to say that was a first for me."

I tapped my ash onto the ground. "Wanna talk about it?"

He glanced over. "I'd rather talk about what the hell happened to you last night. Did that fucking perv hurt you?"

Shit. How could I explain to Nick what had spooked me? "No, he didn't hurt me. But I . . . I didn't realize until after I got there that something was off about him. And when I tried to leave, he shoved me against the door and wouldn't let me go."

"Jesus, Sasha . . ."

"Then, I called you."

"What do you mean by 'something was off' about him? What scared you to begin with?"

"Um, it's hard to explain . . ." *His condo gave me psychic visions from what he did to others in the past.*

"Try."

I took another drag on my cigarette before answering. "I was sick. And I thought he had a knife."

"You were sick? You okay now?"

I nodded. "It was . . . temporary."

He gave me a heavy stare. "What aren't you telling me?"

"You wouldn't believe me." The only person I'd ever tried to tell besides my zayde was Justin, but he'd thought I was screwing with him, so I'd let it go.

"What did I tell you about assuming shit about me? I might look like a meathead, but I think I'm fairly open-minded."

"I don't think you're a meathead."

"So why not lay it all out here? What's said in the truck stays in the truck. You can trust me."

"I know I can, it's just . . ."

"Just nothing. Go for it. I'm all ears."

I tossed the cigarette butt out onto the pavement and turned in my seat to face him. A little knot of worry wrinkles formed between his brows, and I had to clench my fist to keep from reaching up to smooth them away.

"Fine. You ask me a question, and then I get to ask you one. And no arguing with each other. We listen and accept the answers as truth."

"A bit cheesy, but I'm game. I go first. What did you mean that you were sick?"

"I'm kind of . . . psychic. I get visions and feel emotional energy from spaces like rooms and houses. I was fine until I walked in Trevor's condo, but once inside, I was overcome with the bad vibes, and it made me weak and queasy. My turn now."

"What? No, it's not your turn! What do you mean you're psychic?"

"Not until it's your turn again, cheater. So, tell me, do you regret kissing me?"

"No."

"No? That's it?"

Nick smirked. "Guess you'll have to wait until it's your turn to get more answers. Now you tell me, specifically this time, what you mean by psychic visions."

"You don't have to believe me. I understand—"

"Did I say I didn't believe you? Answer the question."

"Fine." Dang, this was hard. "Okay, remember the day I told you about the brick wall supporting the house? Well, I knew it was there because it was originally planned to be the exterior wall. My best guess is that the builder decided to make the home larger sometime after construction started. Anyway, the bricks were exposed until the nineteen twenties, when they plastered it up."

"And you know this from a vision?"

"Yes. I don't see them all the time. Memories sort of imprint on a place when something emotional happens. Every house or building or room I walk into has its own emotional signature depending on what sort of memories it has. Most of the time I only get a feeling. The visions come when the space is really agitated. And if they're extremely intense, the emotions seep into me. Last night, when I was in Trevor's condo, the atmosphere of sexual violence was so strong, it made me want to hurt him. Scared the shit out of me."

Nick's jaw worked back and forth. I scrutinized him for signs he was going to kick me out of his truck, but didn't see any. He seemed lost in thought.

"Can you please say something, because I can't tell what you're thinking?"

"Sorry," he said, with a small shrug. "Is this why when you walk through an empty room, you hug the walls like you're avoiding furniture?"

"You noticed that?"

"Well, yeah." He admitted. "And is this also how you knew about the leak in the bathtub drain?"

"Yes . . . in a way. I didn't know what exactly we'd find when you opened the wall, but the house showed me a vision of that wall with a red spot on it, like it was sore or something." I paused a moment to let it sink in. "Back to my turn. Tell me why you kissed me. And no one-word answers this time."

He scrubbed a hand over his head. "I guess I just like you. I don't know why. I don't think I'm gay. Not really. It's not like I don't think women are still hot. Maybe I'm bi or something? I don't know." He stopped meeting my eyes and started talking to the water. If that made this easier on him, I was okay with it. "It's not just that you're nice looking. Well, that's definitely true, but you're . . . more. Funny and friendly and smart." He picked at the seat upholstery. "And you get me. All I hear from people constantly is why I can't or shouldn't do things. Not only with the house, but with my business, my personal life, everything. I know that I take a lot of risks, but hell it's paid off for me before, and I know I can get back there again. It's nice to have a friend who isn't always telling me no. It means a lot to me." He paused. "And you sort of smell good."

I laughed at that. "I do? Most of the time we're together, I'm either smoking or sweating!"

"Yeah, but you still smell good. I don't know how to describe it. It's just you." Nick lifted his hand hesitantly and then reached for mine. He folded it in both of his, stroking the back of my thumb with his blunt fingertip. The warmth of his skin in the cool night air beckoned to me, making the hair on my neck stand up.

"Nick Cooper, you are one sexy man, and I can honestly say that you do it for me too. What do you want to do about it?"

"Isn't it my turn to ask a question?"

"Fuck the game. We both want this answer."

"Then I don't know. I liked kissing you, but I don't know about the other stuff."

"Well, what do you say we start with that, then?"

I stretched my free hand across the back of the bench seat and touched his shoulder, then ran my fingers up the soft, warm skin of his neck and traced his ear. Nick leaned into my hand like a cat needing a scratch. Taking that as a green light, I moved closer, letting my fingernails lightly scrape through his shorn hair.

"God, Sasha," he sighed. "You drive me crazy."

"Feeling's mutual," I whispered, close enough for him to feel my breath on his ear.

With an unintelligible groan, Nick turned his head and took my mouth in a fierce kiss. His tongue wrapped around mine, making my heart stutter with want. The scent and taste of the cinnamon gum he was always chewing flooded my senses and went straight to my stiffening cock.

We licked and nibbled and sucked for several minutes before he tunneled one hand into my hair and used the other to guide me down. If I'd been smaller, the move would've had me on my back with him on top of me. Unfortunately, I was over six feet tall. Between my legs getting tangled up in the gear shift and then bonking my head on the window, this wasn't going to work.

"Sorry." Nick chuckled, touching the sore spot on my skull.

"It's fine. Why don't you take me somewhere more comfortable, and we can try this again?"

Nick was off me and starting the truck in a flash. He was backing out of the parking lot before I'd even gotten my seat belt rebuckled.

"In a hurry?" I laughed.

"Fuck, yes. Mind going to my place? It's closer."

"Well, considering my place doesn't have any actual furniture, I think that's a good idea. How far it is?"

"Not far. Ten minutes or so."

"Ten minutes is plenty of time for you to cool off and change your mind about me."

He squeezed the lump in his pants. "Do I look like I'm cooling down?"

"Mmm, that's sexy. You gonna let me touch it?"

The truck made a funny lurch as if his foot slipped off the gas pedal, and he shot me a glare. "If you don't want to end up wrapped around a telephone pole, I suggest you behave while I'm driving."

"Fine," I said with an exaggerated sigh. We crossed the river and entered a working-class neighborhood lined with single-family homes. I was curious to see where Nick lived. I expected an apartment complex, but was surprised when he pulled into the driveway of a cozy post-WWII bungalow.

"I could have sworn you told me you lived in a studio apartment."

"It is a studio," he answered as he cut the ignition. "Follow me."

We climbed out of the truck. Then I followed Nick around the side of a detached garage, where there was a rickety set of stairs going up the side.

"A garage apartment? That's cool!"

"Don't get all impressed yet. It's small."

After he opened the door and flipped on the light, I stepped in and looked around. He wasn't kidding. It appeared to be one open room, with a bathroom tucked into the corner. Beside the bathroom was a tiny galley kitchen, separated from the living area by a breakfast bar with two stools. It had a refrigerator, but no stove—he must have a hot plate stashed somewhere. The living area contained a leather sofa, cracked with age but comfortable, and a low shelf of books. A wood stove in the corner appeared to be the only heater. Nick crossed to the unit and began to build a fire using kindling and a fat log.

I couldn't get much of an emotional read on the place. Nick was probably one of the first full-time occupants.

"No TV?" I asked.

"Nah. Can't afford cable or any of those streaming services, so there's no point."

For a man who owned his own business, he sure lived like he didn't have a dime to his name. The room was clean, but sparse.

"Do you sleep on the couch?" I asked, not seeing a bed.

Nick grinned. "No. I sleep there." He pointed up to a loft with a ladder.

"Are you serious?" I climbed the ladder to see over the ledge. The loft fit a king-size mattress and not much else. There wasn't even enough room to stand. I crawled in and laughed. "Holy shit! You have your own fort! I would've loved this when I was six."

Nick stood on the ladder and watched me rolling around on his bed. "Looks like you're loving it now."

"Sorry," I said, sitting up. "I didn't mean to just jump into your bed." I moved to leave, but he waved me off.

"No, please stay. You saved me the trouble of trying to coax you up here." His eyes glittered with mischief.

"As nice as this is, I don't think I want to lay here alone."

He kicked his shoes off, and they dropped to the floor below with hard *plunk*s. Then he climbed in beside me. I toed my shoes off too, and they dropped into a foot-wide crevice at the end of the mattress. The only light was what bled up from the kitchen beneath us. I couldn't think of a more perfect place to be alone with Nick.

"Come here," I said, pulling him closer so he was stretched out beside me, propped up on one elbow.

Nick's expression was both eager and scared, and his fingers trembled as he stroked the side of my face.

"It's okay," I assured him. "We don't have to do anything you're not comfortable with. I'm happy to lie here and talk if you want."

"I don't know what I want. I just know that I haven't wanted anyone in my bed so much in a very long time." He kissed me on the mouth. Then he laughed. "I'm kissing someone with a beard!"

"Sorry. Would you prefer I shaved?"

"No, I like it." Then he kissed lower, on my chin and along my jaw. "It's soft."

I let my hands roam over the powerful muscles of his back. I'd never been with a guy this built before; Nick Cooper was a wet dream on legs. When he draped a thigh between my legs, I let out a groan and pressed against it. He gave me a light nip on my earlobe before he moved back to my mouth.

The pace of our kissing grew more frantic, even if it was a little clumsy. In his eagerness, Nick's erection grazed my thigh, and he jerked his hips back. I examined his expression, making sure he was still with me. At the first hint of gun-shyness, I needed to be able to pull away. His eyes were glazed and lustful, but the way his hands wandered, barely touching me, betrayed his awkwardness.

"Still okay?"

"Yeah, just . . . not sure what to do."

"I meant it when I said we can stop anytime. Got it?"

He nodded.

"Want to stop now?"

"Hell no."

"Shirt off, then," I said, tugging at his hem. "I want to touch you."

Nick reached behind his neck and yanked his T-shirt over his head, tossing it to the side. His skin was smooth and sprinkled with a dusting of hair on his well-defined chest. I traced his ribs, but he knocked my hand away.

"Not yet. Your turn." He popped the pearl snaps on my shirt open one by one, taking his time. I lifted to slide out of the sleeves, and then lay back with one hand under my head, allowing him to look as much as he wanted. Lightly, he ran a finger over my chest, avoiding my puckering nipples. "Fuck, Sasha, you're perfect."

"I'm nowhere near as built as you."

He shook his head. "You don't need to be. You're so . . . sexy." He flattened his rough palm over my abdomen, and then touched the trail of hair leading down from my navel. "I've been lying in bed picturing this spot right here all week."

So, he did check me out that day in the kitchen after all.

Nick dipped his head to place openmouthed kisses on my collarbone. My cock throbbed, begging for friction, but it was important to let him lead. He nibbled up my jaw to my mouth again. His fingers ran through my hair and clutched, holding me in place.

We made out like that for several minutes, Nick taking more liberties to explore my skin with his fingers. It drove me fucking crazy.

"Trust me?" I asked.

He nodded.

I turned Nick over, straddled his hips, and tongue-fucked his mouth, rocking my body in rhythm with the kiss.

His hands drifted down my spine to grip my ass. I arched back and then rolled forward, running our clothed erections against each other.

"Oh, holy fuck," he moaned.

I did the move again, eliciting the same rumble from him.

My jeans were getting restrictive but freeing my cock now might be too much too fast for him. If I ever wanted to have a repeat of this night, I had to make this good for him. I pulled away from his mouth, and shifted down his body to lick the groove between his pecks. His body had a faint scent of soap. I kissed and licked across his chest to the nipple, where I latched on and sucked.

"Jesus . . . Sasha . . ."

I transferred my attention to the other side. When both nipples were wet and pebbled, I explored the ridges in his abs, my fingers brushing his sides. Nick squirmed.

"You're ticklish?" I grinned.

"A little."

"Don't think I'm not filing that information away for later."

I left his ribs to lavish attention on his navel. The rosy tip of his cock poked out from the waistband of his jeans, a bead of pre-come balling in the slit. I peered up to meet Nick's hooded gaze.

"Still with me?" I asked.

He took a deep breath and nodded.

I flashed him my best wicked grin. "Can I suck you now?"

CHAPTER 15
NICK

My hips shifted eagerly, and I gave a brisk nod.

Sasha moved down my legs, yanking my jeans and underwear off. He took off his jeans too, but left his boxers on. I admit, I was glad for that. This was going fast, and I still wasn't sure how far I wanted it to go. Each time I paused to think, I couldn't believe how crazy this was. Me and Sasha? But then he'd give me a look, or touch my skin, and the electricity between us would ignite some spot inside me that I hadn't known was there. I owed it to both of us to explore this strange new attraction.

I peeled my socks off and leaned back.

Sasha stared down at me with carnal hunger in his eyes. His skin shone in the dim light. He didn't have a lot of body hair, only that delicious trail leading down to his tented shorts. *One sexy man.*

Unable to help myself, I stroked my cock. Sasha glared playfully and knocked my hand away as he settled between my legs. He pressed his nose in next to my balls and inhaled deeply.

"I could get drunk on your scent," he whispered. Then he licked the base of my cock, before dragging his wet tongue up the vein to the tip. He swirled around the cut head before drawing it into his mouth. I gripped the comforter in my fist and willed my hips not to buck.

Slowly, he dipped his head lower, taking me into the back of his throat, before he hollowed his cheeks and drew back.

"Fuck . . ." I hissed, placing a heavy hand on the back of his head and grabbing a fistful of his curls. He sped up his rhythm, still taking me so deep that the blunt head of my cock knocked the back of his throat with each stroke. He reached down to cup and tug my balls, sending tingles up my shaft.

Soft grunts escaped me, and soon Sasha was echoing with short hums.

"Christ, you have to stop. I don't want to come yet."

He withdrew from my cock with a *pop* and grinned up at me. "Mmm...I could do that all day."

He crawled up my body and took my mouth with his. I could taste myself on him a little, and I wondered if that was how he'd taste. I wasn't quite up to finding out yet, but I wanted to reciprocate somehow.

Well, carpe diem and all that shit.

With nervous fingers, I fiddled with the elastic of his boxers, before slipping inside to brush against his erection. At his moan, I wrapped my hand around his shaft and gave an experimental tug.

"Yes . . ."

The feel of him was both familiar and completely fucking foreign. So different from my own equipment. I'd seen plenty of cocks in my life—in locker rooms, in porn—but had never considered how powerful it would feel to hold another man's most vulnerable part in my palms.

Sasha fucked into my fist and panted against my neck. After a minute though, he pulled away and sat back on his heels. "I need to come, and so do you. Still with me?"

"Yeah." And I meant it too. Maybe tomorrow I'd have second thoughts, but tonight, I needed more.

He leaned over to his discarded jeans and fished something out of the pocket. Then he shucked off his boxers. His cock wasn't quite as thick as mine, but a little longer. My heart skipped, and I swallowed hard. I was really doing this. With Sasha.

Sasha straddled my thighs and ripped open a packet with his teeth. I thought it might be a condom at first, but instead he poured out lube into his palm. After tossing the empty packet, he slicked the lube over first my cock, then his.

"Give me your hand," he said, his voice rough.

He took my right hand in his and ran the oil over my palm. Once all was sufficiently coated, Sasha shifted his hips closer, settling in with his cock touching mine. Then he wrapped our entwined hands around both shafts at once. Slowly, he began to jack us while rocking his hips, so the underside of his cock slid along mine.

"Holy shit . . ." I groaned. Hot sparks shot out from the base of my spine, and I bucked into our fists with him.

"Like that, Nick?"

"Fuck, yes . . . so good."

Sasha flicked his thumb out to rub the tip of my head with every upstroke, eliciting unintelligible grunts from me.

"I'm gonna come," I warned.

"Do it," he urged. "I want to see you let go."

I thrust faster. Then with a shout, I spurted all over my stomach. A few pumps later, Sasha groaned, and came on my chest in several powerful spasms.

When my mind cleared, I looked up to see Sasha sitting back on my thighs, panting. His face flushed with exertion, he was the most beautiful thing I'd ever seen. I sat up, wrapped my arms around his waist, and nuzzled his chest.

He stroked my head with his non-lubed hand, lightly scraping his short nails over my scalp, sending warm tingles down my neck.

We held each other like that a minute, our breaths slowing, the come between us growing cool and sticky.

"Stay with me tonight?" I asked. "I promise to get you back home early enough to open the coffee shop."

He didn't answer immediately. Had I overstepped?

"Or I can take you home. I'm not usually much for sleepovers either. I just thought . . ."

He tilted my face up to meet his gaze. "Of course, I want to stay here tonight. And not only because you have a real mattress. What kind of girl do you take me for?"

I shoved him off me with a chuckle and reached for my T-shirt, which I used to wipe the mess from my hand and belly. We crawled under the covers, and Sasha snuggled in with his head on my chest. I was almost asleep when he spoke.

"Hey, Nick? I lost my job at the coffee shop. That's why I was home early yesterday. Business hasn't been so good, and I had the least seniority."

Shit, can't he ever get a break? I wrapped my arms around him tighter and kissed the top of his head. "Don't worry about it right now. We'll figure something out tomorrow."

CHAPTER 16
SASHA

I woke up in the morning wrapped in Nick-scented sheets and fingers tangled in the hair on the back of my head. The memory of falling asleep with him petting me like a kitten filled me with comforting warmth. I rolled over to face him, surprised to find him awake and staring at the ceiling in the early-morning light.

"Hey," I said in a voice rusted by sleep. "Good morning."

His mouth turned into a wicked grin. "A very good morning."

"Not freaking out about waking up with a guy in your bed?"

A growl rumbled in his throat, and he climbed on top of me, settling between my legs and nipping my bottom lip. "I've been debating waking you up for round two for the last half hour."

Ignoring our morning breath, I drew him in for a deep kiss. I loved kissing. Most guys I'd been with had been so focused on getting off quick that kissing had fallen by the wayside. It'd been a long time since I'd truly made out with someone, and Nick used his mouth with the creativity of an artist.

Things were just getting heated when Nick's cell phone rang. He ignored it and bent to explore my chest with his tongue. A moment after the ringing stopped, it started up again. Nick swore against my skin.

"Answer it," I groaned. "No one calls this early unless it's important."

Nick reached over the side of the mattress and answered his phone with a gruff "Yeah."

The sheet slipped, exposing his wide back and the top swell of his ass. What I wouldn't give to spend all day in bed exploring him inch by inch. Unfortunately, given what I could make out from the one-sided conversation, today wouldn't be that day.

"Are you kidding me? That's going set the schedule back at least another week . . . No . . . no, I'll be there soon."

He rolled back, phone still clutched in his fist.

"Rain check?" I asked.

"It's one of my paying jobs, and I can't afford to blow it off, no matter how much I want to."

I placed a soft kiss on his shoulder. "It's okay. What time is it?"

"About seven. I need a shower. I'd invite you in with me, but it's barely big enough for me to fit."

"No problem. I'll shower at home. I don't have any clean clothes here anyway."

"Mmm . . . bet we could both fit in your shower."

"Yeah, but if I had you naked and soaped up, no way would either of us make it to work today."

"Fine," he grumbled, sitting up, then he descended the ladder before stalking off naked toward the bathroom.

Grinning like an idiot, I crawled into my clothes. Remembering that the bed had been made when we'd gotten into it last night, I did my best to straighten the covers. I'd heard somewhere once that successful people always made their beds. I didn't know how true that was. If they were successful enough, they probably got other people to make their beds for them. But in any case, I made sure to set mine to rights every morning. I balanced from knee to knee on Nick's mattress trying to minimize the wrinkles, which wasn't easy. By the time it was good enough, Nick was back, dressed in his typical jeans and T-shirt, his hair damp.

"Ready?" he asked.

In the truck on the way to the house, Nick laid out the timeline for the day's work.

"You can continue stripping the doors this morning. That should keep you busy until I can get back. My friend Jeff is coming over this afternoon to measure the place for tile. With three full bathrooms to do, I don't have the patience for it. Best to subcontract it out. You should see the deal he got us on discontinued travertine for the master."

I let him ramble on, loving how excited the planning made him. If he could pull off half of what he wanted to, it would be amazing.

The guy had vision, that was for sure. Different from my visions, but a wonder just the same.

After he dropped me off, I took a quick shower and changed into work clothes before heading to the garage. I was prying open a can of turpentine when my phone rang. Another unrecognizable number. I sighed and answered, "Yeah?"

"May I speak to Sasha Michaels please?" asked a high-pitched voice.

"That's me."

"I'm calling from St. Luke's Medical Center. We have your mother here. She'll be all right, but she came in this morning in a lot of pain, and we're admitting her." The woman continued to explain how my mom had been found by a neighbor walking his dog in her front yard beaten and unconscious.

I was already rushing back inside to get my wallet. I'd have to call a cab. A bus would be too slow. "I'll be there as soon as I can. Tell her . . . I don't know. . . tell her I'm on my way."

Wallet, keys, and phone in hand, I barreled out the door, nearly mowing Damien down as he came up the porch steps.

"Whoa, hold up!"

"Sorry." I smiled sheepishly. "I'm in a hurry."

"I can see that. What's wrong?"

I scrolled through my phone, searching for the number of a cab company. "My mom's in the hospital. I need to get a cab to take me over."

"She gonna be okay?"

"Yeah, someone roughed her up. I don't know too many details yet. They said she's stable, but they need to keep her for observation."

"Want me to take you?"

A ride would be nice, but I didn't want him to feel he had to sit with me at the hospital. It was bad enough that Nick had seen the shit-show of my family life. I didn't need his brother exposed to it too.

"No, I don't want to take up your time. A cab is fine."

"Do you have a license?"

I leveled a gaze on him like he was stupid. "Of course I have a license. But I don't have a car."

Damien fished his keys out of his pants pocket and handed them to me. "Take mine. It's parked in the driveway. I'm going to be working around here most of the day, so I won't need it."

Jesus, these Cooper men were nice. "Any other time I would say no, but I really do need to get to the hospital. Thanks, man."

"No problem. Call me if you need anything."

Nick phoned while I was driving to the hospital, and I filled him in on what I knew, which wasn't much. He wanted to meet me there, but I downplayed the situation to convince him to stay put. His timeline was tight enough without taking a day off for my mother's bullshit.

The initial panic I'd felt when I got the call had faded into anger by the time I got to St. Luke's. Anger not just at whoever did this to her, but if I were being honest, at her too. Not that I blamed the victim. She didn't deserve to be beaten up by anyone, no matter what. But I was pissed because her shitty life decisions were going to kill her one of these days, and there was nothing I could do about it.

In the hospital, the receptionist directed me to a room on the third floor. With a deep breath, I knocked and poked my head inside. My mother lay in bed, staring at the ceiling. Her face was purple, one eye completely swollen shut. She had tape stuck to her face holding the set of her broken nose. Her right arm was in a sling, resting against her chest. She didn't look at me as I pulled a chair up beside her bed and sat down.

"Hey," I said, needing to speak, but not really knowing what to say. "How're you feeling?"

She rolled her one open eye and didn't answer.

If it were anyone else in the bed, I'd probably hold their hand. But my mother and I didn't have that sort of relationship.

"Jerry do this to you?"

She sighed like a sullen teenager. "I'm not pressing charges. Don't need cops in my business."

"I never asked you to. I asked if Jerry beat the shit out of you and left you on the front lawn."

Her silence was answer enough. My fingers longed to wrap around his scrawny little neck.

A knock on the door warned us a moment before a nurse walked in. "Hi. You must be Sasha. I'm Alice. The nurse who called you."

"Yeah . . . thanks for that."

"I have to get your vitals again, Rina. This will only take a minute, and then I'll let you get back to your visit." Her cheery tone sounded out of place in the tense room. "Blood pressure's good. How do you feel?"

"Nine."

My mother's answer confused me until I noticed the pain scale on the wall. Nine out of ten. That couldn't be good.

The nurse checked the IV that dripped clear liquid into a tube in my mother's arm.

"What's in there?" I asked.

"Just some fluids. She was dehydrated when they brought her in. We've also put her on a low dose of morphine for the pain."

"Bet she's loving that," I muttered.

Mom glared at me.

I kept my trap shut after that until the nurse left the room. Once she was out of ear shot, I asked, "So give me the damage. I see your nose is broken. What's up with the sling? Did he break your arm too?"

"It's my shoulder. Torn rotator cuff."

Ouch. I wasn't a hundred percent certain what the rotator cuff was, but it sounded bad. "Does that require surgery?"

"Physical therapy." She pressed the button on her bed to raise herself up. "They're making me go to rehab."

She wasn't talking about rehab for her arm. My mother had tried the rehab route twice before. Neither time stuck. The first time had been shortly after I was born. I was born with drugs in my system, and she would have lost me if Zayde hadn't stepped in. The social worker from CPS agreed to let me go home with him if my mom would commit to getting clean. She was on the state health insurance because her income was so low. It had only paid for her to do an outpatient program, which meant she still had her loser friends hanging around. She'd done okay for the first few weeks, but then it must have gotten too hard. The lure of the high was too tempting. That was the first time she split, leaving me with my zayde. I was eight weeks old.

The second time she went to rehab, I'd been thirteen. Justin and I had come home from school to find my mom on the floor of Zayde's bathroom in the middle of an overdose. The whole time we waited for the ambulance to come, I held her convulsing head to keep it from banging the floor and prayed she would pull through. I had thought for sure this would be the wake-up call she needed. Zayde had too. He'd immediately begun looking into an inpatient program for her. The one everybody recommended had been called Woodland Acres—a secluded place in rural Tennessee. A representative from the program met with us in the hospital waiting room while Mom was detoxing. I'd flipped through the glossy brochure with pictures of manicured gardens with tree-covered mountains in the distance, while the man had explained the program to Zayde.

"We believe in treating the whole person. Addiction is not just a psychological condition. You can't heal the mind without healing the body as well. In addition to our therapists, we employ world-class personal trainers and nutritionists. It's a very holistic approach. We have an open bed, so if Rina will agree, I can drive her down when she is released."

"And how long is this program? Thirty days?"

"We prefer not to place a time limit on the program. Each guest works with an addiction counselor to create an individualized plan with attainable goals based on their specific needs. Most guests stay sixty to ninety days. Then we help coordinate aftercare treatment for when the patient returns home."

I glanced up from a picture of a smiling group of people doing what looked like yoga on the lawn in front of an ivy-covered building to see Zayde's eyes shining with hope.

"This sounds perfect for Rina. She needs to be away from Milwaukee for a while. How much is this program? She only has the state health care."

The man gave a sympathetic frown. "Yes, I know. Unfortunately, since ours is a private clinic, the state care won't pay anything. She would need to pay for it out of pocket, but really, when it comes to your loved one's health, isn't it worth it?"

"How much?"

"Twenty-five thousand dollars per month."

All hope sucked out of the room, and Zayde lowered his eyes. "I see."

"I understand Rina may not have that kind of money. Most addicts don't."

"So how do they pay for it? Is there some assistance she can apply for?"

"I'm sorry, but no. Ours is a private facility, so we don't get government subsidies. Most of our guests' stays are covered by their relatives. How is your financial situation, Mr. Michaels? Are you able to take out a second mortgage on your home maybe? Or perhaps you have a 401(k) savings plan that you could borrow from?"

Zayde's face was ashen, and I could tell that he was struggling over his desire to help his only child and mortgaging his retirement away. "I must think on this."

It was a dismissal, but the rep didn't take the hint. "How about your other family? Sometimes a group of family members will pool their resources to lessen the financial burden."

"There is no one else."

Zayde stood and left the waiting room, leaving me with the suited representative. I cleared my throat and handed the brochure back to him. "I don't think we're going to be needing this, mister."

The man gave me a sad smile, one that he must have practiced in the mirror for times like this. "You keep that, son. Woodland will always be here if your mother needs us."

Mom had ended up coming home from the hospital under the condition that she had to attend Narcotics Anonymous meetings in the basement of a neighborhood church. She'd gone for about two weeks before she was caught snorting Adderall in the bathroom with one of her former dealers and was asked not to come back.

Looking at my mother all battered and bandaged in the narrow bed, I really did want to see her get better. I just didn't have a lot of faith that the types of rehab available to her would get the job done. The way she was going, she would either have to wake up and work the program or end up dead before she reached fifty.

I said at last, "That's good, Mom. But you don't have health insurance anymore, do you? How are you going to pay for it?"

"The social worker said I can get in on a state program for battered women. Since I'm on probation already, I either go to rehab or jail. Not like it's gonna work anyway."

I had my doubts too, but it would at least give her time to dry out and heal from her injuries before she went back to her old ways.

We talked for a few minutes about the rehab program. It would be a thirty-day check-in, with the option of longer as needed. They were going to keep her in the hospital overnight to monitor her concussion, and the social worker would drive her out to Waukesha in the morning for rehab.

"Sasha, baby. Can you do me a favor?"

If she was going to ask for money, she could forget it. I couldn't give up any of my meager stash. "What is it?"

"There's a spare key under the mat on the back doorstep. Can you make sure Jerry's gone before I come back?"

I swallowed the lump in my throat and nodded. "He'll be out of the house today."

CHAPTER 17
NICK

"I think I might be bisexual," I announced as I burst into Steven's office.

A sputter of diet soda escaped my brother's lips, showering the papers on his mahogany desk. He snatched a couple of tissues from a holder and blotted them. "You're what?"

I sat in front of him. "I'm bisexual. I think. I mean, I've always sort of been attracted to guys—watched gay porn a couple of times, and it was hot enough—but I figured if I never acted on it, I was straight, right? Well, now I've acted on it. I'm bi, and you're the first person I'm coming out to."

Steven did that annoying one-eyebrow-raise thing. "Sasha?"

My knees bounced with pent-up energy, and I had to grip the armrests to keep from jumping up and pacing. "Yeah, man. It was fucking amazing. Well, we didn't do much. We only—"

He lifted his hand to stop me. "I really don't want to know the details."

"You don't seem surprised though?"

"I'm not." He sighed. "You could hardly take your eyes off him at dinner last night. I know you loved Melissa, but I never saw you look at her that way. Though I figured it would take you longer to come around. And don't think I forgot the time I caught you whacking off to that Jean-Claude Van Damme movie."

"Hey, I was thirteen. I whacked off to everyone then." Hadn't we all? I wasn't so sure now. Maybe that should have been my first clue I was bi. I studied Steven's face; a deep crease crinkled between his brows. Steven didn't do creases. "You're not happy for me?"

He rubbed his forehead with a groan. "Sorry. Yeah. I'm happy for you. You know I only want the best for you, and Sasha seems like a nice guy. I'm just distracted." He paused. "Tod left last night."

I swallowed down a whoop of joy. "Dude, I'm sorry. Is this a temporary thing?"

"No. That little show he put on at dinner wasn't about Sasha at all. He's been acting like an ass since he came back from California. We had it out in the car on the way home, and he admitted that while he was out there, he went to a party, got high on X, and let a couple of guys fuck him bareback. Of course, he tells me this after sleeping with me, and we've been off condoms for years."

I shot out of my chair like my knees were springs. "I'm gonna kill him!"

"Sit down. I got tested this morning, though if I am infected with anything, it might be too early to know. But HIV came back as negative today. I'll have to get tested again in a few months."

I started to pace. I couldn't help it. I'd gone from excited to pissed off in seconds, and if my body stopped moving, I'd have to put a fist through something. "Jesus, Steven. Tod's a dick, but how could he be so stupid? How could he risk your health like that? Or his for that matter?"

"I don't know," he replied, his tone full of defeat. "Things have been bad for a while. I think some part of him did it on purpose to force a clean break."

"What's wrong with 'Hey, I'm not feeling it anymore. Let's break up.'?"

Steven leaned back in his chair and stared at a spot on the ceiling. I took to pacing again.

My brother and I had always had a complicated relationship. Even though he was only a year older, he bossed me around constantly. Not surprisingly, I'd resisted. We'd scrapped over his bossiness so many times as kids, our dad had given us boxing gloves for Christmas when I was eight. But fuck if I was going to let someone shit on him like this. I clenched my fists, envisioning Tod's neck in their grasp.

"Whatever you're working yourself up to, stop it." Steven stood and rounded the desk. "Don't worry about me. This breakup has been a long time coming. I don't want any drama. I just want him to get the rest of his belongings out of our place, so I can work on getting on with my life."

"But Steven—"

"No. I appreciate your outrage on my behalf, but seriously. Let it go. You have this great new thing starting with Sasha. Enjoy it."

My neck and shoulders relaxed at the thought of Sasha. The guy really did have some sort of hold on me. Maybe I *was* gay? I pictured the old Claudia Schiffer poster I had on my bedroom door as a teen: tight jeans, lace bra, parted lips. Boobs. God, I loved boobs. No, definitely not gay. Then I pictured Sasha as he was last night while straddling my hips. Bare chest, lean muscles, parted lips. Bi, then. Definitely bi.

"See," Steven squeezed my shoulder, "you're grinning."

"Am I? Sorry."

"Don't be. Sasha seems great, and he's hot." I glared, and Steven chuckled. "Well, he is, but don't worry, I'm not ready to jump back in the market just yet." His grin faded again, and the crease returned.

It sucked that my brother and I were going through such completely different mornings.

"So, do you have any questions for me?" he asked. "About dating a man?"

I smirked at him. "Are you trying to offer me sex advice, big brother?"

"Sure, why not? If I suddenly wanted to have sex with a woman, I'd be so nervous, I'd have to ask Damey what to do."

"Damey? Why not me?"

"Are you kidding? The kid's got game. You don't."

I moved to cuff him alongside the head, but he ducked out of my reach. "Jackass. Fine, what is this sage advice you want to give me?"

"That's easy. Use lube. Lots of it."

"Fuck you. I got work to do. Catch ya later."

Steven gave me a one-armed bro-hug. "Tell Sasha I'm sorry about last night. And seriously, if you need anything, don't hesitate to ask."

"Will do."

A couple of hours later, I was leaving the jobsite of one of my paying prospects when I got a call from Sasha asking for a recommendation for a cheap locksmith. Hell, he didn't need to pay anyone. I could swap out a lock. I swung my truck into a Home Depot, bought new hardware, and headed to meet Sasha at his mother's house.

When I pulled my truck into the driveway, there were several black garbage bags piled on the front porch alongside a cardboard box. I peeked in. Short stack of Tarantino DVDs, some opened mail in Jerry's name, a black bong. Well, Sasha was being thorough in his house cleaning.

I let myself in the front door. Last time we were here, I'd been too nervous to really look the place over. In the light of day, I saw it was a nice-sized ranch home. Perfect for a family, if it hadn't been trashed by its latest occupants. Nice neighborhood, a block from the elementary school. In fact, with some cleaning and paint, the house could fetch good money if Sasha's mom decided to sell it. I quickly put that thought out of my head. Sasha probably wanted the house to stay in the family.

I followed the sound of rummaging to a bedroom halfway down the hall. The lavender curtains and girly quilt on the bed let me know this was his mother's room. Interesting that she hadn't taken over the master after her father died. Sasha stood by the dresser, where he dumped a drawer of dingy tighty-whities into a bag. Out with them tumbled a strip of condoms, a roach clip, and a handful of photos that I knew better than to examine too closely. His expression was pissed off and maybe a little scared.

"What are you doing here by yourself? What if that sleazeball and his gun-toting friend come back?"

Sasha glared at no one in particular. "He'll be lying low for a few days, at least. You should've seen the damage he did to my mom. Her face looks like an eggplant. He probably assumes there's a warrant out on him now."

"And is there?"

He shook his head in disgust. "She won't give his name to the cops. She's claiming an unknown attacker."

"But he needs to be jailed!"

"It's no use. She won't turn him in. No telling what he has on her. All I care about is that he never steps foot in this house again."

"You want me to take his things to the dump?"

"No," he sighed. "I'd love to get rid of it all, but I don't want to give him an excuse to cause trouble for us. He'll see it stacked on the porch when he crawls out of whatever hole he's hiding in."

"Okay." I itched to touch him. To offer some sort of comfort. But at that moment, Sasha seemed like he'd bite anyone who got too close. Maybe I should give him space. "I'm gonna fix the locks. Once this place is secure, we'll both feel better."

Sasha grunted and moved toward the bedside table, sweeping things into the trash bag.

I spared him one last glance, then walked to my truck to get my toolbox. A few minutes later, I set to switching out the locks on the front door. I'd bought a new dead bolt assembly that was keyed to match the lock on the new knob.

I tended to do my best thinking while working. My mind wandered, and it was easy to slip into daydreams while my hands were busy performing tasks they'd done a million times. Most days, I liked this quiet time in my head. Now, not so much.

Last night with Sasha had felt so right. We'd slept together, yeah, but it had seemed like more than that. We'd shared something beyond just a quick jerk-off together. I didn't know what it was exactly, but it had been completely unexpected. Today though . . . Well, I didn't regret it. Not like I'd feared I would, waking up with another dude drooling on my pillow. Christ, thinking of waking up to Sasha so peaceful in the soft dawn light had made my chest swell all over again. My brain kept roiling between excitement and apprehension and something like dread, but dread in the most wonderful sense of the word.

Now, I wasn't sure what to do going forward. Since my divorce, I'd perfected the polite-distance thing designed to let women know I appreciated spending time with them but was not in the market for anything more. As long as they knew the score up front, no one got hurt. But with Sasha, hell . . . last night had been different. It had been as natural as coming home after a long trip.

And isn't that just a load of poetic bullshit.

Admitting to myself that I was bisexual was weird, but it felt right. After all, why should a person's biology matter if you cared about them? And Sasha was so easy to care for. No, the surprising thing was that I was out on this porch screwing in a dead bolt and contemplating my feelings for another person at all. What the fuck was wrong with me?

I wrapped up the front locks and headed to the back door to start on those locks when I spotted Sasha standing in the backyard smoking a cigarette and staring at a tree. I set my toolbox on the stoop and went to stand beside him.

"Nice tree. It's very . . . tall."

Sasha cut a glance at me and exhaled a cloud of smoke. "That's deep."

I took his slight grin as encouragement. "Yeah. Leafy. And big."

"Shut up." He stamped out his smoke and reached for me. I curled my arms around him, and he rested his head in the crook of my neck. It was oddly comfortable hugging a person my same height. I buried my nose in his curls and inhaled my new favorite scent.

"I had to get out of there for a while. The negative energy is overwhelming."

Ah, the psychic thing. I'd sort of forgotten about that. Honestly, I wasn't sure what to make of it. If it were anyone else, I'd think they were blowing smoke up my ass, but Sasha didn't seem to be messing around.

When I was a kid, I used to watch TV shows like *In Search Of* with Leonard Nimoy and *Ripley's Believe It or Not!*, and I would be transfixed by the idea of aliens and Bigfoot and the Loch Ness Monster. I'd known these creatures didn't exist, but I'd wanted them to be real so bad. I'd dreamed of one day flying in the Bermuda Triangle or joining the CIA Stargate Project. Steven, a pragmatist even at age ten, had scoffed and teased me, but I hadn't cared. So maybe there was part of me that was predisposed to believe Sasha. He'd given me plenty of evidence of his abilities. I believed Sasha wouldn't lie to me. And hell, I'd known there was something different from the start.

"What's it feel like? Does it hurt?"

He pulled away and dropped down on his ass under the tree, facing the house. "Not really. Or maybe a little. I don't know. It's hard to explain."

I sat down in the grass next to him. Needed to know more. To understand. To get an explanation. "I'm listening."

Sasha lit another cigarette and took a deep drag. "I don't want to talk about it right now, okay? It's hard."

My brain buzzed with questions, but he'd been through a shitty day and looked like a wire about to snap. I counted to ten and forced myself not to badger him.

After about four hundred years, Sasha ground out his cigarette and sighed. "Guess I better get back to work. I think I've got most of Jerry's stuff bagged up, but I need to do a complete search of the house for drugs. You don't have to stick around if you don't want to. I know you have a shit-ton of work to do at your place. Sorry I bailed on work today."

"No worries," I said, accepting his hand to pull me to my feet. "You got your own crap to deal with. I can stick around a while longer. Help you search or whatever."

We carried the rest of Jerry's things out to the front porch. Then Sasha's face took on a determined expression. His eyes didn't close, just got a far-off gaze to them, as if he were listening to a voice only he could hear. Could he hear voices? I wanted to ask, but knew better than to interrupt. Still, when he set off to the kitchen, I followed, curious.

Sasha held his palm out toward the cabinets, scanning. His arm swung to a small pantry cabinet, where he opened the door and studied the shelves carefully. After a moment, his hand landed on an old coffee can. He popped off the lid and dumped the contents on the table, and out tumbled a small baggie of weed, a soot-blackened pipe, and an empty packet of Zig-Zag rolling papers.

"Huh. You're like a drug-sniffing dog. Think you can help me find my lost truck keys?"

Sasha smirked, and I mentally patted myself on the back for lightening his mood.

For the next ten minutes, I followed Sasha around the house in complete fascination as whatever inner voice he heard led him around. A few times, I saw him pull toward the closed door to what I assumed was the master bedroom at the end of the hall, but each time he'd snap alert and turn in another direction.

"My zayde helped build this house," Sasha explained as we searched. "He came here from the Soviet Union in the early seventies.

His first job was with a construction company doing grunt work." He gave me a slight grin. "Kind of like I do for you."

"Wasn't it hard for him to get out the U.S.S.R. during the cold war?"

"It wasn't as hard for Jews. He knew some people in Israel, and it was much easier to emigrate there."

"How long did he stay in Israel?"

"Not long. His goal always was to go to the United States. Zayde was always proud of his Jewish heritage, but like a lot of people born shortly after World War II, he never really developed the faith. His parents were young, and both barely made it out of the camps alive. They latched on to each other because they had no family left. I met them once. When I was six, Zayde took me back with him for a visit."

"Wow, and you remember them?"

"I remember the plane better. Zayde warned me on the way over not to say anything about the numbers tattooed on their arms. So of course, I spent the whole time trying to peek up their sleeves to get a glimpse."

I wasn't sure what to say about that. I'd never known anyone affected by the Holocaust, let alone a close family member.

"They gone now? Your great-grandparents?"

"Yeah. They died a long time ago." He opened the linen closet and pried up a loose floor board and withdrew a dingy baggie with two white rocks. "So yeah, Zayde worked on a lot of the houses in this neighborhood, and when they were built, he bought this one. Not long after that, he took the janitor job at the high school, and the rest is history."

Once Sasha had finished scouring the other rooms on the main floor, and had done a cursory scan of the basement, we examined the haul on the kitchen table. I didn't know much about drug paraphernalia, never having been a user myself.

"What's this?" I asked, picking up something the size and shape of a smartphone, but wasn't.

"A scale. For weighing purchases." Sasha opened a half-empty vodka bottle and began pouring it down the drain.

I set the scale down beside a pill cutter. "Your mom does pills too?"

"She'll do anything she can get her hands on. Mostly weed and meth, because they're cheap. Pills are more expensive, but I'm sure she manages to score them now and then." He turned to place the empty bottle on the table and noticed where my eyes were focused. "Actually, I think that pill cutter belonged to my zayde, but well, I was drawn to it, so I assume someone's been using it."

"What should we do with this stuff? Can it go in the garbage?"

He snatched up the baggie of weed and dumped it in the sink, where he ran it down the disposal. "I don't want to put it in the trash here. I'll bag it up and toss it in a dumpster somewhere. We should break the pipes though, so no one can stumble across them and use them again."

We took the two glass pipes out to the back patio. I stepped on them with my work boots, and Sasha scooped the glass up with a dustpan.

"Can I ask you a question?" I asked.

"Of course."

"Why did you avoid the room at the end of the hall?"

His grin faded. "I need to get in there. I'm just procrastinating."

"Was it your zayde's room?" I asked, testing the Yiddish term on my tongue.

He nodded. "Yeah, but that's not the problem. Not really."

I waited for him to continue, but he didn't. I couldn't help it. I pressed. "Is it because his personal items are still in there?"

He blew a curl off his face. "No, most of his clothes are in boxes in the basement. Let's just say there are things my mother's done in that room for drugs that no son should have to stomach. I tried to go in this morning, and had to turn right back around. The house keeps pulling me back there, but I just can't."

I was dying to ask him how the house was pulling him, but he was already walking away to empty the dustpan.

"You want me to do it? Search that back room? I think I know what I'm looking for."

He started to shake his head but then gave a reluctant groan. "Okay, yeah. Maybe if you can just get any obvious paraphernalia out of there, I'll work on getting the rest of it tomorrow. Pretty much everything has to go."

"I got this." I rubbed his shoulder, snatched a garbage bag out of the box on the counter, and headed to the back of the house. For the hundredth time today, I cursed Sasha's mom. She didn't deserve such a good son.

I paused at the door. That night when Jerry's buddy had come stumbling out with the gun, I'd been pretty sure he'd come out of this room. There better not be a sex swing or anything in there. I squared my shoulders and turned the knob.

No sex swing. That might have been amusing. No, what I found was infinitely sadder. The room smelled of stale sweat, unwashed sheets, and a hint of burnt shower curtain. Low light filtering in from the closed blinds cast a sickly yellow glow over the air. The bed took up most of the side wall, and the half-exposed mattress was stained with god knows what, but my eye was immediately drawn to a low coffee table on the far side of the room. Someone had shoved the dressers into a corner to make room for it. Scattered around were misshapen and stained couch cushions, presumably where people would sit at the table. And on top were the remnants of some sort of a party: cheap lighters, an overflowing ashtray, burnt scraps of aluminum foil, and a single residue-clouded pipe. Didn't see any drugs, but I did spot a few empty snack-sized Ziploc baggies discarded on the floor. Couldn't blame Sasha for not wanting to come in here. I wasn't psychic, and even I could feel the despair hanging like a cloud.

Garbage bag in hand, I picked up the ashtray and dumped the mound of cigarette butts in the bag, then thought better of it and dropped the whole tray in. Sasha was right. It all had to go. The sweet and sour scent of what I assumed to be meth coated everything, making me wish I had gloves on. I considered running out to my truck for a pair, but just wanted to get this over with.

When the tabletop was clear, I tossed the cushions onto the bed and picked up the floor. The carpet was rank. Not only did it stink, but there was a hardened spot near the bathroom door that looked like a puker hadn't quite made it to the toilet.

I swallowed the lump in my throat and stepped into the bathroom. It had probably been a nice room once upon a time. It had been remodeled in recent years with a stylishly tiled shower/tub combo and matching fixtures with brushed-nickel hardware. Unfortunately, it was filthier than a bus station men's room during a janitorial strike. Grime had turned the white porcelain to gray, and the soles of my shoes stuck to the floor tiles. The wastebasket was overflowing, so I tipped the contents in my trash bag. On to the medicine cabinet. I'd figured anything of street value would be long gone, and I was right. A couple of cruddy tooth brushes, a jar of Vicks VapoRub that looked as old as I was, and a rusty can of Barbasol. I was about to shut the door, when I spotted some stuff tucked behind a container of cotton swabs. A burnt spoon, a frayed shoe lace, and a plastic syringe.

Remembering what Sasha had said about junkies getting into garbage, I stomped on the syringe to break it before tossing it in the bag. The spoon caught my interest though. It was small, a baby spoon, with etched Hebrew script along the handle and a Star of David on the end. The metal was badly tarnished, indicating it was something nicer than stainless steel. It didn't feel right to throw it out.

Spoon in hand, I returned to the bedroom and did another search, checking behind furniture and in the heat register. The dresser drawers were mostly cleaned out. The top of one was littered with unopened bills. I picked up the top one addressed to Sasha's grandfather and stamped with a red *PAST DUE* on the envelope. What happens to a person's bills when they died? Presumably a responsible beneficiary would pay them off, but nothing I'd seen of Sasha's mom yet evidenced any sort of integrity.

What would happen to my debt if I couldn't repay? My mouth went dry. Truthfully, I hadn't given serious thought to the consequences when I'd originally taken it out. I'd told myself failure wasn't an option, so it wasn't worth worrying about. Part of me wanted to believe Frank wasn't *that* bad. This wasn't *The Sopranos*. I'd figured intimidation was a game all loan sharks played to make sure you remembered who was the boss. After all, physically harming me wouldn't get his money back any faster.

But then Frank had mentioned Marty. I wondered how much he was into Frank for.

I dropped the bills back on the pile and wandered out to the kitchen.

Sasha had scooped all the items from the table into a large trash can dragged in from the garage, and now stood in front of the open refrigerator, chucking its contents.

"All clear." I disposed of my small bag into his bin. "You're right. Everything in that room has to go, including the carpet. I cracked the windows and opened the blinds to help clear the funk. And look what I found. It might be able to be cleaned."

I held the spoon out to Sasha. His jaw tensed, and clearly he was struggling to maintain a hold on his anger. He took the spoon from my hand and examined the handle, eyes reddening with unshed tears.

"This is real silver. My grandfather's baby spoon. It was one of the few items he was able to bring with him when he moved to the US." He scrapped his nail along the blackened scoop. "Now my mother is letting people use it to shoot heroin."

The spoon dropped from his fingers into the garbage, and Sasha stalked off to the bathroom.

I wanted to hold him. Comfort him. Something. It was what I'd have done if Sasha had been a woman I was sleeping with. But he wasn't a woman, and he didn't seem to want to be vulnerable in front of me. So I didn't go after him. Instead, I reached into the trash and retrieved the spoon.

CHAPTER 18
SASHA

B*reathe in. Breathe out. Clear your thoughts. Brace for the pain ...*
As I'd done every night for the last few weeks, I unclenched my fists and lightly rested my fingertips on the living room carpet where I sat cross-legged. My breath caught with the rush of vibrating energy filling me. My thoughts tumbled like my brain had its spin cycle set on high, and it took a moment for me to feel upright again. Once steady, I imagined a hollow place inside me, big and deep. When the cavern had been established, I reached out to the house and sucked in as much of the hurt and misery as I could, filling the empty space. The energy buzzed through my limbs like my veins were live wires, and I had to resist breaking the connection to scratch my skin off.

When the hollow was filled with roiling energy, I leaped to my feet on popping knees and rushed out to the dark backyard, where I dropped at the base of the tree. I heaved, emptying my mind along with my guts, sending the poison into the earth. Leaves withered and rained down on my head from the branches above. As my dry heaves stopped and the hollow rang empty, I rolled to a sitting position and buried my head in my hands.

I was spent, in body and mind. I felt two hundred years old and crumbling apart, and there was nothing to be done about it. I'd made it my mission to heal Zayde's house before Mom returned. Which as it happened, could be anytime, since after only three days into her rehab stint, she'd checked herself out of the center and disappeared on the back of some guy's motorcycle. But this was Zayde's house. The one he'd built with love and care to be a home for his family. I just wasn't ready to give up on it.

So, yeah, I had a serious time crunch to deal with. On top of the loan-shark enforced deadline at Nick's house. If he got his legs broken over that stupid loan because I was too wrapped up in my own shit to help him, I'd never be able to live with myself.

And that was why I was getting up at dawn every morning to start working on Nick's house, and then taking the hour-long bus ride to Oak Creek to work here each night. I rarely made it home before midnight, where all I was able to do was take a quick shower and fall onto my bed pallet. The meager sleep I did manage to get was marred with bizarre and scary dreams, the kind that made me feel more tired when I woke than I'd been when I'd gone to sleep. A side effect of freebasing on bad juju for days on end.

Things with Nick had cooled, but not from a lack of interest, just a lack of time. We worked beside each other every day, but usually Damien, Kelly, or some subcontractor was around and their presence prevented any real conversation. He offered almost every day to go to Oak Creek with me, but I didn't want an audience for what I was doing. I had a feeling he wouldn't like my method of healing the house. Maybe I'd let him help once the time came to make the minor repairs. I'd cleaned most of the place up and had even painted several of the rooms, but the plastic-covered window in the kitchen from where the glass had been shot out needed to be replaced, and the back bedroom needed . . . well, a nuclear bomb.

Ignoring my sore abs, I stood to wipe the prematurely dead leaves from my jeans and made my way back inside. I'd have to book it if I was going to catch the last bus home. I scooped up my hoodie and began turning out lights. The house felt noticeably lighter than it had when I'd started working on it. It wasn't done yet, but we were getting there. I made a pit stop in the bathroom and was washing my hands when there was a familiar tug on my arm.

"Christ, not again," I muttered. A heaviness settled on my left arm, pulling me in the direction of the back bedroom. I'd thought Nick's sweeping it might've helped, but no, it had only gotten worse. The house wanted me to go back there something fierce. I had no intention of spending more time in the room that had been so badly defiled by my mom. The residual sexual energy made me want to tear my hair out. Not to mention that anxious, itchy feeling from all the meth smoked back there.

The house yanked at my arm again.

"What?" I asked a little too loudly for someone addressing an inanimate object. "Why do you want me in that room?"

The only reply was more of the nudging.

"Fine!" Frustration propelled me back to the room, where I flung open the door and switched on the light.

Immediately, my vision fogged with conflicting images. On top of the room's depressing reality, I could see the ghost of how it had been the whole time I grew up. Bed made with an old quilt, a black-and-white TV perched on top of the dresser, Zayde's work uniform draped over a chair, his work keys on the dresser beside some loose change. If that was the only vision I saw, I'd hang out in this room every day. But it wasn't. Overlaying everything was a vision of the sickness of the last year. Acrid smoke in the air, ashes ground into the carpet, a used condom discarded next to the bed. The cycling of the competing visions was disorienting. My mouth started to water again, belly began filling with acid. I squeezed my eyes shut to block the images.

"What is it?" I yelled, "I'm here! What do you want from me?"

The house tried to pull me farther into the room, but I clutched the doorframe to stay put. My arms tingled with the sensation of crawling bugs, remnants of The Ghosts of Tweakers Past. I released the frame to scratch them away.

With a deep breath, I opened my eyes. "Show me."

The heaviness tugged me, and I gave in, walking past the bed to the far corner where two mail-covered dressers were shoved. The pulling stopped, and I tried to focus through the visions and make sense of what the house was trying to tell me, but my thoughts were bouncing in different directions at once. *Miss Grandpa. Gonna puke. Rock bottom. Ant arms. Hate life. Need Nick.*

"What? What do you want me to see?" I shouted.

My limbs shook, and I lost my balance, hip-checking the dresser hard, sending part of a stack of mail skittering to the floor. The pain of the drawer handle punching my flesh gathered my thoughts back together. I had to get out of here. I spun on my heel and ran for the door.

It wasn't until I'd plunked down on the bus stop bench that I noticed the bleeding claw marks on my arms.

CHAPTER 19
NICK

"Watch the woodwork," I warned the installers as they carried the new cabinets in the front door. I'd gotten an incredible discount on a discontinued style at a manufacturer's outlet. The dark stain paired with the quartz countertops I'd splurged on would be amazing. Kelly had suggested we echo the same materials in the bathrooms to make the home cohesive. Better listen to her while I had her, because once she graduated, I wouldn't be able to afford her services.

I followed the cabinet guys to the kitchen. The new floor had gone in a couple of days before, and I prayed no one would drop a hammer or something and break a tile.

"Starting to look like a real kitchen," said Damien, from behind me.

"Hey, man. Yeah, it's shaping up."

"You just get here?"

I nodded. "Finished up a big deck for that house out by the zoo this morning. The one with the sunken hot tub in it. It's so cool. Here, I have some pics." I handed Damey my phone so he could scroll through. "Once the landscapers are done doing their thing, this will be the best yard in the neighborhood."

"Did you do that brickwork on the barbeque yourself?"

"Yeah. And Jeff did the mosaic tile countertop. Speaking of Jeff, he's starting the tile in the bathrooms here this afternoon. Should be around any minute. Can you believe how quick this is going? At this rate, Steven might be able to put it on the market early next month. Part of me is going to hate to see it go, but the sooner it sells the better."

The whirring of the installers' drills roared to life. Damien motioned for me to follow him to the living room, where he leaned on the newly exposed and tuck-pointed brick wall in front of the half-finished fireplace. It was still noisy from where Sasha must be running the floor sander upstairs. I hadn't seen him yet, but as always, I was painfully aware of his presence.

"What's Sasha going to do when this place sells? He have a place lined up yet?"

I ran my hand along my shorn scalp, not even wanting to think about the question. After our night together, I had half a mind to invite Sasha to move in with me. I knew it was stupid fast, and I didn't have a lot of room in my garage loft, but then Sasha didn't have much in the way of belongings. Waking up with him in my arms that morning had been the closest to perfect I'd ever felt. For weeks, every time we'd been in the same room, my heart would speed up and I'd get all nervous and twitchy, consumed with the desire to wrap him in my arms. When he wasn't around, all I did was obsess over him like a teenager with his first crush. It was surprising I hadn't resorted to writing his name surrounded by hearts all over my notepad. I'd been heading fast into the L-word territory, but then the shit had happened with his mom, and he'd gone all distant on me.

And then there was the other reason I couldn't ask him to move in with me. If I didn't get out from under Frank Diamond, I might end up sleeping in the shelter with him.

The whir of the sander signaled a change of direction above us. "Don't know. I haven't asked him lately."

My brother looked at me like I was the stupidest human being he'd ever met. "What do you mean you haven't asked him? Too busy acting like horny teenagers to have a decent conversation?" The expression on my face must have given my disappointment away, because he stood up straight. "What's wrong? You do something to piss him off?"

"Of course not. He's just been busy lately with work at his grandfather's house. We haven't spent any time together."

"How come you don't help him?"

"Doesn't want my help. Trust me. I've offered."

To be honest, it pissed me off that Sasha was going to his grandfather's house every night and not letting me give him a hand. I was a contractor for fuck's sake! I worked on houses for a living.

But he didn't want me around, and made half-ass excuses about having to do it himself.

And then there was the other issue. I'd thought Sasha had had as good of a time that night as I had, but he hadn't touched me since. The few times I'd managed to get him alone and steal some kisses, he'd felt distant, like his mind was a million miles away. Whether it was because he was too exhausted from the hours he was putting into both places, or if he wasn't into it because of me, I didn't know. I'd never had any complaints from the women I'd been with, but what if I was supposed to be different with guys? Kiss them differently or something? Hell, I didn't know. And no matter how cool Steven was, there was no way I could ask him about it. Was this Sasha freezing me out? I sure as shit hoped not.

"You can't just sell the house out from under him and send him back to a park bench. Have you asked Steven for any apartment leads?"

"He said he'd keep an eye out, but the places in Sasha's price range probably won't open up until the end of the summer when the student leases become available. Look, Sasha's not going to sleep in a park. We'll figure it out."

I ducked my gaze to avoid Damien's stare. Clearly, he wanted to ask more about Sasha and me, but unlike Steven, Damey knew when to back off.

"Fine. Well, let me know if you need any help. I actually came over here to talk to Sasha. The band I had lined up for tonight at the bar broke up over some love-triangle drama, so I'm suddenly without music. Think Sasha would be interested in picking up a few bucks playing?"

"You can ask him. He's upstairs."

I followed Damien up the steps, inspecting the newly sanded floors in the bedrooms as I went. No gouges, good. We'd have to take a hand sander to the edges, but the hardwood was cleaning up beautifully.

We found Sasha in the master bedroom. When he spotted us, he raised a finger for us to wait while he finished up the last couple of passes with the industrial sander I'd rented for the job. I took advantage of his distraction to watch him walk behind the big machine, his worn jeans riding his hips just right. He wore a mask over his face to keep from breathing the wood dust. A couple of those unruly curls had escaped from the knot at the back of his head and bobbed around his ears happily. I wanted to touch his hair, touch him. A mental snapshot of him naked and straddling me flashed through my mind, as it had fifty times a day for the past several weeks. I wanted him that way again. Soon. Whatever the problem was between us, I needed to get it fixed ASAP.

Damien smacked me on the chest. He looked at me knowingly and motioned for me to wipe the drool from my mouth. I flipped him off.

Sasha reached the end of the room and turned off the machine. He yanked the mask down around his neck. "Coming up to inspect my work, boss? What do you think?"

"I couldn't've done any better," I replied. "Once the bathroom cabinets and fixtures are in, we can get the floors stained and sealed."

Sasha retrieved a water bottle from the windowsill and took a long pull. His Adam's apple bobbed and the skin was flushed from exertion. My pulse thumped and I remembered how I'd kissed and sucked that skin. I wondered if he'd let me make a video of him swallowing sometime.

"So," Damien said, "I was telling Nick that the band I lined up for tonight canceled on me. You interested in filling in?"

Sasha's eyes flicked to me with a spark of excitement before it slowly faded. "I don't know. I'd love to, really, but I have so much work to do down at my grandfather's house before my mom shows back up."

"Work that Nick can help you with if you just stop being stubborn and let him. The big dope is itching to pay you back for all you've done around here. Do us all a favor and give him a chance to show his appreciation."

Leave it to my brother to say what I couldn't. I cuffed him on the arm for his trouble.

Sasha glanced to me again, this time with hesitation in his eyes. "Okay. I guess that would be fine."

"What do you say? Fifty bucks plus whatever you manage in tips? Weeknights don't pull in a huge crowd, but once the bowling league gets done at Ten Pin Alley, things usually pick up for an hour or two."

"Uh, sure. Okay. I'll be there at seven."

"Come early, and I'll feed you." Damien headed for the door with a wave.

Sasha and I stood there listening to Damey's clomping steps fade away, not exactly meeting each other's eyes. How had things gotten so uncomfortable between us?

"You really going to let me give you a hand at your grandfather's house? I'm happy to do it, you know."

"Yeah. I know. It's just that it's sort of my problem."

"It doesn't have to be," I said, taking a tentative step closer. He stiffened slightly, and my chest squeezed at the rejection. "Why don't you tell me?"

He lifted the dangling mask from around his neck and tossed it down next to the water bottle on the windowsill. Then he yanked the band out of his hair and reknot it. Classic killing-time moves to keep from having to talk. How had I ended up on the other end of this game?

I opened my mouth to ask him to level with me, but the marks on his arms derailed my thoughts. "What's up with your arms?"

He ran one palm over his forearm as if noticing the long red scratches for the first time. "Oh, these. I scratched myself."

I reached to examine the marks more closely. "On what? It looks like you got into a fight with a litter of kittens."

"It's nothing," he said, drawing his arm out of my grasp.

I was about to protest, when a clatter sounded behind me. We turned to see Jeff and his crew carrying in boxes of tile for the two upstairs bathrooms.

"Yo, Nick. How's it hangin'?"

"Good. You?"

Jeff was one of my oldest friends and the best tile guy I knew. A real artist. He slapped me on the back with a meaty paw.

"Can't complain, man."

Jeff directed the guys to the bathrooms and called out a few orders for them in his booming but friendly voice. There was some confusion over which design was going in the master shower, but I helped to straighten it out.

Once the guys started mixing up the mortar, Jeff turned back to me. "The house is finally starting to look habitable, thank god.

I thought you were nuts buying it. Houses get funny when they're left vacant too long. Place looked haunted or something."

"No ghosts here." I grinned, wondering if I needed to confirm that with Sasha later. I turned to introduce them, and found the space where Sasha'd been standing empty. Damn it! When had I become the one who got given the slip?

CHAPTER 20
SASHA

BZZZZT!!!! "Sorry!" Damien turned the volume down on the old guitar amp that he'd dug up from somewhere in the bar's back room. "It's old, but it works."

Well, beggars couldn't be choosers, and looking at the size of Damien's bar—a converted Catholic schoolhouse located next door to Saint Norbert Church—I was going to need some sort of amplification, or no one would hear me over the clanking of pool balls. I plugged the old amp into the pickup on my guitar and strummed a chord. Not bad for equipment older than me. A moment of nostalgia came over me with the memory of the Fender amp my grandfather had bought me for Christmas when I was sixteen. I'd loved that thing. Owning it had made me feel like a real musician, one that could play music for a living. Then, one afternoon, I'd come home from school to find the amp missing from my room. Mom had pawned it.

It took a few months, but Zayde had replaced the amp. He'd even helped me find a hiding spot for it in the basement where Mom would never think to look. But it hadn't been the same, and I'd ended up having to pawn the second one myself when I'd decided to prioritize eating over my rock star dreams.

I grinned at Damien. "Sounds fine. I can work with this."

Damien grinned and clapped his hands. "All right, then. Let me know when you're ready and I'll introduce you."

I tuned my strings. As I did so, I inventoried the crowd. This was a neighborhood bar that looked like a popular after-work hangout. The kind of place that sponsored softball and bowling teams. Ages ranged a little older than the college bars I used to play. Most patrons were in the thirty-to-fifty range. My mind flipped through my repertoire. I should sprinkle in some eighties tunes into my set.

Just then, Nick walked through the door and waved at me. He'd changed into a clean pair of dark jeans and a long-sleeved Henley. I lifted my hand to wave back. His presence added a layer of nerves over my usually cool stage demeanor. I wanted Nick to like my music. And not only like it. If this thing between us was going to continue, I needed him to experience the same thrill listening as I did playing.

As Nick ordered a beer, I motioned for Damien. He bounded up onto the tiny stage and artfully flipped the messy hair from his eyes in a way that had every female in the place sit up and take notice.

"Welcome to the Communion Bar, Milwaukee's most holy watering hole. Don't believe me? Ask Deacon Dave nursing his pint at the bar."

An older gentleman dressed in business casual raised his glass with a smile while the small crowd applauded.

"We've got a special treat for you tonight. As the former front man of Stomping Erebus, he played all the best venues in Wisconsin, including Summer Fest. Put your hands together for my friend and all around good guy . . . Sasha Michaels!"

Mildly curious applause sounded, and Damien returned to his place behind the bar.

I stepped forward and tapped the mic. Skipping opening remarks, I started right in with a crowd favorite, "Brown Eyed Girl." It was a good warm-up, and something I could play in my sleep. As was my habit with this song, I quickly located a woman, about my mother's age, with large brown eyes sitting at one of the front tables. I made eye contact with her as I sang the chorus. She and her friends twittered over my blatant flirting, and sang along with the "tra, la, las" with enthusiasm. This was one of my favorite things about performing: interacting with strangers in a way that was fun and socially acceptable without awkwardness.

When the song finished, I gave the woman a wink and glanced back to Nick. He was sitting on the edge of his barstool, staring at me intently. When he caught my glance, a gigantic grin spread across his face, and then he began clapping and whistling loudly, encouraging the rest of the bar to applaud with a little more enthusiasm.

I played covers for about an hour, gradually drawing the crowd out of their shells to have a good time. I even took a request from the ladies at the front table to play "Every Rose Has Its Thorn," a song I hated, but which went over well with the middle-age set. At some point, Nick worked his way up to a seat directly in front of the stage, where I couldn't help but see his grinning face mouthing the words along with me. Seeing him there, supporting me and truly enjoying himself, filled me with warmth that almost certainly shone on my face.

I wiped the dampness off my brow with my sleeve. "Whooo, that was fun, but I need a break. Stick around, and I'll be back in twenty."

Damien turned the jukebox on, and I sucked down half a bottle of water. *Man, I miss playing.* Before I had a chance to check my tip jar, Nick stepped onto the stage, took me by the hand, and dragged me into the store room. He slammed the door and pinned me up against it with his big body, heat dancing in his eyes.

"You were so fucking sexy up there."

I grasped the back of his head and pulled him in for a deep kiss. Nick stiffened at my sudden affection, but recovered quickly, becoming an enthusiastic participant. Performing made me horny, and based on the lump in his jeans, watching me perform had the same effect on him. My hands trailed down his spine, grasped the globes of his ass, and dragged him tight against my groin, pinging all my pleasure centers.

"You're amazing. A natural," he muttered as he nuzzled my beard. "I'm officially your number-one fan."

"Of my singing? Or my guitar playing?"

"Of everything. You can do no wrong."

Our kisses grew more rough and heated. My lips followed his jawline and sucked on his earlobe that had the scar of an old piercing. Christ, I'd missed him. Exhausted or not, I needed him.

"Want you so bad." Nick leaned in, licking and nipping at my collarbone, and my head dropped back against the door as I reveled in the way his hands roamed my body.

When his palm wrapped around the bulge in my jeans, I groaned. "Oh, fuck, Nick. I can't start this now. I have to go on stage in like fifteen minutes."

He lifted his head and looked me in the eyes with heat and the spark of something more. "No worries. Let me take care of you."

His hands slid down my body, and he slowly sank to his knees.

"Nick! You don't have to do that."

He glanced up at me with hooded eyes. "'Have to'? Shit, I've been thinking about this for weeks." He teethed his lower lip as he undid my jeans.

Well, fuck. Who was I to protest?

Nick's hands trembled as he drew out my cock. I loosened my stance. He gave me a few strokes with his hand, obviously reacquainting himself with the feel of me. I squeezed my fists and let him take his time exploring with his gaze and hands. Curiosity and lust shone in his eyes, and tenderness rolled through me. That he would choose me for his first experiences with a man was a gift I wasn't sure I deserved. Unable to stop myself, I reached for his face, running my palm down his cheek and under his chin, tilting it up so he'd meet my gaze.

"If you don't like it, you can stop anytime."

He nodded and gave an experimental tug on my ballsack, sending a rumbling groan through my chest. The noise of the bar faded away, and the only thing left in the world was Nick Cooper.

After a couple of more strokes, Nick leaned in with parted lips and licked around my cockhead. His mouth was tentative and slow, but so warm. Clearly gaining in bravery, he took in my length and sucked.

"Shit . . ." I hissed, pressing my palms on the door.

Nick popped off. "Am I doing it right?"

"You're perfect. You okay with this?"

"You kidding? I think I found my new favorite hobby."

And with that, he sucked my cock with a little too much enthusiasm, choking a little. He couldn't take it deep, but he kept up a fierce rhythm. I dropped my head on the door and gave myself over to him. Much sooner than I'd have liked, my balls tightened up and the impending orgasm rose.

"I'm gonna come," I warned.

Rather than pulling off and finishing me with his hand, Nick doubled down on the suction. I exploded and pulsed so hard I saw sparkles. Nick swallowed my come like a champ before resting his forehead on my hip and wrapping his arms around my thighs.

"How was it?" he asked hoarsely.

I drew him up and held him tight, still breathing like I'd run a marathon. "Fishing for compliments now? It was incredible, and you know it."

"Not fishing, just . . . unsure."

His voice sounded hesitant. I glanced up to see worry in his eyes.

"Stop that," I said, tapping his lips with my finger. "What's that look for?"

"I know I don't know what I'm doing with you, and I appreciate you giving me a chance . . ."

"What are you talking about?"

He stepped away and turned his back to me. I buttoned my jeans and slid up behind him, leaning on his broad body. "What is it? What's bothering you? Didn't you like it?"

"Like it? I loved it. It was different to be on the giving end, but also kind of amazing to make you come apart like that."

"So what's the problem?"

He groaned and rounded to face me. "I'm worried that I'm screwing this whole thing up. I don't know how to be with a guy. You gotta tell me what I'm doing wrong."

"Who says you're doing anything wrong?"

He fixed his gaze on mine. "Look, that night at my house was one of the best nights I've spent in a long time. I thought you were into me. But then you pulled away like you weren't interested, and we've hardly talked since. If I did something wrong, if I didn't make you feel good or something, can you just tell me so I can learn?"

And now I felt like an asshole. The whole time I'd been wallowing in my family drama, Nick had been beating himself up, thinking he wasn't good in the sack. Was that what this whole seduction scene had been about, him trying to please me? I didn't like the one-sidedness of that idea.

"Hey, look at me," I said. "You're the best thing I've got going on right now. I understand I've been distant lately, but honestly, it's only because I'm crazy exhausted from working so much. I'm getting about half the sleep I should be, and all I do is run from one task to another without a break. I guess I took it for granted that you understood it wasn't you."

"You've been shutting me out."

"Yeah, I'm sorry. I didn't think it would take me so long to deal with my zayde's house."

"It's taking so long because you won't let me help."

"That's because you *can't* help. I'm not only clearing out the junk. I'm trying to heal the damage my mom has done to the home's psyche."

Nick's brow knit up in confusion. "You what? How?"

I wasn't used to talking about this stuff, and I wished I hadn't said anything. How could I explain it? He seemed to be handling my freakiness so far, but what if this pushed him over the edge?

"Forget it. It's nothing."

"Don't do that," he pleaded. "Stop shutting me out. I thought we were in this together."

Were we? In it together? I weighed the idea in my mind. It felt like I'd been on my own for centuries. Did I even know how to be a partner to someone else? I wasn't sure I was any good at it, but for Nick, I was willing to try.

"Fine. You're right. I'm sorry. Tomorrow after we finish up at your place, let's go down to Oak Creek and I'll show you what I'm up to, okay?"

"Thank you." He leaned in for a tender, but too-brief kiss. "Now get out there before your new fans storm the stage."

CHAPTER 21
NICK

My hands tapped the steering wheel to the beat of the classic rock station as I pulled up in front of Sasha's grandpa's house. I'd been high as the moon all day after reconnecting with Sasha last night. I still couldn't believe I'd sucked him off . . . and that I liked it. Couldn't wait to do it again.

"Jerry come for his things?" I asked, spotting the empty porch.

Sasha unbuckled his seat belt and climbed out of the truck. "I assume so. One day his shit was gone and the words 'fuck you' were carved into the floor boards. I sanded them out."

I winced and followed Sasha inside.

"Wow! It's totally different in here." Everything was clean and in its place. A fresh coat of paint brightened up the room, and it smelled like the carpets had been shampooed. The living room was still missing a couch, but Sasha had arranged a couple of recliners in front of the TV so that it seemed intentional. "What more do you have to do?"

Sasha blew out a sigh and considered the space. "I cleaned and painted every room except the back bedroom. Still can't go in there. I was hoping that if I could heal the house enough, I'd be able to deal with it."

"I can take care of that room for you, but I need you to bring me up to speed on this house-healing you're doing."

Sasha sank into one of the recliners and closed his eyes. "I don't know how to talk about it."

"Then show me."

He looked up at me in consideration. "You sure? Don't you think I'm some sort of a whack job?"

"No. I don't." Yes, my brain was buzzing with questions about the whole psychic thing, but it was curiosity, not concern. I sat in the other recliner and motioned for him to continue.

"When I got here the day after Mom and Jerry had their big blowout, I couldn't even get through the front door. I don't know everything that went down, but the violence coming off the place was too much for my head."

"But you did go in."

"Yeah, but only after I spent a half hour draining the bad juju away from the front porch."

I choked on a laugh. "I'm sorry, 'bad juju'?"

"I don't know the technical term. You get what I mean."

"Okay, so how does this bad juju stuff work?"

"Whatever went down here imprinted on the house. Not just the violence of that night, but an accumulation of nastiness that has been growing since Zayde died. Have you ever walked into a room where people were fighting and felt a heaviness in the air?"

"Yeah. Actually, I have."

"Well, it's like that for me all the time, only with all kinds of emotions. When I got here, the house was so filled with violence and anger I couldn't get past the porch without my heart speeding into palpitations and my breath going all asthmatic."

"Jesus, Sasha. Are you sure you should be here?"

He clasped my hand. "Yeah, I'll be okay. I turned down the worst of it when I first got here."

"What do you mean by 'turned down'?"

"How do I explain?" He paused. "Say you have a spectrum of emotions ranging from manic to completely depressed. Neither extreme is really good, you know. The stable emotions are the neutral ones in the middle of the spectrum. So when I open myself up to the emotions of a house, I just kind of nudge them to a more neutral place on the spectrum. Turn down the intensity."

"Where did you learn to do this?" I asked, envisioning some sort of Hogwarts for psychics.

"When I was a kid, Zayde told me stories about his mother who had a gift similar to mine. She was an empath with an emotional affinity with people in much the same way I have with spaces. Zayde told me about how she could manipulate emotions of people around her to calm down heated situations. He thought I might be able to do the same kind of thing. It was part of the reason he took me to meet her when I was a kid. I was young, and we were only there for two weeks, but she did her best to teach me how to meditate and tune in to the energy around me. I admit, I wasn't a good student. But I liked the feeling of oneness when I let the energy fill me. As I grew older, I began to experiment with the meditation. I wish now that she had lived long enough for me to visit again. I'm sure there are more things I'm capable of that I don't know about."

"Okay, so how does this emotion thing work?"

"Um . . . let me try to show you." Sasha moved to sit cross-legged in the middle of the floor, rested his fingertips on the carpet beside his thighs and let his eyes drift closed. He took a deep breath and let it out slowly, then grinned. "Never done this with an audience before."

"No worries. I'm not judging, only curious."

He let his grin fade and took a couple of more breaths.

"I sort of meditate on the emotions of the space, setting whatever I'm feeling aside and let them fill me."

I leaned forward with my elbows on my knees.

For several minutes, Sasha didn't say anything, just breathed. Without thinking about it, I slid down to the floor and mirrored him. When I'd been married, Melissa had talked me into going to a meditation center with her once. She'd said it would help with my ADD. It didn't. I spent an hour kneeling in a room with a bunch of hippies, my mind racing a million miles an hour and my foot falling asleep.

What Sasha did was like meditation, but with more purpose. I breathed in and out in the same rhythm as he did, but didn't feel any emotional connection with the room. Instead, I watched him, his eyes closed, lips parted. Just his presence calmed me in a way no one else's ever had.

"Okay," Sasha said softly. "I'm fully connected now."

"What's it like?"

"Like energy coursing through my veins. My stomach is a little queasy and my neck muscles are tightening. I'll probably get a headache soon."

"So are you going to turn the volume down or whatever?"

He gave a slight shake of his head. "No. There is too much going on here for that to do any good. I need to open myself up and absorb as much of the bad juju as I can to remove it from the house altogether."

"Is that safe?"

"Shhh . . ."

I watched and waited. The tiny wrinkles in Sasha's brow deepened, and his cheeks began to flush pink. The minutes ticked by at a snail's pace, and I had to sit on my hands to keep from fidgeting and wrecking his concentration.

When his breathing grew rapid, I stopped mirroring him. And when the beads of sweat appeared on his brow, my worry cranked up ten notches. I wanted to stop him, but feared hurting him. Whatever he was doing seemed to take deep focus, and I was afraid of what would happen to all that energy if I broke his fragile connection.

I let my eyes drift closed and attempted to feel something again. The air seemed lighter, but that was probably just my imagination. I believed in what Sasha could do, but didn't fool myself into thinking I had any more psychic ability than a rock.

The sound of Sasha shifting made my eyes pop open. His face was red now and a line of sweat dripped from his temple down his neck. His body trembled, and I almost reached for him.

"You okay, Sash?" I whispered.

He gave one quick nod and opened his eyes; they were bloodshot and distant. Without a word, he scrambled to his feet and lurched toward the back door. I followed him out, clenching my fists to keep from grabbing his shoulders. Sasha fell to his hands and knees on the overgrown grass and heaved out his lunch. I rushed back into the kitchen to get a glass of water, and then carried it and a paper towel to where he knelt, drooling on the lawn.

I squatted beside him, set the glass on the ground, and rubbed his back in slow circles until he stilled.

"You all right?"

He spat again and then sat back on his heels. "Yeah."

I handed him the paper towel to wipe his mouth and followed with the water so he could rinse. Exhaustion was written all over his face. As he caught his breath, I brushed the curls off his sweaty brow and examined him for signs that he might be sick again.

"Don't stare at me like that. I'm okay."

"All right." I held my hand out to help him up, and as he got to his feet, I noticed something strange. The four areas of grass that had been directly under his hands and knees were brown and crispy as if all the moisture had been sucked out of those points in the otherwise lush yard. I shifted my focus, expanding my view of the property. Dotted around in similar groups of four were dozens of other burnt-brown spots. The tree in the back of the yard held nothing but dead leaves, not unusual for October, but this was coming up on June.

I turned to meet Sasha's eyes, where I was met with guilt and shame mixed with determination.

"Sasha, honey, what did you do?"

CHAPTER 22
SASHA

I dreamed I was being smothered by a bear. When I awoke, Nick was sprawled across my chest and his beefy leg was slung over my thighs. I groaned and pushed at him, which made him curl his arm and leg around me tighter.

"You're hot," I complained without conviction.

"Um, not so bad yourself." He kissed my shoulder, and snuggled into my neck.

Setting aside the invasion of my space, I relaxed in his embrace and listened to the morning rain trickling on the roof above. We were curled up on my floor pallet because when he'd brought me home last night, Nick had refused to leave me alone. I guess my demonstration had messed with his head. I'd known it would. On a normal night, I would have performed the clearing act two or three times, but Nick had refused to let me continue. Instead, he'd insisted on driving me to Denny's to get something to eat, and then home to rest. Not gonna lie. It was nice to be taken care of.

"This floor is killing me," Nick groaned. "How can you stand it?"

I stroked the hair on his arm. "It works better when you sleep flat on your back."

Nick sat up, massaging his shoulder. "But then I can't hold you."

I grinned at his pouty morning face, his short hair sticking up in funny tufts. The words came out before I had a chance to think about them. "I don't care where I sleep as long as I get to wake up with you."

Nick's expression melted into a smile. He rolled over and landed on top of me, sending my breath out with an "Oof!"

"You mean it? You like waking up together? 'Cause I was thinking, maybe you should move into my place. With me. Like for real."

The blood rushed to my face and the atmosphere in the room thickened. I pushed Nick off and sat up, rubbing my forehead. It wasn't that I didn't want to be with Nick. Of course, I wanted to be with him. I knew which direction my feelings were heading in. But would he even ask if I wasn't homeless? The imbalance in our situations weighed on me, and for the millionth time, I wished I brought more to this relationship. If I ever did decide to shack up with someone, I'd need to be one hundred perfect certain it was because we wanted to be together, and not out of our financial need.

Not to mention, this was all moving crazy fast. The guy had only recently discovered he liked dick. What if some woman came around and caught his interest? Or another guy for that matter. What if I got all comfortable in his life and he changed his mind about me?

"Well?"

I shrugged, my mouth suddenly dry. The house filled with a weird energy, as if it were also waiting for my answer.

Nick scooted up next to me and slung his arm around my shoulders. "Look, I know this is quick, but Christ, it's never been like this for me before. This needing to touch someone all the time. Needing to understand someone and wanting them to understand me."

I felt the sincerity of his words, even felt them back, but I wasn't sure I could take a chance on them yet. "Can I think about it?"

"You have to think about whether to sleep on the floor alone or in a comfortable bed with me?" He said it jokingly, but couldn't disguise the hurt in his tone.

"It's more than that and you know it." I ducked out of his hold and turned to face him. "I might be in a desperate situation, but this is a big step for me. For us."

"I know."

"Do you? Why do you want me to live with you, Nick? Tell me."

"A million reasons. You want me to list them all?"

"Top three."

He swore under his breath, and then reached for my hands. Looking in my eyes, he counted off. "One. I like sleeping with you. It feels right. Two. I care about you. I don't care if that freaks you out or what. It's the truth. Three. I think we make a good team. We're friends and partners and lovers. And I want to continue that way for a good long time. There. Satisfied?"

I searched his face, finding no deception, only naked emotion, as if he'd laid his heart out on the ground and was praying I wouldn't stomp on it.

"So it's not because you feel guilty for kicking me out of here in a few weeks? Or because I'm gonna end up back on the streets again soon?"

"Of course not! If easing my guilt was all it was, I'd ask Damien to house you until you got on your feet. I'm not asking you to be my roommate, Sasha. I'm asking you to share my life."

I hated to bring it up so early in the morning, but it had to be said. "And how can we do that with Frank Diamond hanging over your head? You might think I'm overly cautious, but what would we do if you defaulted on your loan? Are you even going to have a place to go home to?"

Nick scrubbed his hands down his stubbly face in frustration. "I don't know, okay? I can't think about that right now. I need to stay focused on getting the project finished so I can pay him off and give my business a jump start."

I rested my hand on his forearm, trying to say this as gently as I could. "It would be worse for both of us to start something together only to have it blow up in our faces. I have my own plan. When you sell this place, I'm going back to the shelter for a while until a room opens up at the Michigan Inn. I'm already on the waiting list."

"No way! I'm not going to just sit back and let you live in a shelter."

"You may not have a choice. Do you really think a guy like Diamond is going to renegotiate a payment plan based on a sliding scale of your income? Fuck no. He's not running a charity. He's gonna come after you with all he's got. Especially knowing you have a nice, middle-class family who loves you and would mortgage themselves to the teeth in order to bail you out of trouble."

Nick's face blanched and his eyes moistened.

"Jesus, Sasha. He's gonna go after my family, isn't he? He knows Steven and Damien are my brothers, and that they both own businesses. My parents have their retirement savings, but they need that to live on. I can't let him go after them. I won't."

I cupped his trembling fingers in my hands and gave him what I hoped would be a reassuring smile. "I'm gonna help you as much as I can so that doesn't happen. But we need to be realistic here."

I let that hang in the air a moment, giving him time to absorb. Then, I reached up to rub slow circles over his back, the tension in his body slowly eased.

"You believe I can do it, right?"

I answered honestly. "If I had any money, I'd bet it all on you."

"I don't know why you have so much faith in me, but I'm grateful for it."

"Well, I think I care about you too."

His eyes lit up and he failed to keep the smirk off his face. "You think?"

"Yeah. I think. But I still need a little time to ponder on the whole moving-in-together thing. I've never been in a serious relationship before, and I don't want to screw it up just because you're too impulsive for your own good."

He pulled me in for a deep kiss, and before I knew it, I was pinned under him. "We could start out at my place, but once this house sells, we can look for something bigger."

"I didn't agree to anything—"

There was a lurch in the atmosphere. Loneliness and a deep sense of loss filled me. I pushed Nick away and sat up, opening myself up to the house. Its emotions began to swirl and roll.

"I know, I know," Nick continued, not realizing what was happening. "You didn't agree yet. But I can still plan for when you do. How about a place in my parents' neighborhood? Not next door. Christ, that would be a nightmare. I'm just thinking that part of town. Bet we could rent a little bungalow for cheap."

My body went hot and cold at the same time, making me break into a cold sweat.

"Stop," I said, placing a damp palm on Nick's arm. "Stop talking a minute."

He sat up, studied my face, and pressed a hand to my forehead. "Do you have a fever? You're all flushed."

"Not me. The house."

"The house has a fever?"

"No. The house is upset with us talking of moving out. It doesn't want to be alone again."

Silently, I attempted to soothe the house. I pictured a family eating dinner in the new kitchen in the hopes it would see the potential. It didn't. Instead, a vision of phantom furniture rose around me from some point in the past. I tried not to be disconcerted with the fact there was now a desktop cutting through my neck, decapitating me, and I examined the vision to see what the house was trying to tell me.

The room was a mess. The bed was unmade and heaps of clothes piled around an overflowing hamper in the corner. A gigantic tower of beer cans stood stacked against one wall, and a blue bong sat on the floor next to the bed. The Dave Matthews Band and Cake CDs stacked on the desk next to me gave me a rough time period for the vision. This must have been the room of one of the college guys who'd trashed the house when they left it.

"Nick's not going to sell you to someone who will use you as student housing. Why would he put all this work into you if he was going to just let you get trashed again? Right, Nick?"

Nick looked startled, but then he cleared his throat and said, "Uh, yeah. I'll make sure you go to a good family."

You.

I groaned. "House, I can't stay here. Even if Nick gave me a deal, I can't afford you."

The air around me vibrated angrily. *You.*

"No, House. You know I gotta move on soon. You knew when I came here that it was temporary."

Suddenly, the energy of the house rolled, and a groan and a *crack* sounded above us.

"That wasn't thunder," Nick said, hopping up to look out the window at the falling rain.

"Oh shit," I muttered. I hopped to my feet and went for the attic steps. Careful not to step on anything stabby with my bare feet, I walked back to the general area over my room. There were several steady drips of water leaking in from the roof.

"Are you fucking kidding me?!" Nick yelled. "The roof was fine. Why's it leaking?"

Because the house made it leak.

"What happened?" He leveled his narrowed eyes on me. "Why did the roof suddenly spring a leak? It was that talk about you moving out, wasn't it?"

I nodded, embarrassed that it was my fault. "I'm sorry, Nick. I knew the house was attached to me, but I didn't think it would do this."

His face went pale. "I don't believe it. I totally buy into what you can do with the whole psychic-communication thing, but I never thought the house could do something so . . . real."

"You mean affect the physical world? Unfortunately, it can. Ever heard of poltergeists?"

"Like pissed off ghosts who throw shit? Yeah, I saw the movie."

"Same concept."

"The house did this?"

"Yes, but it takes a hell of a lot of energy. It's completely closed itself off to me right now. It should be quiet for a while. Look, I'll get a couple of those five-gallon buckets from downstairs to catch the drips." I turned back toward the attic steps.

"Fuck! I'll have to run to the hardware store for a tarp."

We went back down to the bedroom to pull on some clothes.

"The rain is supposed to let up this morning sometime," Nick said. "Maybe once the sun comes out, I can climb up there and patch in a few shingles."

I hoped a few shingles was all it would take. Considering my admittedly meager cash reserves, I might be able to pay for a patch. It was the least I could do.

We walked down to the kitchen so I could grab things to catch the leak.

"Wait, Nick," I said, stopping him before he walked out the door. "I'm really sorry. If I'd known this was gonna happen, I would've done something to stop it."

"Hey, it's not your fault." He pulled me close, and I felt his heart racing. "I'm the stupid one who kept pushing the issue. I'm in shock. It scares the shit out of me that the house has this kind of power. But I'm glad you're safe. And I can deal with a few shingles."

He gave me a peck on the mouth, and left out the back door.

I expected to hear Nick's truck start, but instead he called me outside. I poked my head out the back door to see Nick standing in the drizzle, glaring up.

"Come 'ere."

I walked out and looked up where he pointed, expecting to see a shingle or two loosened or sluffed off. But no. Every shingle on the entire rear slope of the house was shrunken up and curled like crispy bacon left in the pan too long.

"Fuck, Nick. That's not just a patch job, is it?"

CHAPTER 23
NICK

Unable to look at the damage anymore, I began to pace like a caged animal. How many times had I said that it was a good thing I didn't have to replace the roof? It hadn't been perfect, but good enough to get me through the sale. Now, the shingles had lifted and curled like the ruffled scales on the back of a pissed-off dragon. What the hell was I going to do? A new roof on a house this size would be over ten grand, and that was with me doing the labor. And my timeline? Blown to shit!

"Do you have insurance?" Sasha asked, his face gone gray. "Maybe they could pay for it."

"An adjuster would take one look at that roof on a house this old, and say it's wear and tear. Fuck, I gotta run to the store. Get those buckets up there."

I stomped off toward my truck, clutching my keys so hard they could've left a permanent imprint in my hand. I didn't glance back at Sasha. I knew he was beating himself up over this, but I didn't have it in me to reassure him right now. If I'd just backed off when he said he needed time to think about moving in together, this never would've happened.

I got in my truck and drove to Home Depot. I grabbed a few tarps and ordered the materials for a new roof using the store credit on my contractor's account. It took all my available credit, which meant I couldn't order the new bathroom fixtures this week like I had planned. Basically, all other work at the house would have to come to a screeching halt until the roof was dealt with and I somehow came up with more cash. The store clerk arranged to deliver the new shingles tomorrow.

Shit. I needed to call my subcontractors to rearrange schedules.

Back in my truck, I noticed the clouds parting. Good. I took out my phone to check the weather for the week. If I got started right away, I should be able to get the new roof on before the next storm was due. I'd need to hire more help, though. Neither Sasha nor Damien had ever installed a roof before. They might be able to strip off shingles, but that was about it.

I called the local Manpower office to see if they had anyone available over the next few days with roofing experience. They agreed to make some calls and get back to me.

Materials and labor taken care of. That just left how to pay for it. I still had money from what I'd borrowed, but it was all earmarked for other things. I'd kept such a tight hold on the budget so far that there was no room to cut any more corners. That left only one option.

A half hour later, I sat in front of Frank Diamond with my proverbial tail between my legs.

"Do I look like an ATM to you?" His face was purple from shouting. "You think I have money lying around and nothing better to do with it? This is a business. I have cash flow to be concerned about, and right now, your little project is sitting on my balance sheet like a massive black hole. Honestly, Nicky, I'm losing faith in your ability to pull this off."

The muscle standing behind me shifted from one foot to the other, making my spine tingle. There were three of them this time. Mountains of men shifting their weight from foot to foot in anticipation of the signal to rip into me.

"Can I just show you something? Let me pull the comps so you can see again what a good investment this is." I opened the browser on my phone and logged into the file with my comp research. "See this house here? It sold two months ago on the same street as my house for two hundred ninety grand. The square footage is slightly higher than I have, but it only has a one-car garage and no yard."

"I'm not interested in your comps! I want my money back with the interest we agreed on."

"I swear to you, Frank. I'm so close."

He examined me through his thick glasses, his jaw tight and cruel.

Sweat beaded on my brow, and I hoped he wouldn't notice. I needed that money. And what Sasha said about Frank was true. If I couldn't pay this back, Frank would put me in the hospital and go after my family for the cash. I squeezed the arms of my chair to keep from running out. I needed this money to make things right. To keep my family safe.

Frank reached in his desk drawer, and I flinched, half expecting him to come out with a gun. But no. Instead, he drew out a ledger book and began to flip through the pages. I held completely still for what felt like an hour. Finally, he slammed the book shut and lit a cigar.

"How much do you need?"

He knew. He just liked to make me to beg. "Fifteen thousand. That would bring our total to one twenty-five." I'd padded the number in case the house decided to get moody again.

"At twenty-five percent, that comes to one sixty."

"Well, more like one fifty-six and change—"

"I don't deal with change. In this business, we round up."

I swallowed and nodded my head. He was going to lend me the money. "Yeah, okay. One sixty. I can do that."

"Not so fast, Mr. Cooper. We still have my cash flow situation to think about. You're not the only person depending on me for financing, you know. And if I want to retain my loyal customers, I need to have the funds available when they need it."

I wasn't sure what he was getting at, but it didn't sound good. "I understand."

"Good!" He smiled in a way that gave me chills. "Then you'll have no problem if we move the timeline up to July first."

My mouth went dry. "But that only gives me three weeks to finish the house, find a buyer, and close the sale!"

"Three weeks and three days. Glad we could come to this compromise, Nicky. I'll have the money to you in the morning. Now, if you don't mind, I have other appointments today." Looking up at the guard on the door, he said, "Get this asshole outta here."

I stood in a daze and felt the hand of a guard on my arm, ready to steer me out. "Wait. What if I can't pay you back or sell the house by the end of the month?"

Frank's eyes hardened to steel. "My associates here would be happy to give you a demonstration."

CHAPTER 24
SASHA

Too bad all the demo was done. I needed to hit something with a hammer. Instead I had to settle on finishing the edges of the wood floor with a hand sander and holding on to my anger tight enough that I didn't gouge the hard wood. I couldn't fucking believe the house had thrown a temper tantrum like a two-year-old and fried its own roof.

"It's not like I want to leave, you know," I said out loud. It could hear me even if it was hiding in on itself. "Believe it or not, I've come to really like you. Well, until that stunt you pulled with your roof. What were you thinking? Do you want to get all moldy? Nick is doing his best by you, and this is the thanks he gets?"

The house for its part felt chastened and remorseful. Not a lot of good that would do Nick now.

The rain let up soon after Nick left, so the leak in the attic tapered off. I soaked the water up with towels and set buckets out in case it started again. When he didn't come back from the hardware store after an hour, I figured he was paying that creep Frank Diamond a visit. I hated that Nick was indebted to him, but I got it. He was just trying to get back into the work he loved, making old homes beautiful. Even if those homes could sometimes be ungrateful.

I sat back on my heels and gazed at the ceiling. "What do you think is going to happen here?" I asked the house. "You know I can't stay. No matter how much I want to. I can't afford to buy you from Nick, and he has to sell you or he's gonna have some nasty guys after him."

And I really did want to stay. It was hard for me to find places that made me feel completely comfortable. This place might be a tad moody, but only because it was afraid of being lonely again. I understood that. The time I'd spent on my own had been rough. People ignored the homeless, staring through them as if they didn't exist. There had been days on end when I hadn't spoken to another human at all. Since I'd met Nick, things had gotten better, but if I had to go back to live alone on the streets again, I might act out too.

"Nick will do right by you. I promise. I'll make sure of it."

The sound of footsteps on the stairs caught my attention, and Kelly popped her head in. Her face went from smiling to puzzled. "I thought I heard voices. Were you talking to someone?"

My face heated. I need to be more careful. Too many people had access to the house right now, and I didn't want them to think I was a nutjob. I flashed her a sheepish grin. "Caught me singing to myself. I do that sometimes when I work alone."

"Oh, yeah. I could see that. You could use some tunes. Want me to get the radio from downstairs?"

I hated the radio. For every decent song played, there would be five horrible ones. "Nah, I'm good. You looking for Nick?" I asked, changing the subject. "He went to the store. Not sure when he'll be back."

"Darn! I wanted his thoughts on this new job I'm working on." Her bottom lip pushed out in frustration. I didn't know why some girls did that fake-pouty thing. It wasn't cute.

"Aren't you still in school?"

"I graduated last week! I'm working for an interior design company now. It's just entry level, but my boss asked me to put together some ideas on a new commission. I really want to impress him, so I'd like Nick's opinion before I present it."

"Wait, you don't work for Nick anymore? You're here all the time."

"Not all the time." She play-slapped my shoulder. "It didn't feel right to bail just because my final grades were in, you know? Nick's done a lot for me these last three years."

I sat back on my heels and wiped my brow. "Three years? As an intern?"

"When I first started working for him, I was an actual employee. It was a part-time summer gig. I'd had the vague idea that I wanted to go to design school after finishing my undergrad degree in art, so I thought a few months at a small construction company would be a good place to start."

"You went from employee to an unpaid intern? Don't take this the wrong way, but isn't it supposed to be the other way around?"

Kelly gave me a sad smile. "Last year, Nick let me go. I didn't make much, but even so, he couldn't afford my wages. He thought that was the end of me, but I talked to my advisor at school, she got it cleared for me to work here for class credit."

"I can't imagine working for a whole year unpaid."

"For me, it was worth it. I live with my brother, so don't have a lot of living expenses. And the job experience and the course credit are payment enough. When I started, I didn't know anything at all, and Nick taught me way more about construction than I ever could've learned from a textbook. In fact, I started by doing some of the same tasks you are. He used to say interior design wasn't only about picking pillow fabric. That if I wanted to make it in this industry, I needed to learn from the ground up. After all, how would I be able to truly work with carpenters and subcontractors if I didn't have at least a basic knowledge of what they do? And the best way of doing that is hands-on. I think I'm the only person in my graduating class with first-hand experience installing a toilet."

Huh. I glanced down at the sander in my hand. Look at me. I was refinishing hundred-year-old hardwood floors. Not something I ever expected to know how to do. And more importantly, I liked it. It beat teaching scales to a bunch of bored high school kids. I liked that feeling at the end of the day of looking over my work and seeing the results of my labor. I could rest easy, knowing I'd done something productive. That I'd contributed.

"What's that face for?" Kelly titled her head to study me.

"Nothing. Just thinking."

"Okay, well, I'll let you finish. Tell Nick to call me when he gets back."

I nodded, turned on the sander, and for the first time in forever, I contemplated my future.

CHAPTER 25
NICK

Aches and pains radiated though my entire body. The busted-up face and bruised ribs were bad enough, but I was too fucking old to be sleeping on the floor. I'd have to get Sasha an air mattress or something. If I could afford one anyway.

I peeled the lukewarm, gelatinous cold packs from my skin and tossed them in a pile beside me. When I got back to Sasha's last night, he'd taken one look at my split lip and bloody nose and had turned all Mother Hen, running out to the drugstore and coming back with more first aid supplies than the Red Cross. It had felt good to let him fuss over me, and I'd let the pain relievers he'd forced on me lull me into a dreamless sleep.

I touched my sore side, assessing the damage. It definitely could've been worse. At least nothing was broke. Frank's men knew how to get a point across without inflicting so much damage that I couldn't work. Today wouldn't be fun, but once I got some coffee in me, I should be able to handle it. I had no choice now. I had a house to finish in about half the time I needed to do it.

Fucking Frank! No, scratch that—fuck me. I was the dumbass who'd thought he could handle doing a deal with a loan shark and escape unscathed. I'd never seriously considered that this all might go tits up on me. My mind drifted to Marty with his arms in casts. Then, I pictured me in that hospital bed and my parents gathered around all worried. If they had to bail me out of this, they'd both have to come out of retirement and go back to work. No way was I going to let that happen.

Sasha mumbled something unintelligible and rolled to press against my side. He was warm and his chin hair tickled my collar. I ran my thumb along his jaw, caressed his ear, and twisted a curl around in my fingers. He was probably awake but refusing to open his eyes in a last stubborn attempt to cling to sleep.

I'd been so stupid to introduce him to Frank. It was one thing for his trained apes to come after me, but what if Sasha got caught up in the middle? Another person I needed to protect from the fallout if I failed.

I turned us so I was seated between his thighs. Only then did he open his eyes to smile up at me. I kissed him, slow and soft, careful with my sore lip, then chuckled when his beard hair stuck to my stubble like Velcro.

"Something else that never happened to me before meeting you."

"It's those two days of growth you've got going on."

"You complaining?"

He rocked his hips so that his morning erection ran alongside my cock. "Does it feel like I'm complaining?"

My body was about to respond in kind when someone started pounding on the front door.

"Fuck me," I groaned, rolling off him.

"Careful what you wish for," Sasha said, yanking his jeans on, "I just might take you up on the offer."

Barefoot, he headed down to see who would show up at our door at—I glanced at my phone—6:47 in the morning.

I yanked on my T-shirt from yesterday. It was splattered with rusty blood stains and dirt. I'd have to go home to shower and change before starting work on the roof. Downstairs, I heard Sasha removing the chain and unlocking the door.

"Morning, Steven."

"Nick!" my brother bellowed. "You borrowed money from Frank fucking Diamond?!"

Shit. A dressing-down by my big bro was never fun, but before seven in the morning?

"I told you a million times, when you got ready to get back into the flipping business, I'd help you line up the financing. But no. You'd rather go to a loan shark than ask for help from your own family. You're so goddamn stubborn!"

I came down and sat on the lower steps to pull my socks on. "Cool it, would ya? You'll wake the neighbors."

"Holy shit, what happened to you?" He grasped my chin and turned my face side to side to get a look.

I knocked his hand away. "Just a little bruised is all."

"Did you report this to the police?"

"Report what? My illegal loan? First thing they would make me do is give the money back, and it's already spent, or most of it is, anyway."

"What about the assault?"

"Frank never raised a hand to me. What am I going to do, report his bodyguards? All that is going to do is piss him off. Besides, it looks worse than it is. I'm fine."

"You're not fine. You can't be. Because if you were, you wouldn't have done something so profoundly stupid as take money from a loan shark with the ability to call in favors from every dirty fighter and criminal in the city."

"How'd you find out anyway?"

"How'd I find out? I ran into that piece of shit Diamond at the UFC fight last night. He wanted me to pass on a little message for you."

"Oh yeah? What's that?"

"Just that July first falls on a Saturday this year, so you'll need to have your closing done on the thirtieth in order to get your money to him on time. Doesn't want you counting on having the weekend or anything."

Steven peered around at the construction zone. We were making great progress, but no way could we have the house finished and sold by then.

"How much are you into him for?" Steven asked.

I didn't want to answer, but what was the sense in hiding it at this point? "A buck sixty."

"A hundred and sixty thousand dollars?" He enunciated each syllable like he was pounding nails in my coffin lid.

"Yeah. All in, including the twenty-five percent interest."

Steven walked over to the window to stare daggers out onto the street.

Sasha sat down on the step next to me and folded my hand in his. Well, at least I had one person in my corner.

After a couple of very long minutes, Steven turned back to us. "If I had known about this before Tod left, I could have bailed you out. But now . . . Did I tell you he got a lawyer and froze most of my assets until we can get the condo sold and all of our stuff divided?"

I was torn between hurting for my brother and wanting to hunt Tod down to give him an ass whooping. "How could he do that? You weren't married."

"No, but we had joint accounts and owned the condo and a few investment properties together. Until we get the split worked out, I'm limited to whatever is in my checking account. It probably will only take a few months, but doesn't sound like you have that much time."

I hadn't really given any conscious consideration to asking Steven to bail me out, but hearing that he couldn't be my safety net even if I needed him made my stomach sink. He was the only person in my family who usually had access to that kind of cash. Damien might be able to scrape together a few thousand dollars, but that would be nowhere near enough to make a difference.

The world felt like it was shrinking in on me, and if I didn't keep moving forward, I'd be trapped.

"Thanks anyway, bro," I said, struggling to keep the defeat out of my tone. "I'll work it out."

"How? Where else are you going to come up with the cash by the end of the month? Even if you worked on this place twenty-four hours a day, you'd never get it sold by the end of the month."

"I'll get the money."

"Where? You gonna rob a bank? Start turning tricks? I hate to break it to you, but your ass is too old to get much on the street."

I leaped to my feet, clenching my fists. "I said, I'll get it! I don't need Saint Steven to ride in on his white horse and save me all the goddamn time. This is not your problem."

"Oh yeah? It'll be my problem when Mom and Dad are torn up over their son getting dragged out of Lake Michigan by his cement shoes. But fine. You want to handle it all by yourself? Have it your way."

Steven slammed the door so hard that the glass in the window panes rattled.

The house went deadly silent. I turned, half-expecting Sasha to be gone too, but there he sat on the third step, giving me a sad smile.

Fuck. What business did I have trying to start something real with him when I was up to my asshole in debt to a wannabe mobster? And then there was sweet Sasha, not criticizing, not offering me empty platitudes or telling me what to do. Just being supportive. I had to make this right for him. For myself. If we had any chance of building a life together, I'd have to get my head out of my ass and fix this.

CHAPTER 26
SASHA

Sweat rolled off me in waves, and I lifted the hem of my T-shirt to wipe my face. While Nick and some guys he'd hired took care of the roof, I'd spent the rest of the week sanding, prepping, and refinishing the hardwood floors. Not an easy job when over a hundred years of former occupants had worn in stains, drilled holes to run cables, and pounded in random nails, probably in an effort to fix squeaks. We'd wrapped up applying the second coat of finish, and I planned to spend the weekend at Nick's place to allow the floors time to dry.

We were busting our ass to get the house done before Frank called in his loan. Damn, seeing Nick roughed up like that had scared the shit out of me. He talked tough about it, saying he'd been hurt worse in the ring during his fighting days, but I hadn't missed the way he winced when he stood up or rubbed his shoulder when he thought I wasn't paying attention. The first couple of days, he'd let me give him pain relievers, but by day three he'd told me to quit acting like a mother hen, he'd take care of himself. I'd taken his feistiness as a sign that he was feeling better.

Nick strolled into the kitchen from the backyard, where he was instructing a couple of high school kids which bushes he wanted torn out. They'd wandered over from across the street after their mother had gotten sick of them moping around the house. Nick, unable to turn down cheap labor, had been happy to give them a weekend project.

"Shower together or separately?" I asked, rooting in my overnight bag for some clean underwear. I was lucky that the bathroom off the kitchen had a shower, since the rest of the house was off-limits.

"Do you even have to ask?"

"Well, come on, then. I want to get down to Zayde's house before dark." We hadn't been back since Frank had turned up the heat, choosing to spend all our time here, and I was anxious to check on the place.

We hurried through the shower and a couple of soapy handjobs. We'd spent every night together for the last week, sometimes at his place, sometimes here, but our intimacies were usually quick affairs dulled by exhaustion. I wanted to fuck him, or have him fuck me, but while I wasn't the most sentimental guy in the world, it didn't seem right to rush that. I wanted to take my time with Nick. Time to explore each other's bodies without our other worries getting in the way. I just hoped that time would come soon.

After a run through a fast-food drive-thru, we got to Zayde's house. As I worked my key in the lock, a voice called out.

"Hey there, Sasha."

I turned to see the old guy from next door standing in the yard. I couldn't remember his name, but he and my zayde used to stand across the back fence and discuss things like weed control and whether the Packers would make the Super Bowl.

I lifted my hand in a wave. "Hi."

"Say, I don't know what's going on, but I've seen you over here cleaning up the place. I thought you should know your mother was here this morning trying to get in. Didn't mean to eavesdrop, but she got angry when her key didn't work."

Shit. The blood ran out of my head all at once. Why'd she have to come back? Couldn't she go somewhere else to screw up her life?

"Was she alone?"

The man shook his head. "No, she was with a girl. 'Bout your age, brown hair. The girl wanted to bust through a window, but your mom said she knows someone who's good with locks."

Nick and I exchanged a glance.

"Thank you," I said. "I appreciate you letting me know."

The neighbor began to turn away, but stopped himself. "Listen, Sasha. I'm sorry about your grandfather. He was a good man. I think he'd be proud of you for helping out around here like this."

All I could do was nod my thanks.

Nick took the keys from me and let us inside.

I dropped into a recliner and buried my face in my hands. The news of my mother combined with fatigue nearly overwhelmed me. "What am I gonna do? She's gonna come back here and turn this place into a shithole again. And God help the place if she starts cooking meth in here. She's been busted for it before. The house will end up condemned if she doesn't blow it up first."

Nick paced back and forth the length of the room. He really didn't need my drama to amp up his anxiety. After a few minutes of silence, he knelt in front of me and took my hands.

"You've been killing yourself over this place, Sash, and I'm afraid it's going to all be for nothing. Your mom's going to come back in and mess up your hard work. I know you don't want to hear this, but maybe it's time for you to walk away. Let her do with it what she wants."

He was right, but when the atmosphere in the room rippled and swirled at his words, I wasn't sure I could simply walk away. This house might just be a cleverly pieced together stack of building materials to Nick, but to me it was sentient. It had a personality. I didn't necessarily want to live here—it was too far from the city center for a guy with no car. And anyway, it was too big for me. But I still felt a responsibility to do right by the place.

"This is so frustrating!"

"I know, babe, but the way I see it, you only have two choices . . . turn over the keys and walk away, or stay and fight. And while I'm not really one to shy from a fight, as long as Rina owns this place, you don't have much to stand on."

An invisible pull began to yank on me in the direction of the back bedroom. "Not this again," I muttered.

"What?"

"Nothing. The house is all agitated from this talk of Mom coming back, and it's trying to pull me into the back room." I looked around. "House, just relax. We'll find a solution."

"Does that help? Talking to it?"

"Not lately."

Nick stood. "Well, we should get on with what we came here for. I'll clear out the back bedroom and you can do your magic in here.

If your mom shows up, we'll deal with her then. Is it going to bother you if I make noise?"

"I should be all right. It's not a deep meditation or anything."

"And everything goes?"

I thought over what I'd seen in the room. "Yeah, everything except the mail. I better go through it. Looks like Mom was stacking up whatever she didn't want to deal with. Let me know when you get to the heavier furniture, and I'll help load it on your truck to take to the dump."

"Sure thing." Nick gave me a kiss on the forehead and walked away. As he did so, the pull of the house shifted from me, and probably over to him. I rolled my shoulders, grateful for the reprieve. The house could tug on Nick all it wanted, he'd never know.

With both Nick and the house occupied for the moment, I moved down to the floor, hoping to get at least one cleansing completed before my mother showed up. I tried to clear my mind, to concentrate on what needed to be done, but it was impossible. Instead, I considered what Nick had said about walking away. I probably should. After all, if Zayde had cared so much about this place, he would've written a will and left it to me or to charity or to anyone but his derelict daughter.

I shook my hands out and rested them on the floor. No sense getting frustrated over what he should've done. I deepened my breathing and tried to relax. Just as I began to tap into the house though, a sharp wave of elation rolled through me. My heart jumped and my cheeks flushed. Then, the house's tension began to fade away.

What the hell?

"Sasha!"

I opened my eyes to see Nick rushing down the hall with an envelope and letter in his hand. "What is it?"

"The reason the house wanted you in that room."

CHAPTER 27
NICK

I shoved the *Past Due* notice at Sasha, my heart racing. I'd had no intention of going through the mail—only wanted to stack it out of the way so it didn't get lost in the shuffle. As soon as I saw the top envelope, though, my stomach had dropped. I'd bought and sold so many properties over the years that I'd realized immediately what I held.

"So," Sasha said. "Mom hasn't paid the property taxes. I would've been more surprised if she had."

"That's not it. Look who it's addressed to."

"Dear Mr. and/or Mrs. Michaels . . . Did Zayde forget to tell them when Bubbe died?"

Frustrated, I stepped forward and pointed. "Not that, this. See the address. Bernard and/or Sasha Michaels."

His brow furrowed, and he didn't say anything.

"What was your grandmother's name?"

"Elizabeth."

"So not Sasha."

"Of course not. Where we come from, Sasha is a male name, you know."

"Yes, but don't you see? The property taxes come in the name of whoever is titled on the house." I held up my phone. "I just checked the City Assessor's website on my phone. Your grandfather put your name on the title. It's been like that for at least ten years."

"But he didn't have a will."

"It doesn't matter. You own this property. Without a will, everything else he had goes to your mom. Everything except the house. Once he died, it became yours alone."

Sasha's face paled, and he steadied himself with the wall. "I own it? Not my mom?"

"No, Sash. It's yours. She has no rights here. All you have to do is take a copy of the death certificate downtown and have his name removed from the deed."

"Shit, I don't know what to say." He tugged at the crown of his hair.

"I know! It's wild, huh?"

"I own a house. Without a mortgage. No more sleeping on the streets!"

I drew him into my arms and placed a kiss on his shoulder. "Never again, baby."

We held each other for a long moment, both reeling from this turn of fortune. I was so damn happy for him.

"Oh, no!" he exclaimed suddenly, eyes growing wide. "I'll have to come up with something to pay the taxes. How am I gonna do that?"

"Don't worry about that now. It's only one year of taxes, and you aren't far behind. The city isn't like the banks. They don't want to foreclose on properties unless they have no other choice. Too much hassle. I've seen homes with a decade of unpaid taxes, and the pencil pushers downtown don't do anything about them. Call the Assessor's Office on Monday. Explain the situation. I'm sure they'll work with you on some sort of payment plan."

Sasha placed a hand on the wall. His lips moved silently as if in a private conversation with the house. I averted my gaze to give him a moment. When he again turned to me, unshed tears had welled in his eyes and a smile split his face.

The naked emotion tugged at my chest. I'd seen this man as low as anyone could get, and rather than turning to crime or drugs, somehow he'd kept finding the strength to pick himself up and plunge forward. And now, finally, something good had happened. His grandfather hadn't forgotten about him. The man had actually taken steps to ensure that Sasha always had a home. The heaviness that weighed on him was gone. He stood straighter, his head held a little higher. Before me stood, I suspected, the real Sasha.

I grinned and held my arms out to him. He rushed at me so hard he had me pinned against the wall with his tongue in my mouth before

I could think about it. There was nothing sweet about this kiss. It was desperate and rough. Exactly how I liked it.

My hands snaked around to grab his ass and pull him tight against my groin. We were both growing hard. When he wrapped his leg around mine and rutted against my hip, that was all I could take. I needed him. He needed me. Our lives weren't perfect, but fuck, he'd just gotten some incredible news, and we deserved to celebrate. BJ's and handies were nice, but we both needed more.

"Ever have a guy over in your bedroom?"

He laughed. "Not since I was a kid. Once Zayde found out I was gay, that put an end to the sleepovers. Why do you ask?"

I scraped my teeth along his neck, making his skin bump up. "Because I want you, and I don't think I can wait until we get back to my house."

"Mmm . . . well, you're in luck. I know where there's a bed."

I locked the dead bolt on the front door in case Rina returned, and followed Sasha down to his basement bedroom. As I descended, my anxiety rose. It had been a long time since I'd felt like a virgin when it came to anything with sex, but suddenly, my guts hummed with self-doubt. Not about Sasha. No, I wanted to be with Sasha in every way possible. But what if I wasn't good enough in the sack to keep him happy?

Sasha turned on a bedside lamp, rather than the harsh overhead light. I'd seen the room before, but now it was clean, mostly bare of personal belongings, except for the poster on the back of the door. A pale man with wild black hair stood on a stage holding a guitar. He was beautiful, and had a bit of the same brooding expression Sasha got whenever he concentrated on something hard.

"Who's this?" I asked.

"Jack White, formerly of the White Stripes. He's solo now. My favorite guitar player."

I'd heard of the band, but wouldn't recognize any of their songs. Truth was, my musical knowledge stopped right around the time Nirvana had. All Melissa had ever wanted to listen to had been Top 40 bullshit, so I'd gotten to the point where I hated the radio.

"I know he's cute, but are you gonna stare at him all night, or are you gonna come down here with me?"

I turned away to see Sasha stripped to his boxers and lying on the light-blue sheets of his narrow twin bed. Christ, his body looked like it'd been chiseled from marble by one of those ancient Greek dudes. I wasn't a religious man, but in that moment, I wanted to worship him.

I shucked my shoes and pants and stretched out on top of Sasha. The bed was way too tiny for the both of us, but when he lifted his legs and wrapped them around my hips, I set that aside to resume the fierce kissing we'd started upstairs.

Sasha pulled on the back of my shirt. I yanked it off and knocked my elbow into the wall, sending a zing up my funny bone.

"Sorry. This bed sucks," Sasha said.

"I don't care how small it is as long as you're in it." I bent to his neck and sucked on the skin above his collar.

We hadn't talked about things like who would top and who would bottom, but I'd been giving it some serious thought these last few weeks. The easy thing for me to do would be to ask to top. I'd had anal sex a couple of times with women, and I knew the drill, though I'd never gotten the feeling that they'd enjoyed it. Not like the guys I'd seen in porn. Yeah, yeah, porn wasn't like real sex, but I did happen to know a bit about biology and prostates, and I had an older brother who'd assured me many times that getting fucked by another man was sexy as hell. There was something in the way those guys in the videos looked when they were getting plowed by another man that made me hot . . . and made me want to try it.

I took my time touching and kissing Sasha down his chest to his belly. He smelled like salt and soap from his shower, and tasted like clean man. He filled my senses, and my anxiety began to ebb. This was Sasha, and there was no one in the world I'd rather be with. When my exploring mouth reached his waist, I bit the band of his shorts and pulled.

"Here," Sasha grinned, "let me help you with that."

We both stripped our shorts off, and I went back to traveling his body. Hip, thighs . . . When I licked his knee, Sasha squirmed and bucked.

"Stop that!" he laughed. "You're not the only one who's ticklish. If you don't behave, you'll have to leave."

"You wouldn't make me go home," I said, my bravado coming back. I moved up to kiss along his jaw. "Not when I'm about to give you the best night of your life."

"Pretty confident there. Sure you're ready to fuck a man?"

I rocked my hips so our cocks slid together. Sasha moaned and pushed up against me, chasing friction.

"As much as I would love that," I said, pausing to gaze into his eyes, "tonight, I want you in me."

CHAPTER 28
SASHA

I froze and stared Nick in the eyes. "Are you sure? I can go either way."

His cheeks flushed, making the fading bruises stand out. "Yeah. I'm ready. I trust you."

My chest swelled, and I swallowed past the lump in my throat. "I'm . . . honored, I guess. I mean, I just hope I can make it good for you."

"I'm sure you will." He smirked. "Now, shut up and have your way with me."

With a little awkward maneuvering, I flipped us over, positioning myself on top. Nick grinned up at me. Damn, he was gorgeous. And he wanted me. How did I ever get so lucky? I sucked his full bottom lip into my mouth and gave it a playful nip. Nick answered by grasping the back of my head and drawing me into a deep, almost frantic, kiss.

I was painfully hard, and judging by how Nick was rutting against my body, he was as eager as I was to move things along. I tried to retrieve the condom from my wallet and almost fell off the tiny bed.

"Damn it," I muttered, standing up. I found the condom, and then got out the economy-sized bottle of lube from the nightstand drawer.

"Thought you never brought guys here," Nick teased, looking pointedly at the huge bottle.

"I didn't, but after I chafed myself beating off, I learned pretty quick how to take better care of my equipment."

"The Jack White poster?"

I grinned wickedly. "You wouldn't believe how he handles a guitar." I tossed him a fat pillow. "Here, turn over and lay your stomach across this."

Nick's brows raised with intrigue, and he did as I instructed.

The position sent his ass into the air, open and exposed. I kneeled on the bed behind him and gripped the globes of his cheeks. His ass was perfect. Muscular, but squeezable. I kissed down his lower spine to the top of his crack, making him squirm. I sure hoped Nick was up for this, because I was so ready to be inside him, to finally make him mine.

I flipped open the lube and slicked my finger. Then I began to massage it into his hole. He was tense at first, the ring of his muscles tightening at the invasion. I whispered and massaged until he relaxed. Then, he bore down on my finger eagerly.

"Is this okay?" I asked.

"Yeah, give me another one," he said, his shaky voice betraying his nerves.

Slowly, I added a second finger and scissored them to open him inside. His muscles loosened around me. Then, I curled my fingers to press against his gland. I could almost feel the zing go through his body, and he made a sound that was a cross between a groan and a yelp.

"Holy shit . . . Yeah, do that again." He pushed back onto my hand, but I withdrew. I needed to be inside him. To show him how much I wanted him.

"You ready for me?"

He peered over his shoulder to see me lubing up my condom-sheathed cock. "If you can do that with your dick, you may never get me out of this bed."

I leaned over his back to kiss his shoulder. "Challenge accepted."

He reached behind to spread himself wider.

"Fuck, you're hot," I muttered. With great restraint, I pushed inside inch by inch, until I was fully seated. I didn't move, giving him time to acclimate himself to the invasion. "Breathe, Nick. Relax into it."

He took a deep breath and the tension in his body eased. "This is so weird. And perfect. But weird."

"Does it hurt? You gotta tell me if it hurts."

"A little. Mostly, it's just different." He rocked back onto me, stretching around my cock.

When I couldn't take it anymore, I began to move, shallowly at first, then when I sensed he wanted more, deeper, but still slow. With every thrust, he grew bolder, pushing back to meet my strokes. I wound my arm around his chest and bit into the meat of his shoulder, letting the taste and scent of his clean sweat fill my senses. Being inside Nick was like nothing I'd ever experienced before. His body was so strong and powerful and, god, I needed him. Even pressed against his naked back, I couldn't get close enough.

We rocked together like that for several minutes, panting and moaning in unison. Then I eased out.

"Hey, we're not done yet," he complained.

"Not leaving, adjusting. Turn over, and put that pillow under your hips."

"Bossy."

I had to stand so he could roll over in the narrow space. Once he was situated, I positioned myself between his legs. I bent to lick his cock from root to tip before lifting his legs with my arms and entering him again. This time my cock nudged right into his P-spot, and he shouted. Chasing Nick's pleasure, I sped up my strokes, reveling in the way he bit his lip as he moaned.

"God, Nick," I panted. "You're perfect."

He answered with a wink, then hooked his ankles behind my ass to draw me closer. We traded sloppy kisses as I slid back and forth over his sweat-slicked body.

"Touch yourself," I begged. "I want to see you come."

The way his dick was leaking, it'd be over quick. Never taking his gaze from mine, he stroked himself until the combination sent him spurting. The sight of his pulsing cock sent me over the edge with a guttural moan.

We clutched each other, chests heaving. When our breaths calmed, I gently pulled out and turned to dispose of the condom. He tugged the pillow out from under his hips, yanked off the case, and used it to mop up the come on his chest before dropping it on the floor. I returned to cuddle up behind him, my hand lazily stroking his chest. Then we did what men do best after good sex. We fell asleep.

CHAPTER 29
SASHA

A shift in the room's atmosphere woke me. I yawned and checked the clock. We'd only been dozing for an hour or so. I tuned in to the house and sensed an uneasy stirring. Something was up. I slid out of bed and pulled on my jeans.

"Where're you going?" Nick mumbled, still half-asleep.

"Upstairs. I'll be right back."

I gave him a peck on the mouth before scooping up my T-shirt and heading upstairs. I'd just entered the living room when I heard it—the *click* and scrape of metal. Someone was trying to pick the door lock.

Mom.

Just who I wanted to speak to.

I flipped the dead bolt and flung the door open. In fell Jerry, on his knees and still holding the Swiss army knife he'd been using on the lock. My mom stood behind him, mouth gaping open with obvious shock. She recovered quickly though, pushing past Jerry and coming inside. I let her. We had some things to discuss.

"Sasha! I had no idea you were here." She laughed and scanned the dim room with rapid eye movements. Scabs littered her forearms where she'd been picking, and her hair hung in greasy hunks. I could tell she was high by the way she talked with her hands, waving them around in wide arcs. "Thank you for keeping an eye on the house for me. Oh, and it looks like you cleaned! Such a good boy."

"Mom, we need to talk. Jerry, get the fuck out of here before I have you arrested for trying to break in." I pulled the phone out of my pocket to drive my point home.

Jerry scrambled to his feet. "I wasn't breaking in! I was helping my woman get back into her house after you changed the locks. Go ahead, call the cops! We'll have *you* arrested."

I picked up the notice from the City Assessor's Office and shook it. "Oh yeah? Well, per the city, I own this property. Isn't that right, Mom?"

Jerry looked to Mom as if for support. Her expression shifted from shock to guilt and into resolve. "Jerry, go wait in the car. I need to speak with my son."

He fumed at the dismissal, but when she didn't give in, he took his tools and stomped off.

I switched on a table lamp. Mom squinted in the light, but her dilated pupils didn't shrink. I really didn't want to have this conversation with her when she was high, but if I waited for a better time, it might never come.

"I appreciate all your help around here." Mom smiled, clearly thinking she could smooth things over between us. "Now, give me the keys so I can swap out the old ones."

"Are you crazy? I'm not giving you keys."

"Don't be silly, Sasha. I'm home now."

"This isn't your home. It hasn't been since you were eighteen and you abandoned me here." I held the tax notice out again. "Besides, I found the secret you've been keeping from me."

She crossed her arms and gave me a *So what?* look.

"I own this place, Mom. Me. Not you. And you knew about it this whole time, didn't you?" My voice broke with emotion. When Nick first showed me the notice, I'd thought there was no way my mother could have known that the deed was in my name. It was one thing for your adult child to leave home because they didn't want to live under your roof, but it was a whole other thing to kick them out of their own house and force them to live in the streets while you trashed the place. My mother was messed up and selfish, but I'd never thought she was malicious.

"Of course, I knew. Do you think I'm stupid? But why should I live in one roach-infested apartment after another? With the old man gone, I could finally live here without his nagging."

"But it's my house!"

"And I'm your mother! You have no respect for me. Neither of you ever did. This house should've been mine, but my father always chose you. From the time you could talk, you sucked up to him. And he got off on it. 'Oh, Sasha has such good grades. Oh, did you know Sasha's the best musician in his school?' He always loved you more!"

"He was keeping you informed about your child."

"He was rubbing it in my face! And then he goes and gives you the house. He didn't care at all what happened to me."

"And what the hell did you think was happening to me for the last year? I've been sleeping in parks, in shelters, in doorways, in abandoned houses. Cold. Hungry. Scared. Where the fuck were you when I needed you, huh? You knew I had a perfectly good bed right here, and you kept me from it."

"You never would have let me stay here."

"Maybe I would've, maybe not. We'll never know now." I ran my hands through my hair and gripped tightly. It wasn't worth fighting with her like this. "If you would just clean yourself up, get a real job, stay out of trouble—"

"I will not be lectured by my own kid," she yelled. "Who's the parent here, huh? You think you're so much better than me, is that it?"

She was spiraling into a hissy fit, and I needed to get her back on track. "Mom, can't we have one serious conversation about this? The last thing I want to do to anyone is kick them out of their home, but I won't live with the drugs. How about we work together to get you clean? I'll go to meetings with you. I'll go with you to that free mental health clinic and see about getting you some counseling. Or better yet, maybe you could go back to that rehab place and give it an honest chance."

"I've tried, Sasha!" Her tiny fists were clenched and shaking at her side. "How many times have I told you and Abba those state rehabs don't work. They're as dirty and corrupt as the streets. Last time I was in there, a male nurse was sneaking in pills in exchange for blowjobs from the female patients. And then there was the ex-con bitch who was pimping out patients to the night janitor in order to supply her in-house heroin ring. Hell, I met Jerry at an NA meeting three years ago. He goes sometimes when his weed sales are down."

"I'm sorry the last year has been uncomfortable for you, but my life has been nothing but shit for the last twenty-five years. I'd love to get clean, Sasha. Get clean, finish my GED, get a job, find a stable relationship with a man who has his shit together . . . but that kind of life is only for people with means that I don't have. I'm doing my best here. I've got it under control."

We glared at each other, her visibly trembling with her anger.

"Okay," I said. "You have everything under control. Is that why your skin is all pockmarked and scabby? Why your teeth are gray and rotting? Why you smell like—"

"Stop it! You can't talk to me like that."

"Actually, I can. This is my house. And if you want to live here, you know what you need to do."

Her lip shook. "My stuff—"

"You can come by when you're sober and go through the house to take what you want. I'm not dealing with you anymore when you're high. Go on. Get out. I'm done."

Rina hitched her ratty purse onto her shoulder and stalked out, head held high like it was her idea to leave. I slammed the door on her ass and flipped the bolt home. Pressing my forehead to the cool door, I let out a shuddering breath.

"You okay?" came Nick's voice. I turned to see him leaning in the kitchen doorway, his arms crossed over his bare chest.

I nodded. "Yeah, I think so. How much of that did you hear?"

"Enough."

I shoved off the door and crossed to him. Wrapping my arms around his waist, I buried my face in his neck. His arms embraced me, and he sank one hand into my hair where he always played with my curls.

This is home to me. Not the house, but Nick.

When had that happened? When had this man come to mean more to me than where I slept at night?

"I'm sorry about your mom."

"No. She's just Rina now. I have no mom. Never really did."

CHAPTER 30
NICK

"Hey, Dad," I said wearily, patting him on the back as he sat belly-up to Damey's bar, eating a cheeseburger and chili-cheese fries.

"Good to see you, son. Jesus, Nick! What did you do to your face?"

I touched the faded, yellow bruise beneath my eye. "Just a stupid accident."

"Looks like you accidentally fell into somebody's fist."

"No worries, Dad. A little disagreement."

"And it looks like you haven't slept in days. You're not working yourself too hard, are you? Maybe you should take a few days off."

"I'm fine."

He was right; I'd barely slept and had spent every waking moment I could working on that damn house. And all morning, I'd felt like I was on autopilot. Earlier, my mind had been so preoccupied with my task list that I'd stumbled over a small stack of lumber and almost face-planted. Sasha had insisted I take a break and go pick up lunch. Now, I perched on the stool beside my dad with my knee bouncing, frustrated with wasting time when I could be finishing the built-in bookshelves.

Damien stepped out of the swinging door from the kitchen and refilled the glasses of a couple of old men at the end of the bar. I nodded a greeting to him.

The lunch order probably had a few more minutes before it was ready, so I tried to will my exhausted body to relax a moment. I wanted to lay my head down on the bar, but feared I'd fall asleep.

Now that the roof was done, I'd decided to keep the Manpower guys on in a hopeless attempt to get back on schedule. In addition to my skeleton crew, Steven had talked a couple of his friends into coming over to donate some labor. They were skilled guys and I'd take any help I could get, but they could only be there a few hours in the evenings. Steven had probably promised to pay them on the side, but I was too embarrassed to ask. Maybe if I got the house sold, I'd be able to pay him back.

If I was smart, I'd pack up my things and leave town.

Damien typed into the register and ripped off a bill, slapping it onto the bar in front of me.

I slid my credit card to him. "Don't forget the family discount."

Damien swiped my card and passed the slip to me to sign. "You mean like the one you gave me when you replaced my electrical panel?"

"That was a hell of a lot of work, and I did give you a discount, remember?"

"Yeah, that minus three cents you wrote on my invoice was hilarious."

"Quit bickering, you two," Dad said with a mouth half-full of burger. "Always were embarrassing me in public."

Damien and I exchanged grins. It was only our way of messing around. He knew I had actually charged him half of my normal labor rate on that electrical panel, just as I noticed he hadn't charged me for the bottles of soda he always included in the bags.

I signed the slip with a messy scribble, adding a three-cent tip for the hell of it, and handed it back.

Damien glared at it and muttered, "Asshole."

The door behind us opened. Damien glanced up, and his expression turned from welcoming to concerned. I looked over my shoulder, and my stomach dropped. In the door stood two track-suited giants and one bug-eyed man who only came up to their chests. Frank fucking Diamond.

"Nicky! I'm surprised to see you here. Thought for sure you had too much work for leisurely lunch breaks."

The tracksuits positioned themselves to block my exits and stood with their hands clasped in front of themselves like Secret Service agents on duty. Out the window of the front door, there was another one stationed on guard, presumably to prevent anyone else from entering the bar. I could hold my own in a regulation jiujitsu match, but as I'd learned last week, my fighting skills were nothing against multiple guys who didn't worry about fighting fair.

I sat up straighter on my stool, trying to project a confidence I didn't feel. Every nerve in my body was on edge. Out of the corner of my eye, I saw Damien grasp the handle of the baseball bat he had tucked under the bar. My father glanced from Frank to me, obviously trying to figure out what was going on.

With a grin that could only be described as *menacing*, Frank stepped forward. "You must be Mr. Cooper. I'm Frank Diamond, a business associate of Nick's."

My father nodded, not offering a hand. It didn't take a PhD to look at overconfident Frank and his Wall of Traveling Muscle to know exactly what kind of man he was. Thankfully, Dad didn't ask any questions, just sat up a bit straighter, probably trying to accentuate his height, which wasn't nearly as impressive as it had been in his youth.

"And this must be your brother. Damien, is it?"

Damien studied Frank wearily. Somewhere under the counter was an alarm that reported to the police department. I wasn't sure if it was within his reaching distance, but it made me feel better knowing it was there.

Frank maintained a creepily pleasant smile while he glanced around the room, presumably noting the position of the two security cameras up in the corners. Then, he turned his cold gaze on me.

My heart pounded so hard it hurt. This was all a message to me. That he could get to my family. He knew who they were and where they hung out. I felt like a tightrope walker navigating above a pit of crocodiles in the dark. I had to get Frank away from them.

"Something I can help you with, Frank? Maybe we can go outside and talk."

"No, no. It's all right. I saw your truck outside and thought I'd come ask how our house is coming."

"Good," I said, my voice pitched too high to be natural. "Picking up some lunch for the crew. I gotta get back soon. Lots of work to do." Thank fuck I hadn't brought Sasha with me today. Frank didn't seem to have realized that Sasha was more important to me than an employee.

"That there is." Frank wandered over to one of the two stained glass windows that flanked the bar. This window showed a scene of old-timey monks getting merry with barrels of ale. "Beautiful job restoring this place. You have these windows made locally? They look too delicate for a tavern. You know, when these break, they shatter into a million pieces."

Damien watched as Frank pressed a finger to the glass. "This is a friendly neighborhood place. I don't tolerate roughhousing in here."

"You must have good security."

"The best. It helps that the cop shop is just down on the next block. Any trouble, and they can be here in an instant."

He chuckled softly and held his hands up. "Good thing I mean no trouble. Well, Nicky, don't spend too much time lollygagging around. July first will be here before you know it."

I gave a tight nod.

Frank waved to his men and they left, taking most of the oxygen in the room with them.

When the door shut, I let out a heavy sigh and dropped my head into my hands.

"Who the fuck was that, Nick?" Damien's eyes blazed with a deadly combination of anger and fear.

"Son?" Dad said, resting a hand on my arm. "You in trouble?"

"No, Dad, it's nothing."

"Sure it is," Damey huffed. "What was that 'our house' business?"

Dad clasped my forearm and gave me a look that I hadn't seen since high school. "Nick, tell me what's going on. What did he mean by 'business associate'?"

"Really, Dad. It's nothing. He's a local boxing promoter, runs a gym."

"Quit dodging my questions. You doing some sort of business with his guy? Is it drugs?"

"No, of course not."

"And what's all this 'Nicky' bullshit?" Damien demanded. "You never let anyone call you that, even when we were kids. What's he got on you? Oh, shit! Don't tell me . . . He's the one financing your house flip."

Before I had a chance to answer, Tasha, the lunch cook, came out from the kitchen carrying two big bags of boxed lunches.

"Here you go, Nick. Six burgers with the works and extra fries."

"Thanks, Tasha." I stood, gathered the bags and patted my dad on the back. "Don't worry, Dad. I'm not in trouble. He's just a little man who is constantly surrounded by men twice his size. He tries to intimidate everyone. Now, give Mom a kiss from me. See ya."

I turned and, somehow, made my way out of the bar on shaking legs, ignoring my dad's call behind me. I'd barely made it to my truck when someone grabbed my sleeve, startling my heart up into my throat.

"Not so fast," Damien said, glaring. "I was right, wasn't I? You borrow money from that guy?"

I stared at my brother, trying to come up with an answer that wouldn't make him freak out further. I must have taken too long.

"Oh shit! It *is* money! It's that goddamned house, isn't it? That's who you got the money from."

I nodded, staring at the brick wall of the bar, rather than look my brother in the eye.

"Fuck, Nick, how could you? And what was that about July first?"

"The expiration date on my loan."

Damien stood there, pale and with his mouth open, clearly processing exactly how fucked his big brother was.

CHAPTER 31
SASHA

I lay in bed, staring at the drop ceiling of my old bedroom while Nick snored softly beside me in my too-small-for-two-grown-adults bed. He'd been quiet this afternoon, after returning with lunch, but when I asked him what was up, he smiled and assured me he was fine. The unattainable time-crunch we were in was probably getting to him, and I wished there was something, anything, I could do to make this Frank Diamond problem go away.

After busting our asses all day at work, we'd come down to Zayde's house—my house—to get the paperwork to change the deed over to my name, which I planned to do before Rina concocted a scheme to fight me on it. Of course, once we'd gotten here, and I'd noticed how red Nick's eyes were from three eighteen-hour workdays in a row, we'd decided to call it a night and sleep here.

Nick had been out before his head hit the pillow. He always was a good sleeper. Me, I couldn't stop thinking. *This house is mine!* Really mine. As long as I kept the taxes paid, no one would ever be able to take it from me. No more wearing my entire wardrobe in layers to keep the chill out. No more sleeping on park benches. Hell, I didn't even have to sleep on the floor at Nick's flip if I didn't want to. But every time I let myself feel too happy about it, I'd remember the trouble Nick was in, and the anxiety would creep in again.

I climbed out of bed and drew on a pair of flannel pajama pants that had been hiding in the back of the drawer since I'd left home, along with the other discarded remnants of my high school wardrobe. They were a little short, but fit my waist well enough to let me step out for a cigarette. I scooped up my pack and headed to the back porch.

The night was clear but still. The city lights blotted out all but the most determined stars. I sat on the cement stoop and lit up. I should quit, or one of these days I'd end up with a singing voice like Al Pacino. Now that my housing crisis was over and I owned a home, maybe it was a good time to grow up and make responsible decisions like that.

So I guess I'll have to move back to Oak Creek. I groaned softly and then felt guilty for it. I should've been fucking happy. After all, this was the first time I'd felt secure since Zayde died. And while contentment was my favorite emotion, security ran a close second.

So why was I dreading living here?

Honestly, I'd never seen myself living in Oak Creek as an adult. The jobs were all in the city, so I'd always assumed I would stay in Milwaukee after college. And since I didn't have a car, commuting wasn't a viable option.

And then there was the house itself. This was a family home. A place for kids and maybe a dog. There was a reason the house always showed visions of my childhood. It missed those days of hustle and bustle. It wouldn't get that with me, not even if Nick moved in. I was a quiet person with few friends. I'd rather read a book than throw a party. And as outgoing as Nick was, I thought he'd feel the same.

But what about the memories?

I finished my smoke and headed back inside. The kitchen was lit by the stove light, the same way it had burned every night of my childhood. Nightlights such as this and the one that used to be in the bathroom were how my zayde had made me feel safe. I'd never worried about monsters in the dark when I'd had to get a drink of water or use the toilet. But Zayde wasn't here to protect me anymore, and truthfully, I could fight my own monsters now.

I wandered into the living room where yellow light from the street lamp streamed in through the picture window. I'd spent so many hours in front of the TV playing with my Matchbox cars. It used to be hard to run them on the shag carpet, so one day, Zayde had bought me a plastic track set. What happened to my cars and that track? I supposed, like the shag carpeting, they'd been erased by time.

Running my hand along the textured drywall, I reached out to feel the psychic connection with the house. There was a low neutral hum as the house was relaxing from its year of pain and frustration. It had never liked Rina, at least not as long as I could remember. She was too volatile and disrespectful. It had always been clear when she showed up by the shudder in the atmosphere. Now that she was gone, the house wouldn't have to worry about that anymore.

I stepped into the hall and peeked into Rina's room. I'd have to pack her clothes up. Technically, all the furniture in the house was hers too. She could have it if she wanted, but I doubted she had any place to keep it. Probably once I cooled down a bit, I'd let her walk through and take anything she wanted. But not now. I wasn't ready to see her yet. Of course, once she took her stuff, I could paint over that godawful purple.

That got me thinking about other things I'd have to change to make this house livable for me.

I crossed to the bathroom and looked around. I hated the shower in here. After I crossed the five-foot-nine mark, I'd had to stoop just to wash my hair. Nick would have the same problem. The shower in the master was better, but the thought of turning Zayde's room into my bedroom made me queasy. I didn't want to be haunted by the visions of my mother's debauchery for the rest of my life. Plus, that part of the house held too much of Zayde's essence. It was one thing to remember your loved ones and another to be haunted by their memories. I'd basically have to block off this whole back part of the house and leave it unused. What a waste. But then I didn't want to sleep in my little kid room either, not now. Nick and I would need a king-sized bed for sure, and the basement bedroom would never accommodate it.

Nick. Well, it hadn't taken as long for me to warm to the idea of shacking up with him as I'd thought it would. Yes, it was a big step, but one I felt ready for. Now that my housing situation wasn't so dire, I could finally meet him on a more-or-less even ground. If he moved in here with me, it wouldn't be like him saving me or me saving him. I brought a whole house to the table now.

I might be a little young to be thinking about settling down, but my time on the streets had aged me inside. Most guys my age were still bouncing from party to party and bed to bed. I didn't want any of that. I just wanted a warm, safe place to sleep at night and Nick by my side. But would he be happy living here?

If he doesn't get out from this mess with Diamond, he might not be living anywhere.

I chilled at the thought.

Now that my housing woes were over, I needed to find a way to help Nick. Each time I had closed my eyes over the last few days, I'd seen his battered face. The thought of him under that guy's thumb had me terrified. As much as it pained me to think about, maybe Nick should leave Milwaukee.

The spark of an idea tickled my brain, and I gasped.

I needed the internet. Now. Rina had pawned the old desktop that had gotten me through high school, but Nick had a smartphone. I crept back downstairs. He was sprawled across the mattress on his stomach, taking up the entire bed. The tangled sheet was wound around his legs, exposing one bare butt cheek.

"Hey, Nick," I whispered, not wanting to alarm him. "Can I use your phone?"

He muttered something like an affirmation into his pillow. I dug the phone out of his jeans pocket.

"What's the password?"

"Birthday."

I punched in the month and day of his birthday, and the phone came to life.

"Thanks."

Back in the kitchen, I poked around on the web for a good hour, scribbling notes on scratch paper. Then I brought the mail out from the bedroom and began to comb through it. I organized the bills into manageable stacks. Some could be dispatched with a copy of Zayde's death certificate. Others should be paid. The birds were waking up by the time I was finished, but man, I hadn't felt this motivated in a long time. I had a plan. A good one.

I yawned, but I had one last thing to do before turning in. I scrolled through Nick's contacts and found Steven's work number. I pressed it. A voice recording picked up and I fidgeted as it ran through the office hours and fax number. When the tone beeped for me to leave a message, I took a deep breath.

"Steven. This is Sasha. I think I found a way to help Nick."

CHAPTER 32
NICK

"Shit!" I yelled, sticking my thumb in my mouth to soothe the pain from where I'd clipped it with the drill. Working this fast and tired was making me sloppy. The bruises on my legs and large scratch on my forearm were a testament to that. But, fuck, I had to keep going.

"You need to slow down," Kelly said, as she watched me installing the shelves in what Sasha called the library. She was only pointing out the obvious, but I glared at her anyway. "Do you want a bandage?"

"I'm good." I returned to my work. When done, there would be two large shelving units on the sides with a credenza in the middle for extra storage. Above the credenza, I'd wired in a space for a flat screen. It was exactly what I wanted in my home someday—a casual place to kick back and relax. After weeks of nonstop work, the thought of relaxing seemed like an impossible dream.

"I got an email this morning that the bedroom window coverings have to be shipped from another warehouse. They'll take about two weeks."

"Two weeks? I don't have two weeks! I need this house sold in ten days."

As it always did when I thought about the calendar, my gut filled with acid. Most of the big stuff was done, but there was still close to a month of work left to get the house ready to list. Time I didn't have, and my budget didn't allow for me to hire any more labor. My mouth went dry. *Shit, I'm not going to make it.* I squeezed my eyes shut and willed the water filling them to back the fuck off.

"We could always cancel the order and let the buyers purchase their own."

As tempting as that was, I couldn't do that. "Window coverings are expensive, and the last thing buyers want to sink money into after purchasing a home are blinds. If I want to sell fast, I need to make it as turnkey as possible. See if you can find a different style that's in stock. Keep it neutral. And for Christ's sake, keep in budget. Please."

"I'll see what I can do." Kelly jotted notes on her tablet. "Is Sasha around?"

I wish. I could have used him to strip the paint from the porches. "Nah. He had stuff to do this morning."

My voice cracked on that last bit. He was being cagey about something. Had said he had to run out to do laundry this morning, but had somehow left without taking his bag. Even though we spent every night together sacked out on the floor upstairs, he still hadn't answered me about moving in, and now it didn't feel right to bring it up since that would basically mean inviting myself to move in with him. On top of everything, I didn't have enough money to pay the rent on my apartment.

Homeowner now or not, Sasha was still camping out here, probably because the commute to Oak Creek was inconvenient without a car. So while I was curious about what he was up to, I had more important things to figure out. Like which Central American country to hide out in once I missed Frank Diamond's drop-dead date.

"I like him. Sasha."

"What?" I glared at Kelly. She was leaning against the wall wearing a pink sundress that matched the streaks newly added to her hair.

She laughed. "You should see the look on your face! I meant that I like him . . . for you."

I schooled myself into my best neutral expression. Talking about Sasha and my bisexuality with my brothers was one thing. They were my best friends. But I thought we'd been doing a pretty good job staying professional when my employees were around.

"Oh, come on, Nick. How long have we been friends now? Even with as stressed as you've been lately, when Sasha walks in the room, your eyes light up. I know love when I see it."

"Love? It's not . . . you know . . ." I hated that word. I'd only ever said it to Melissa, and even then, rarely. Looking back on our marriage now, I didn't think I'd really meant it. Mostly, I'd loved the idea of

Melissa. Having someone to come home to and talk to about my day. And Melissa had been a damn good listener. Until she'd stopped. And then I'd realized I hadn't been listening to her at all.

But being with Sasha was different. I loved listening to him. Whether he went on and on about past gigs he played or stories about the trouble he and his friend Justin had gotten into as kids. I even loved to listen to him hum as he worked, a habit he didn't seem to be aware of.

The conversation was eating up precious time, so I returned to my installation work. Kelly was not deterred.

"All I'm saying is it's obvious to anyone who knows you that you two are crazy about each other. I didn't even know you two were gay until I saw those moony looks you give each other when you think no one is paying attention."

"I'm not gay. I'm bi."

"That's cool. My older brother, Patrick, is gay. I'm probably bi too. Made out with a girl in my dorm freshman year. I generally date guys, but after her, I think I'd be open to another girl."

I cleared my throat and focused on the work at hand, super uncomfortable with how the thought of Kelly making out with a chick on her dorm bed made me feel. "Well, that's good. I guess. So you should probably be on your way now. To fix the blinds problem, I mean."

She giggled knowingly. "Sure thing, Nick. I'll text you when I figure it out."

Kelly left, and I immediately regretted sending her off. Alone, I couldn't stop my mind from tracking back to the Frank Diamond problem, making my stomach sink again.

I heard a car pull into the driveway. I glanced out the window at Steven's BMW, and then did a double take when Sasha climbed out of the passenger seat. Did Sasha call my brother for a ride? They were friendly enough to each other, but I'd always thought Sasha got along better with Damien. Or hell, me.

"If you needed a ride, you could have called me," I said when Sasha walked in the door. I scowled at Steven. This only made him laugh.

"Settle down, bro." Steven opened his man-purse—okay fine, attaché—and started rooting around.

In an uncharacteristic move, Sasha grasped my head and laid a short but toe-curling kiss on me. When we separated, his smile and eyes lit up with naked emotion. It was . . . stunning.

Steven cleared his throat. "Sasha, do you have something you want to discuss with Nick?"

"Yeah," he said, his expression fading to serious. "Nick, I have a proposal for you."

"You're proposing!" Gay marriage might be legal now, but that didn't mean I wanted one. Not right now anyway.

"Come on, Nick. If we were going to run headfirst into marriage, we both know it would be you dragging me along. No, I have a proposal, like a deal, to offer you."

"A deal?"

"Yes." He motioned to Steven, who handed him a small packet of familiar papers. Sasha took a deep breath and passed them to me.

I stared at them, not quite believing what I saw. My face flushed and hands started to shake. "You want to buy this place?"

Steven spoke up. "Cash offer. It might not be as much as you hoped for, but I think the offer is fair. Especially since I'm waiving my commission to make it work. The offer is contingent on two things. The closing must be complete by June thirtieth, and you have to complete the following repairs within the next twelve months."

The repairs requested were basically just the remaining work on my task list. In fact, they suspiciously looked copy-and-pasted from my project form.

For a moment, all I could do was stand there with my mouth gaping open. "What's going on here, Sash? Where's this money coming from?"

"I sold Zayde's house. It has a lot of memories for me, but I don't really want to live there. It doesn't fit me anymore, and besides, there are too many memories that I want to forget. Steven has some first-time home buyers who want a house near a grade school to raise their kids. We don't close for a month or so, but Steven set me up with one of those bridge loans so I could pay you for this place now."

I sat down on a step stool and stared at the offer in my hands. The words blurred together, and I blinked fast to hold the stupid tears back. Two hundred thirty thousand dollars. It was a little low, but I could pay off Diamond and still have some profit to get started on my next project.

"I don't know what to say. Are you sure you want to live here? It's a big house for one guy."

He crouched down and placed his hands on my knees. "I've never been surer about anything. I love this house, and fortunately, it loves me too. It drew me here for a reason. And anyway, I don't have to live here alone. You'll be with me, won't you?"

A lump formed in my throat, and I pulled him in tight, burying my face in his hair. I couldn't stop a few tears from leaking as I held him. No way could this be real. It was all too much. Frank Diamond, the endless scramble of work, the crush of disappointment I'd seen in my brothers' eyes since I'd confessed my mess. And now Sasha—sweet, beautiful Sasha—had not only offered me a way out from the crushing debt, but had offered to share his life with me as well.

"Yes. To all of it." I gave him a quick kiss. "This is the perfect home for us to start our life together."

"You sure? The house offer isn't contingent on you moving in with me."

"Of course, I'm sure. I love you. There's nowhere I'd rather be."

His cheeks pinkened. "I love you too."

Steven waved the paperwork at us. "Ahem! Sealing the deal with a kiss is sweet, but I really need Nick's signature so I can get this filed."

Sasha pulled away laughing, and Steven handed me a pen.

"But what about your grandfather's house? You were so happy when you found out it was yours."

"I was happy, but it's not practical for me." He dropped his voice and gave me a serious look. "I can't live in that house anymore. Not after my mom . . . well, I can't risk envisioning . . . things. You get me?"

"Yeah, I get you." I gave him another peck on the mouth. "Okay, let's do this."

I pressed the offer against the wall and signed my name.

Steven took the paperwork and said to Sasha, "Sir, you have an accepted offer. Congratulations on purchasing your first home. It's beautiful." Then he turned to hug me. "You have an amazing man here. Pay Diamond off and don't go near him again."

"I won't. Promise."

"I'll see you both at the bank at eight Friday morning to close."

When Steven left, I drew Sasha into an embrace and squeezed. "Thank you. Thank you so much."

"We're never going to own enough furniture to fill this house up."

I laughed. "No, not for a while."

"And, Nick. One more thing."

"Yeah?"

Worry lines cut between his brows. "So I sold Zayde's house for three hundred and twenty thousand dollars. I'm going to have to settle the taxes, but I had an idea for the rest."

"You got three twenty and still gave me a low-ball offer?" I joked. "That's awesome. You deserve the cash. Think you might want to go back to school?"

"Nah. I never really wanted to be a music teacher. I like playing music, and I can do that without a degree." He studied his shoes. "What I was thinking was maybe—only if you want to—I could go into business with you. Flipping houses." He glanced up and met my eyes. "I know I don't know anything, but I want to learn. I have it on good authority that you're an awesome teacher. And I could help you too. I can read the homes. Control the emotions. Look for hidden defects and such. What do you think?"

I was speechless. I'd never had a partner before, never wanted one, but Sasha and I worked great together. And his unique gifts brought something completely new to the table.

He ran his hands down his beard. "You hate the idea, don't you? It's okay. I won't feel bad if—"

I squeezed his shoulders. "I love it. I love the idea of working with you. Of being partners. In every sense. Let's do this."

CHAPTER 33
SASHA

The next days flew by in a whirlwind of paper signing and legal jargon, all organized for me by Steven, who had a talent of explaining the steps for real estate transactions in a way I could almost understand. I'd made some big decisions in a short period of time, which was unusual and very scary for me, but regret hadn't set in, and with each day that passed, it seemed more likely that it never would.

"Frank'll see you now," said the bored woman, the gatekeeper to Frank Diamond's office.

I squeezed Nick's hand. "You ready?"

"More than ready."

The woman led us back to the smoky office. It wasn't any better the second time around, but I knew enough to avert my gaze to ignore the phantom blood stains.

Frank sat in his leather chair with his hands steepled in front of him and a gimlet stare fixed on Nick.

"You got one day left Cooper. If it's a time extension you're looking for, you might as well turn right back around."

"Don't need more time." Nick slapped a cashier's check on the desk. "Paid in full."

Frank's brows raised. He picked up the check and examined it intently, inspecting every decimal point with his thick glasses. Apparently satisfied, he drew out his smartphone and snapped a picture to upload the check to his bank account. For a guy who still kept hand-written ledgers, this bit of technical savvy surprised me.

"You impress me, Nicky. I had my doubts that you'd make good on your end."

"Like you, I'm a man of my word."

That was laying it on a little thick, but maybe Nick was not-so-subtly reminding Frank that he was no longer under his thumb.

Frank gave him a hard stare, then nodded once. "Nice working with you. Keep me in mind next time you get in a bind."

We showed ourselves out. When we got into the truck, I said, "You are never borrowing money from that guy again."

"Truth."

We drove home. Our home. My name might be on the deed, but everywhere I looked, from the hardware on the kitchen cabinets to the restored mantel over the fireplace, there was Nick's signature. Technically, we had moved in, though most of the rooms were empty. There was still plenty of work to finish, but with the luxury of time, we could tackle the rest in weekend projects.

We walked inside and collapsed on Nick's couch, the only furniture in our living room. My eyes drifted closed, and I let myself feel the vibrations of the house. To say it was pleased with this new arrangement was an understatement. It was over the moon. We weren't going to have to worry about spontaneous bursting pipes or an unexplained foundation crack anytime soon.

Nick pulled me to him, so my head rested on his chest, and stroked my hair, sending chills down my spine.

"So now what do you want to do?" I asked.

"Chill on the couch and watch the Brewers game."

"We don't have a TV."

He kissed the crown of my head. "So I guess I'll relax with you. It feels like we haven't stopped moving in months. An afternoon with nothing to do sounds perfect."

"Just so I have this straight, are you saying I come in second place to the Brewers?"

He groaned and flipped me around so he was sprawled on top of me, his big body holding me in place. His kiss was warm and filled with the promise of hot things to come as soon as we could motivate ourselves.

After a few minutes, Nick said, "I have something for you." He sat up with some reluctance.

I scooted upright and ran my fingers through my hair. "For me? What?"

"One sec."

Nick took the steps two at a time in his rush upstairs, returning with a small jeweler's box.

I raised a brow in question. "This better not be an engagement ring."

"Don't worry. I know you need time get back on your feet after this last year. Besides, I don't need some piece of paper as long as I get to sleep next to you every night. Open it."

The hinges creaked as I lifted the lid. Inside was Zayde's silver baby spoon. Sort of. It wasn't a spoon anymore. The scoop part had been removed and the intricate handle was curled in on itself, making a ring. It had been polished so the Star of David shone and the Hebrew lettering on the handle ringed around the band.

My heart leaped to my throat. "This is amazing! How did you do this?"

"I liberated it from the garbage. I took it to a jeweler to clean it up, but you were right, the spoon part was all gross. The jeweler suggested turning it into a ring. That's a thing nowadays."

I slipped the ring on my middle finger, where it fit just perfectly. "Guessed right on the sizing."

"I told the guy your fingers were thinner than mine. He said if it didn't fit right, he could size it for you." He paused a moment, and then added, "I won't be offended if you don't want to wear it. I know you're not much of a jewelry guy."

"No, I love it. Really. Thank you." I kissed him softly. "I love you."

Nick's cheeks blushed pink. Neither one of us were big on declaring our feelings all the time. What was more important was knowing that we were in this together. Partners in every sense of the word.

I set the box on the floor and pulled Nick down on top of me again. We kissed leisurely, like two people in love who had all the time in the world.

Well, until my phone rang.

I ignored it, letting the call go to voice mail, but less than a minute later, the ringing returned. With a groan, I dug it out of my pocket and checked the screen.

Rina.

"I better get this," I said with an apologetic look. I pressed the Call button. "Yeah?"

"Sasha, honey. I got your message about selling the house."

I sat up, bracing myself. "Yes, under the circumstances, I thought it was for the best."

"If you didn't want to live there, you could have rented it to me."

I didn't have it in me to fight with her today about what a piss-poor risk that would have been. "The closing is in a couple weeks. You'll need to get your stuff out of there before then. Do you have somewhere you can take it?"

"Yeah. I have a room in a women's home right now, but they have little storage areas you can rent for cheap. It'll do until I can afford a place."

I hadn't expected anything that optimistic. "Does that mean Jerry's out of the picture?"

She took an audible drag on a cigarette. "I guess. He's back to shacking up with his baby-mama. Says there's nothing going on between them, but I'm not stupid. I have no way of hauling the stuff though. Think that guy of yours will help me with his truck?"

I glanced at Nick, who still sat with a worried expression on his face. "Yeah, we can help."

And that was how we found ourselves two hours later loading up the back of Nick's truck with my mother's meager belongings and other sentimental odds and ends.

Rina and I stood in the kitchen doing one last survey while Nick finished battening things down with bungee cords. She was sober today, but the trembling in her hands suggested that she'd be heading off for a fix as soon as we were done. And that made me sad. So fucking sad.

"Sure you don't want any of the furniture?" I asked.

"Nah, I don't really have the room to store it. Besides, this place doesn't hold the same good memories for me as it does for you. When I was a kid, I couldn't wait to escape from here."

I froze. Desperately wanting to ask her what she meant and not wanting her to shut down on me. I'd never known what could've been so awful in her life that she'd had to turn to drugs. I'd asked Zayde a few times, but he'd just blamed it on bad kids at school and had admonished me to stay away from hooligans. Had something happened to her in this home to make her seek comfort elsewhere? Surely, Zayde and Bubbe hadn't been abusive. Zayde had hardly ever raised his voice to me.

I cleared my throat and asked as delicately as I could, "Will you tell me about it?"

Rina's mouth tightened, and when she didn't speak for a long moment, I figured she would shut down completely, but she surprised me. She leaned against the counter and began to speak.

"It all seems silly, now. Think of all the kids out there with real problems—hunger, abuse—I didn't have any of that. I was an only child growing up in a lower-middle-class family, in a middle-class town with stable parents who loved me. But I was a kid, right? All I saw was how different we were. It's not easy growing up in white bread America with immigrant parents."

She fingered the lacey curtains on the patio door that her mother had sewn sometime before I was born. They were yellowed, but Zayde would never have considered replacing them.

"We mostly spoke Russian in the home. Abba could speak English well. Had to. You couldn't get a decent job in this town without it. But Ima didn't work outside the home."

"I thought she had a sewing business," I commented.

"Yeah, she took in sewing, but Abba ran most of the client interactions for her. She never got over feeling self-conscious speaking English in public. She had a hard time letting go of the Old World. She used to make me go with her shopping so I could translate."

"You were embarrassed by her because she spoke Russian?"

Rina shot me a glare. "You don't understand. We spoke *Russian* during the Cold War. Every bad guy on TV back then was Russian. Kids at school were suspicious of us. They used to call me KGB. Of course, that was just kids teasing, but there were plenty of parents who were cautious about having their children play with the Russian-Jewish girl, you know? And it didn't help my popularity any that Ima made my clothes until I went to high school. I looked like I'd come straight from the Eastern Bloc."

I'd seen photos of Rina as a child growing up, so I had a good idea of what she was talking about. My bubbe had loved head scarves, stiff dresses, and fur-lined everything.

"When I got to high school," she continued, "I'd had enough. I told Abba I'd go to school naked if he wouldn't let me shop at the mall like the other girls. After an entire summer of fighting about it, he gave me some money and a ride to Kmart. Happiest day of my childhood."

I took a seat at the table, relishing the opportunity to have a real conversation with my mother when she wasn't angry or inebriated.

Rina hesitated for a moment, but then sat down across from me, pushing a stack of papers out of the way. It was still cluttered from me working to settle Zayde's accounts. I could have let most of them go—he was dead after all—but he wouldn't have liked that. Also on the table was Rina's box from my bedroom ceiling. She'd probably want it. Rina let her fingertips trail across the lid in thought.

I wanted to keep her talking. "Did the new clothes help?"

"A little. I fit in better, but I still didn't have any friends. At least not until I met Sherry Moseley in tenth grade. Do you remember Sherry?"

I did. She'd been pockmarked and so thin that I could make out her skeleton under her skin, which used to frighten me as a child. "She died, didn't she?"

"Yeah. Suicide. She had AIDS back in a time when there wasn't much you could do for it. She ended up ODing when the pain got to be too bad. But she was the first real girlfriend I ever had. Abba and Ima didn't like her because she was constantly running away from home and hanging out on the streets. She had problems, yeah, but she was nice to me."

"And she got you into drugs?"

Rina rolled her eyes. "It's not like she put a gun to my head. I got myself into drugs. Being friends with Sherry just made them easier to get. I thought I was having a good time. And I figured when high school was over, I'd get serious and go to college. But by then it was too late. I was in love with the high. Quit going to classes. Never did graduate." She paused, staring out the window with a faraway look in her eyes. Then she smiled. "And there you have it. The not-so-tragic story of how your mother ended up an addict."

We sat in that moment, neither speaking, or even really looking at each other. Afraid to break this fragile time between bonding and arguing. I was so sick of fighting with her.

The thing that was easy to forget was that when my mother was sober, she wasn't so bad. There had been a brief time when I was about ten when she'd been somewhat stable. She'd rented a small apartment in the city and took a job at the Walgreens in the photo department. I remembered it because it was one of the few times she'd been home for my birthday, and she brought me a cheap camera with a couple of rolls of film. Then, we'd gone out to the backyard and taken pictures of garden slugs and tree bark.

I hadn't thought about that day for a long time. Probably because the next time I'd seen her, she'd shown up tweaking, with no job, with no apartment, and cussing up a wild streak because Zayde wouldn't give her money.

I picked up a pen from the table, and set it back down again. I glanced at the neat stacks of mail on the table, the legal pad where I'd been keeping track of what was paid and what still needed to be settled.

That was when I remembered the brochure that I'd seen in her box. The one from Woodland Acres Rehab Center. The expensive one down south. She'd kept it for a reason. Didn't that mean some little part of her wanted to get better? I opened the lid, unfolded the brochure, and passed it to her.

"I bet this place doesn't have staff that brings in contraband."

Rina looked at the cover and huffed, "I'm sure it doesn't. For what it costs to go there, they can afford to pay their staff enough so they don't have to run sidelines."

"They have an eighty-seven percent success rate."

"What did you do, memorize the thing?" She pushed it across the table back to me.

"I understand how awful those state rehabs are. If a person were serious about getting clean for good, they would go someplace like this. Far away from the negative influences in their life. A place where all they had to do was concentrate on getting healthy."

"Give it up, Sasha. You know I can't afford no magic rehab."

"Nothing magic about it. It's hard work." I paused, unsure if I wanted to lay it all out there. But damn it, this was my mother. Zayde would want me to try. And if she said no? Well, then I could walk away with a clear conscience knowing I'd done what I could. I took a deep breath. I needed to get the offer out there before I came to my senses. "You know, if you're ready to get serious about cleaning yourself up, I'll pay for it."

She stared at me, mouth gaping. I didn't want her to say no.

"Zayde always hoped one day he could afford to send you there. And I made some money from the sale of the house. Not a lot, but enough that I could pay for you to go and get the help you need."

Her expression moved from shocked to skeptical. "Why would you do that? I got a piss-poor track record when it comes to getting clean. You'd be farther ahead to take it to the casino and have a little fun losing it."

"I'm not worried about making a bad bet on you. I think if you're in the right place, this place—" I tapped the brochure "—you can do it. I know you can."

Rina opened and closed her mouth a couple of times, starting to speak but stopping herself.

Encouraged by her lack of outright refusal, I continued, "You always said that the reason you failed those state programs was because they were filled with the same people you knew on the street. I guarantee you won't have history with anybody at Woodland." I opened the brochure to the page with a bullet-pointed program offering. "See, they don't just focus on your addiction, they work to address all your issues, mental and physical. When was the last time you saw a doctor for a checkup? Have you ever had a breast-cancer screening? You're pushing fifty with a short stick. It's time to start making your health a priority."

"Don't remind me." Rina stared at the glossy photos. "They have a pool."

"Yeah, it's a nice place."

"What would your fella think of you spending your nest egg on me like this?"

"He'd be proud of both of you," said Nick from where he leaned in the doorway. "I can't think of a better use for the money."

I smiled at him, and he came forward to sit at the table. He pulled Woodland's website up on his phone, and we spent the next hour answering Rina's questions and hammering out the details. When we finished, I called to reserve a bed for my mother and made a flight reservation for the next day. A representative from the facility would meet her at the Nashville airport and take her directly there. We all thought it best that she come home with us that night. Now that she'd agreed to get help, I wasn't going to take my eyes off her until she was safely in the air.

That night, with my mother settled on the couch and her belongings stored in our basement, I crawled into bed beside Nick, who was propped up on pillows reading a detective novel and looking like a wet dream. Our bed consisted of Nick's king-size mattress from his loft tossed on the floor in the master bedroom. Furniture would come in time. For now, I considered anywhere with Nick a blessing.

"Well, can't say I expected my mother would be our first overnight houseguest. I hope she's still here in the morning."

"She will be." Nick leaned over to place a soft kiss on my shoulder. "She's scared, but I don't think she was faking that expression. She's hopeful."

So was I. And I wasn't sure that was very smart. To my mother, I'd projected all the faith in the world that she could kick the shit for good, but inside, I maintained a healthy skepticism. But if she tried and couldn't do it, I'd have to be okay with that.

Nick set his book aside and opened his arms for me to snuggle on his bare chest. I pressed my cheek to his warm skin and drank in the scent of him, fresh from the shower. His hand settled on the back of my neck, where he could play with my curls.

This. Just this. Contentment. It's what I wanted for the rest of forever.

Then Nick's cell phone rang.

"Are you serious?" he muttered.

Not moving from his position, he answered. "Yeah?"

"Hey," greeted Steven, whose voice was clearly audible.

"Hey, you. What's up? I'm going to sleep."

"It's only nine thirty. You turning into an old man?"

Nick squeezed me a little tighter. "No, but I have a lot of motivation to spend as much time in the sack as possible now."

"Ew. Am I interrupting something? No, don't answer that. I don' want to know."

"Do you think if we were getting it on, I'd answer the phone? What do you need?"

"I just got back from a client meeting. If you're looking for another property flip, I have a new one you might be interested in. I'm going to list it tomorrow, but I'll give you first crack at it. Three bedrooms, two baths, built in fifty-eight. The roof and HVAC have been updated recently, but the inside hasn't been touched. I can get you a good deal; the seller is very motivated. Located in Fox Point."

"Nice neighborhood. They should be able to get top dollar, even on an outdated property. What else is wrong with it?"

"Well, the current owner bought it from an estate. They moved in, but after a couple of weeks, they moved right back out. It's been sitting vacant for almost a year." Steven cleared his throat. "They say it's got a bad vibe."

Nick's eyes flashed to mine, and a slow grin spread across both of our faces. I nodded.

"Sure, Steven," he answered. "We're interested. Text me the address."

Dear Reader,

Thank you for reading Jesi Lea Ryan's *Surreal Estate*!

We know your time is precious and you have many, many entertainment options, so it means a lot that you've chosen to spend your time reading. We really hope you enjoyed it.

We'd be honored if you'd consider posting a review—good or bad—on sites like **Amazon, Barnes & Noble, Kobo, Goodreads, Twitter, Facebook, Tumblr,** and your blog or website. We'd also be honored if you told your friends and family about this book. Word of mouth is a book's lifeblood!

For more information on upcoming releases, author interviews, blog tours, contests, giveaways, and more, please sign up for our weekly, spam-free newsletter and visit us around the web:

Newsletter: riptidepublishing.com/newsletter
Twitter: twitter.com/RiptideBooks
Facebook: facebook.com/RiptidePublishing
Goodreads: tinyurl.com/RiptideOnGoodreads
Tumblr: riptidepublishing.tumblr.com

Thank you so much for Reading the Rainbow!

RiptidePublishing.com

ACKNOWLEDGMENTS

Of the six novels I've published, this book was by far the most challenging to complete. You might think that's because it's my first M/M novel, but that's not why. If anything, I find writing from a male point of view easier. Go figure. It wasn't because of the characters or plot either. I knew right away who Nick and Sasha were. In fact, personality-wise, Nick is more like me than any other character I've written. And Sasha is just the person I would fall in love with.

No, the challenging thing for me was all personal—a string of health issues and a cross-country move sucked the motivation right out of me. There were many times when I thought about walking away from writing altogether. Thankfully, with the encouragement of my husband and my dear friend Jordan, I found it in me to complete this book and find my writing mojo again. Thank you, Steve and Jordan, for being here for me through it all, for not listening to my excuses, for reading the various typo-riddled drafts, for reminding me why I love writing.

There were many other people who assisted me along the way. My critique buddies Jordan Castillo Price, L.C. Giroux, Mark Anderson, and Mercy Loomis, who didn't laugh at my idea of a love story between a house flipper and a squatter. Beta readers Mike Zimmerman, Victoria Grundle, and Dev Bentham, who kept me from making mistakes on construction details or writing characters outside my personal experience. Steve Riggles, who corrected my typos. K.A. Mitchell and Jordan Castillo Price for their assistance with my blurb. My editor, Carole-ann Galloway, who took a chance on this newbie M/M author and challenged me to make this a better book. My cover designer Lou Harper, a true artist. The numerous staff at Riptide Publishing. I thank you all from the bottom of my heart.

ALSO BY
JESI LEA RYAN

Four Thousand Miles
Just a Little Nudge

Young Adult Novels
Arcadia's Gift
Arcadia's Curse
Arcadia's Choice

ABOUT THE
AUTHOR

Jesi Lea Ryan has been kissed by Jimmy Carter, played with a ghost in Gettysburg, can't leave the house without forgetting something, and judges people by their bookshelves. She grew up in Dubuque, Iowa; learned how to adult in Madison, Wisconsin; and now lives in Maricopa, Arizona, with her husband and two exceptionally naughty kitties. She has earned bachelor's degrees in creative writing and literature from Loras College and her MBA from Columbia College. She also holds an assortment of associate's degrees and certificates, because she just couldn't help herself.

Jesi is a social media addict. Hit her up at:

Twitter: @Jesilea

Facebook: facebook.com/jesilea76

Instagram: instagram.com/jesi_lea_ryan

Enjoy more stories like
Surreal Estate
at RiptidePublishing.com!

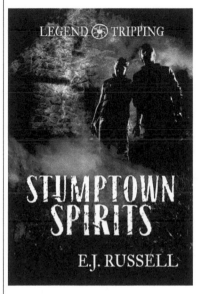

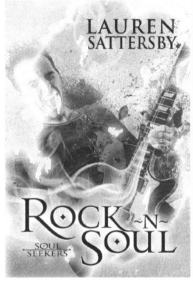

Stumptown Spirits   **Rock N Soul**

Dealing with ghosts puts more   He's a ghost. I'm a bellboy.
than one life on the line.   What could possibly go wrong?

ISBN: 978-1-62649-409-1   ISBN: 978-1-62649-311-7

CPSIA information can be obtained
at www.ICGtesting.com
Printed in the USA
LVHW021558011118
595633LV00003B/491/P